SD

not writing
avoiding exercise   website
michellewillingham.com.

Discover more at millsandboon.co.uk.

THE IRON WARRIOR RETURNS

Michelle Willingham

MILLS & BOON

First Published in Great Britain 2022
by Mills & Boon, an imprint of HarperCollins*Publishers* Ltd,
1 London Bridge Street, London, SE1 9GF

www.harpercollins.co.uk

HarperCollins*Publishers*
1st Floor, Watermarque Building,
Ringsend Road, Dublin 4, Ireland

The Iron Warrior Returns © 2022 Michelle Willingham

ISBN: 978-0-263-30167-0

04/22

MIX
Paper from
responsible sources
FSC
www.fsc.org
FSC® C007454

To Louise, for your bright spirit,
your wonderful conversation,
and for truly being such a fantastic neighbor.

Prologue

England, 1205

All of them were going to die.

Robert of Penrith stared at the other captives. The soldiers had chained four of them together while they journeyed south. A heavy covering atop the wagon shielded them from their surroundings, and the thick door was bolted shut from the other side.

A numbing silence permeated the space, for they were in shock. No one knew if their families had survived the attack, but most of the castle hadn't. Robert would never forget the heavy smoke or the searing heat as the king's soldiers had set it on fire. The stone exterior walls might survive, but the interior had gone up in flames.

The screaming still reverberated in his mind. Men had died, swords piercing their flesh.

Women had cried out in agony before being struck down alongside them. His father's wife, Clarine, had warned him to hide, to stay alive. His stomach twisted with shame, for he'd obeyed. He wasn't a fighter, and now he cursed himself for being a coward. Self-loathing flooded through him, but he'd fled, not knowing what had happened to her. Or any of them now. But Clarine had been right—he owed it to his people to survive and one day claim his vengeance.

Now that the king had attacked and stripped his father, Earl of Penrith of his lands, no doubt Degal was dead. The icy realisation made his throat close up, and Robert closed his eyes.

You don't have the right to feel grief or be afraid. You must be strong and take care of your people.

He breathed in steadily, willing himself to remain calm. There was no time to think of his family's fate. Fear wouldn't help him escape. He needed to study their prison and find a way out.

He'd always been good at taking things apart and putting them back together again. There was no reason he couldn't find a way out of this wagon, as long as he could gain the help of his fellow prisoners. He didn't recognise the young woman or her little brother because he'd spent most of his days isolated in the castle keep. But he knew Piers well enough.

'This was your fault,' his half-brother snapped. 'You're the reason they took us.' He strained against his chains, and Robert didn't doubt that Piers would strangle him if he could. His bastard brother had always worn his anger like an invisible shield, and he was the first to lift his fists, even if he usually lost the fight.

Not that Robert was any better at sparring. As a child, he'd been sickly, and Clarine had forced him to remain indoors. He'd spent his hours surrounded by books, devouring knowledge the way others had trained in swordplay. Now he wished he'd listened to Degal and learned to use a sword or dagger.

'They're not going to kill us,' Robert lied. 'If they were, we'd already be dead.' But in truth, he knew not what would happen or why they'd been captured.

Unless they were the only survivors.

He shook the thought away. Logically, there was no reason to kill the servants or villagers. The king had claimed their castle, and he would need dozens of serfs to tend the land. But why had they taken the young maiden and her brother? Robert hadn't seen them in the castle before, so he didn't know what leverage they would be.

The young woman's dark hair hung against her face and shoulders in waves, as if she'd worn it in braids and it had fallen loose. He couldn't tell much about her, except that she was shivering with her arms crossed. Her clothing was simple, a shapeless undyed woollen kirtle, which meant she was one of the serfs.

Her brother's face grew waxen, as if he expected to die at any moment. He was right to be afraid.

'They're going to torture us,' Piers continued, stretching his chains out as far as he could. 'And then they'll use us to force our father to do whatever the king wants.'

It surprised Robert that his brother believed their father was still alive. After the brutal attack on Penrith, Robert couldn't imagine that Degal was a prisoner. But then again, Piers had a point. It was one thing to defy the king—but quite another to be defiant while someone else was being tortured. The thought wrenched Robert's gut, pricking the fear once more.

'Stop it,' the young woman pleaded. 'You're scaring Brian.'

But it was her own voice that held fear. Robert saw the way she was hunched over, as if guarding herself. There was a raw pain beneath her tone, and he wondered if she'd been hurt during the attack. He wanted to ask if she was all right, but something made him stop. She reminded him of a wounded animal, one that would lash out at someone trying to help her.

'Maybe Brian *should* be scared,' Piers shot back. 'And you should too, Morwenna.'

'Enough,' Robert said quietly. 'Arguing won't get us out of here.'

After that, his brother held his tongue, and the heavy silence only heightened their terror. Somehow, they had to escape this wagon and find sanctuary. It was their only chance of survival.

Robert forced himself to remain calm. They had been travelling for nearly an hour, which meant they were not far from Colford Abbey where his uncle Oswald was the abbot. Outside it was freezing, and he thought he heard the light pattering of snowfall.

His mind began to construct a plan, although the details had not yet taken form. It was too dark to see, but he tried to envision how the wagon doors were constructed. No doubt they were bolted shut from the outside. Could he reach the hinges? The covering rested atop a skeletal frame of wooden bars. If he stretched his arm through the bars, he might be able to loosen that hinge if he could find a way of hammering the pin.

'We need to get the wagon doors off before they stop for the night,' Robert said to the others. 'Then we can hide in the forest and seek sanctuary at the abbey.' Their best chance of escaping was to do it while the wagon was moving.

'And do you plan to use magic for this?' Piers taunted. 'You can't unlock the doors.'

'I'm going to try to take off the hinges. Or at least one of them.' Though he tried to sound confident, he didn't know how he could manage without tools. 'I can loosen the door on the right side.' Truthfully, he had no idea if it would work.

'What about the guards?' Brian's voice cracked as he spoke. 'We don't have weapons.'

'Yes, we do.' Morwenna lifted her chains. Her voice held ice and she said, 'If anyone dares to attack us, I'll strangle him.' The bitterness in her voice spoke of someone who possessed a great deal of hatred.

The young woman didn't look nearly strong enough to battle a soldier, but she did seem strong-willed. She might manage a distraction if nothing else.

'I hope it doesn't come to that,' Robert said. 'But if we don't get out, we're at their mercy.' He didn't voice his fear that they would be killed or tortured as Piers had suggested.

He switched places with Brian and began to examine the hinges. There were only two on that side, and he thought he might be able to remove the pin if he could find something narrow to wedge beneath it.

Again, he tried to picture the hinge in his mind, imagining how he would reach the pin. He looked around and spied a piece of broken wood on the edge of the wagon. Robert grabbed it and twisted the shard. It splintered against his palm, drawing blood, but he managed to break it free. Then he stretched his hand around the outside and jammed the wood below the hinge. The frigid air gusted around his hand, and snow-flakes dampened his skin.

'This isn't going to work,' Piers muttered.

Robert ignored him and used his manacles to hammer at the pin. No, it wasn't likely to work, but it was the only plan he had. He angled the wood and tried again, knocking the hinge over and over. It still wouldn't budge. His hands were freezing, but he centred his focus and soon, he felt the pin begin to slip. Miraculously, it loosened until he was able to pull it free. He was about to try loosening the second one, when the wagon stopped, and the doors opened.

Two soldiers approached, one with a knife drawn. Robert shrank back, keeping the hinge-pin hidden.

'Stop making noise,' the soldier with the knife demanded. He climbed inside and said to the other, 'I'll keep them quiet.'

In the dark, Robert couldn't see the man's face, but his tension heightened. The door closed behind the soldier, but he didn't hear the bolt. For a moment, they all remained silent. Then the horses started, and the wagon began moving once again.

'You're a pretty one, aren't you?' the soldier said to Morwenna. She gave no answer but kept her head down. The man yanked her back by the hair, and she cried out in pain.

Robert gripped the wood in his hand tightly. The soldier was close, but he didn't know if he could do anything to protect her. It was a grave risk, for the man had a blade.

His mind warned him not to get involved. If he tried to interfere, he might infuriate the soldier and cause the young woman to suffer even more. Yet, neither could he stand aside and do nothing.

Robert took a step closer, trying to decide the best way to help. His brain went through each possibility, turning over one idea and then the next. But then he saw the chains clenched in Morwenna's hands. She was prepared for the worst, and he couldn't say whether she would succeed.

He was about to move towards her when a hand stopped him. Piers pointed towards the door, which had loosened even more with the jarring of the wagon. It was nearly open, and now was their chance to get out.

But all of them were chained together. There was no way to escape the wagon unless they all worked together. If one stumbled, it would slow the rest.

'Give us a kiss, then,' the soldier said, reaching for her. 'You wouldn't want me to cut that pretty face, now, would you?'

'Don't touch me,' she whispered.

The soldier backhanded her, and she cried out in pain.

In that moment, Robert despised himself. If he were any sort of man, he would attack the guard and save her. But he'd never had to fight anyone before, and he had no idea what to do.

His fist closed over the splinter of wood. Maybe he could use it as a weapon. He heard the slight jangling noise of the chains Morwenna held. And he suddenly wondered if she was playing a role, luring her attacker closer.

'I'll touch you as much as I want,' the soldier snarled.

The moment he came near, Morwenna wrapped her chains around his throat. But she wasn't strong enough to strangle him, and he wrenched her hands away.

'Stupid bitch,' he gritted out. 'I'll kill you for that.'

Robert could no longer stand by and do nothing—but this was going to end badly. This soldier was trained to kill, whereas Robert had only watched other warriors. His mind spun through the different methods, although he still hadn't decided what to do. Silently, he moved closer.

'No,' Morwenna pleaded when the soldier reached for her gown and tore it open. She fought to hide herself, and in that moment, a cold calmness seized Robert. There was no longer any sense of thought—only action.

In an instant, he raised the shard of wood and stabbed it in the soldier's throat. He felt the warm spurt of blood, and the soldier spun in shock.

Piers reached for the man's knife and stabbed him again, this time in the heart. The soldier staggered to his knees, and Robert was grateful for his half-brother's quick thinking. The soldier was dead, his life's blood spilling over the wood.

For a moment, Robert blinked, stunned at

what had happened. Then he remembered the girl and turned back to her. 'Are you all right?'

Morwenna held the torn edges of her gown together and nodded. 'W-we have to get out of here.'

Though he was still numb about the soldier's death, he had to focus on what lay ahead. Their survival depended on this escape. The door still hung ajar from where the soldier had opened it. Outside, it was too dark to see anything, but they gathered on the edge. They barely had enough time to get out.

'We have to jump together,' Robert warned in a low voice, 'and then we run to the forest.'

'What if we're caught?' Brian asked. His voice cracked on the whisper, as he joined them on the edge.

Piers cleaned the blade on the fallen soldier's tunic before he sheathed it. 'We can't be caught. Or we die.'

Morwenna clutched the torn bodice of her gown, and Robert sobered at the sight. Her expression was pale when she came to stand beside them. He pulled off his cloak, handing it to her.

'Thank you,' she whispered.

She covered herself with it, and then Robert ordered, 'On three, we jump. One, two, three...'

With that, they jumped down from the moving

wagon and fell into the snow and mud. They ran towards the woods, lungs burning as they hurried to escape their captors.

As they disappeared into the night, Robert made a vow of his own. No longer would he be unable to fight or become any man's victim. He might be only eight and ten, but tonight, everything had changed. He would train, night and day, until he turned his back on the coward he'd been.

And, one day, he would claim his vengeance and take back his father's lands.

Chapter One

Two years later

'Who will win, do you think?'

Morwenna turned at the sound of the male voice. She had been watching her brother spar with Piers, but now Robert of Penrith was approaching her. He wore his chainmail armour like a second skin, and his sword rested at his side.

For the past two years, he'd spent every waking hour fighting. He'd filled out, and instead of being lean and swift, he now had arms so thick she couldn't span them with both hands. He could lift a heavy broadsword with one hand, and she'd been fascinated by Robert's transformation. His light-brown hair was tipped with gold, and his brown eyes held a warmth and kindness that made her stomach twist with 'if only's.

Unfortunately, he seemed unaware of her feelings. Or if he was aware, he was kind enough not to tell her that he wasn't interested.

'Piers will win,' she predicted, pushing her idle thoughts away. 'But Brian is getting better.' The two young men continued to spar with one another, and she watched as Piers struck a hard blow against Brian's shield. Her brother stumbled a moment but then struck back with his own attack.

'He's grown stronger, aye. And older.' Robert came to stand beside her, and her shoulder accidentally brushed against his arm. Her cheeks blushed, and she couldn't think of what to say right now. She was entirely too conscious of his nearness.

Don't think of that, she warned herself. *He sees you as a friend, nothing more.*

In two years, he had never once treated her like a woman who had captured his interest. Better to bury the unrequited feelings and act as if it didn't matter.

She stared out at the ruins of Stansbury, the fortress that had once belonged to Lord Penrith. It was a forgotten place where they had fled after they'd left the abbey. Robert's uncle had offered the young men a place to stay among the monks after a few months, but they hadn't wanted her.

Rather than send her to a nunnery, Robert had

come up with the plan for them to come here to train. He'd acquired armour, weapons, and supplies with the help of his uncle. Piers and Brian had welcomed the chance for freedom, and Morwenna had learned to fight alongside them. Somehow, the four of them had become a strange sort of family, staying together to survive.

She wrenched her attention back to her brother and Piers while they sparred. There was a stoic determination about Brian, as if he would never look back on the past. But whenever Piers fought, there was an intensity that went beyond reason. He poured his rage and frustration into fighting until he could no longer stand.

Not like Robert. When he fought, there was no emotion at all—only a quiet, focused demonstration of strength. He seemed to think about every move before he made it.

Morwenna had learned how to defend herself, but she was no match for their strength. She rested her hand on the light dagger at her side. It had once belonged to Robert, but he'd given it to her as a means of protection. There was something about holding a blade that gave her a feeling of power. Not because she wanted to fight... but because it made her feel safe.

A tightness caught in her chest as dark memories assailed her. Never again would she allow a man to attack her. Though she'd mostly pushed the memories aside, there were still moments when she awakened in the middle of the night, terrified by dreams of the soldier tearing her gown and groping her.

She squeezed the hilt of her blade, pushing back the vision. Instead, she studied Robert and saw tension in his stance. Although he'd said nothing, she sensed that something was wrong. 'Is anything the matter?'

His mouth tightened, and he stared off into the distance for a time. 'I have news from my uncle about Penrith.'

From the sound of his voice, the news wasn't good.

'What is it?' She knew he'd been training all these years, hoping to one day retake his lands at Penrith. King John had put a new earl in command, but the lord had many soldiers. It wasn't possible for them to fight an army of that size.

'I've found a way to reclaim the estate,' he said. 'Without bloodshed.'

She didn't know what to think of that—especially since he didn't seem pleased by it. 'How?'

'The earl is hosting a feast at Midsummer. He has invited warriors and lords from across the north for competitions. The winner will wed his daughter—that is, if he gains her consent.'

Her heart nearly stopped with dismay. 'And you…hope to wed this woman?'

Please say no.

But unfortunately, he nodded. 'If I win her favour and her hand in marriage, our sons will be the heirs to Penrith.' He met her gaze, and she felt her heart breaking at the resolution in his eyes. 'It's the best way forward, Morwenna. I'll regain what was lost.'

She knew he was right, but she'd never imagined the invisible pain that slashed her feelings. Though she tried to act as if she supported his decision, it hurt because she was another step closer to losing him.

She didn't delude herself into believing she could ever be with a lord like Robert. Not at all. But these moments living beside him had given her a reason to dream. And she intended to savour his attention for as long as she could.

'Will you walk with me?' he asked. 'There's something I wanted you to have before I go.'

Her heart surged with anticipation. 'Of course. What is it?'

'Well, it's not exactly a gift,' he amended. 'More like something you might need.' He wasn't making eye contact any more, and the awkwardness hung heavily between them.

He led her towards the stables, saying nothing further. As they drew closer, she thought of other possibilities. He might have a new puppy for her or a kitten—something to love when he was gone. Her anticipation heightened as they walked closer to the stalls.

'I thought…you might like it,' he continued.

'What is it?' she asked.

'It's over here,' he said, opening the last stall. She walked inside, and confusion made her frown. There was no ribbon, no kitten. Only a battered wooden shield.

'It's to protect you,' he said, offering a tentative smile.

For a moment, Morwenna could hardly believe what he'd given her. It was the sort of present an older brother might give to a younger brother. Certainly not a woman. What on earth was she supposed to say?

'It's…um…very kind of you.'

'Try it on,' he urged. He lifted the shield and held it out for her to put her arm in the leather straps. The wood was heavy, but the weight of disappointment in her heart was worse.

She tried to form a smile and nodded. 'Thank you.'

He did smile then. 'I thought it might be useful to you. For when you fight.'

She set down the shield and faced him. Did

he mistakenly believe that she loved fighting? 'Robert, I'm not going off into battle.'

'I know you're not. But you do like to spar sometimes.'

She closed her eyes a moment, feeling foolish. The only person she enjoyed sparring with was him. And even then, it was only an excuse to interact with the man she liked. She had no intention of becoming a fighter, and the shield was utterly useless. But then, she didn't want to seem ungrateful for his gift. 'Thank you.'

He gave a nod, but when she studied him more closely, she noted the crease of tension around his eyes. He seemed uncertain about this journey.

'When are you planning to leave for Penrith?' she asked.

He leaned his arm against the horse stall. 'On the morrow. I want to see for myself how things are at the estate. Perhaps even meet the new lord's daughter early if I can.'

The blade of jealousy sliced a little deeper. 'So soon?' Worse was the realisation that she could do nothing to stop him. Robert was going to leave her behind, and it was likely she'd never see him again.

Her brain conjured up all the terrible things that could happen on his journey. The people of Penrith might recognise Robert as the rightful heir, and the earl would want to be rid of him. Or even if he did win the competitions, the earl's daughter might not want to wed him.

To be truthful, she rather hoped the woman would not be interested. Which was ridiculous. Robert had grown more handsome than she'd ever imagined. Stoic and strong, she loved watching him fight. Any woman with eyes in her head would fall in love with him, just as she had.

Her only hope was to be at his side, for as long as she could. And the thought of him leaving shattered the idle dreams in her heart.

'I'm going to win back my lands,' he insisted. 'I owe it to my father's people.'

Without thinking, she reached for his hands and took them. Her palms felt like ice in the warmth of his grasp. His expression turned to pity, and it took all her strength not to crumble.

There was a solemnity to his expression, as if he knew the trials that lay ahead. He reminded her of a soldier about to ride into battle—one who might not return. Her heart clenched at the thought, though she tried not to wear her emotions.

She should have known this day was coming. Over the past two years, he'd done more than transform his strength. He'd spoken to his uncle regularly, learning all that he could about what had happened to his father's estate. And she'd always known he'd been making plans to take his lands back.

'I don't want you to go,' she murmured. The moment he left, he would be surrounded by other men competing for the right to claim Penrith and the nobleman's daughter. It could be dangerous.

He gave her hands a gentle squeeze and then released them. 'I've waited long enough,' he said. 'I acted like a coward on the night the king's men attacked us. I've heard that the new earl has caused hardships for the people of Penrith. I need to know what he's done and how I can make it right.'

In his voice, she heard the yearning for honour. He wanted to reclaim Penrith, and she understood that desire. But she didn't want him to sacrifice everything.

'They took us captive before,' she said quietly. 'If you go back, what will stop the new Lord Penrith from taking you prisoner again?'

He faced her, resting his hand upon the horse stall. 'This earl had nothing to do with the attack. And I cannot hide for ever, Morwenna. That's not the sort of man I want to be.'

She moved closer to him. 'We hid because we didn't have a choice.' Even after they'd left the abbey and taken shelter at the ruined estate, they'd lived with the fear of being discovered by the king's men. They still didn't know why they'd been taken prisoner. Perhaps it didn't matter anymore, but during the past year, they'd slept in a freezing fortress with a leaking roof. The only consolation was that no one had hunted them... and Robert had been with her.

'I have a choice now,' he replied. 'This is what I've trained for. If I defeat the others, I'll win her hand in marriage, and Penrith will be mine again.'

She didn't know what to say, but his determination was clear. He saw this marriage as a prize to be won and a means of reclaiming Penrith.

You knew this would happen, her brain reminded her. Now the moment she'd been dreading was here.

'What about the rest of us?' she asked. 'Should we go with you?' The thought of watching him court another woman was a dagger wrenching in her heart.

'No. I think it's better if I go alone, Morwenna. I don't want to draw too much attention to myself.'

She didn't know how to respond to that. 'Should we wait here?'

He shook his head. 'You should go and live your own lives now.'

It was almost impossible to imagine it, though she'd known they couldn't stay here for ever. Robert had always planned to go back. And for a while, she'd clung to the frail hope of staying with him for as long as he continued to train. But now, it would all come to an end. The thought of her own future terrified her.

'What is there for me, Robert?' she ventured.

'Perhaps you'll find someone to marry.'

When his gaze rested upon her, Morwenna felt self-conscious about the leggings and tunic she'd borrowed from her brother. She was a skinny waif who had hacked the length of her brown hair with a blade until it hung short around her shoulders. Her face was dirty, her skin sweaty. 'No man would have me,' she said quietly. Least of all the man she wanted.

He looked as if he was about to argue with her, but she cut him off saying, 'And besides, I don't think you should go alone to Penrith. It could be dangerous. What if they're still searching for you?'

But the true reason was that she didn't want him to be married.

'I'll be all right, Morwenna. Even if I don't have you to guard my back.' He touched her chin softly, but she sensed the pity in his tone. Her skin burned with embarrassment from the light contact for she knew he did not mean it. For once, she wished she were wearing skirts or even a ribbon in her hair. Something to make him see the woman she longed to be, instead of the awkward one she was.

'I could come if you want me to,' she answered softly. 'I could hide among her ladies.'

His smile dimmed. 'It's probably better if we part ways now, Morwenna. You have your own life to lead.'

He was wrong in that. The only reason she had felt safe during the years of hiding was because of Robert, Brian, and Piers. There was comfort in a place where she was surrounded by protectors. Although she would never be as strong as any of them, she could defend herself and kill a man, if need be. But now they were leaving, and the last thing she wanted was to be abandoned.

'I don't have anywhere else to go,' she admitted. 'I may as well come with you and help if I can. Penrith used to be my home, after all.'

'You have your freedom, Morwenna. Of all the places you could go, why would you return to Penrith?'

Because you would be there, she thought but didn't say it.

Although it was an utter lie, she suggested,

'Perhaps I'll find a husband among the men who don't win the lady's hand in marriage.'

He frowned but couldn't come up with a good reason to refuse her. Then she added, 'There's something else you should consider, Robert. Do you even know how to court a woman?'

'Not really,' he answered. 'But all I have to do is win the fighting competitions.' He rested his hand on his sword hilt.

'Is that what you believe?' Morwenna frowned at him. 'You did say that the new Lord Penrith gave his daughter the choice, did you not? You'll have to do more than win a sword fight to win her consent.' She straightened and regarded him. 'No, I am coming with you. You're going to need my help. Piers and Brian might join us as well.'

He shook his head. 'Piers will go where the wind blows him. He has no interest in helping me gain my birthright. Not when he has his own fortunes to seek.' The two half-brothers had become reluctant allies, even if they would never be friends. They'd fought each other for most of the year before grudgingly admitting that their fighting skills were equal.

But Morwenna clung to hope since he hadn't found a reason to deny her request. 'I'll tell Brian to pack his belongings.'

'Are you certain you want to go back to Penrith?' he asked carefully.

It wasn't about Penrith, she thought. There was nothing there for her. No family, no home. Only the emptiness of a life she didn't want. But the man she *did* want was travelling there, and she intended to make the most of the remaining time.

Morwenna raised her chin and stared at him. Then she lifted her battered shield and said, 'On the morrow, we'll go together.'

And perhaps, if she could find her courage, she might bare her heart to him before it was too late.

It took only a single day of travelling to reach Penrith. They had one horse, and Robert and Brian took turns walking while Morwenna rode. They had few belongings to bring with them, aside from armour and weapons. Brian had outgrown all his clothing, so Robert and Piers had given him what they could.

All of them were dressed simply, and Robert had hidden away his chainmail. For today, he'd been careful to wear only clothing that a serf might wear. His sword was strapped to his back, hidden by a cloak. He wanted to observe his estate and discover what had happened during the past two years before he determined his plan to win the lady's hand in marriage.

In the distance, he saw that the main castle walls had been rebuilt. His instincts sharpened, and although his uncle had told him about it, it felt strange to see the mortar and stones after he'd watched the previous wooden walls burn to the ground. The new Lord Penrith had made changes, and Robert grudgingly admitted that they were good ones.

He shielded his eyes from the sun and saw ripening grain in the fields. It occurred to him that their horse would draw attention, so he avoided the urge to continue onward. Instead, he led the animal into the nearby forest. Morwenna and Brian followed him while he tethered the gelding loosely to a tree near the stream. 'He'll be safe here until we return,' he told them.

'I'll stay with him,' Brian offered.

Robert glanced at Morwenna, but she shook her head. 'I'm coming with you.'

Though he didn't want to endanger her, it occurred to him that they might seem like less of a threat if they walked together. He gave a shrug and murmured his thanks to her brother.

Yet, his uncertainty only deepened as they left the forest. When they had walked a short distance, Robert asked softly, 'How is your brother? He still seems troubled.'

Morwenna kept her gaze fixed ahead. She offered no explanation for her brother's behaviour except to say, 'He feels guilty about what happened to our father that night. He blames himself.'

Robert sensed that there was a great deal she was holding back and didn't push for more answers. The boy had trained as hard as she had, but there was a rigid quality to his fighting— almost as if he doubted himself. Or perhaps it was hidden rage.

Whatever it was, the boy was safe now. No one would harm him or Morwenna again. And yet, Robert knew that they could only rely on themselves.

'Do you think anyone will recognise us?' Morwenna asked when they reached the edge of the forest. She reached for her short hair and tried to smooth it out. Even so, the wind tangled it around her face. He knew she was self-conscious about it, but the brown curls only accentuated her deep green eyes. She reminded him of a wood nymph—a little wild, yet lovely and fierce.

'I suppose they'll know who you are,' he said. 'But as for me? I doubt it. I rarely left the castle keep.'

'Why didn't you?'

'I was ill for many years when I was younger. Even after I got better, it didn't feel right to leave. People stared at me if I did. I think my father didn't want me to leave because he was ashamed of me. I knew nothing of fighting.'

'You know a great deal now,' she said.

But he didn't truly believe that. It was one thing to spar with Brian and Piers. It was quite another to fight against seasoned soldiers who were trained to kill.

He would have to study the other fighters and learn, Robert decided. There was no sense in worrying about the past. Not any more.

As they approached the fields, he saw men guarding the gates at intervals. Uneasiness washed over him as they continued their journey. Who were the soldiers? And what kind of man was the new Lord Penrith? His uncle suggested that there were problems, but it was difficult to say what they were.

Robert felt as if he'd stepped into another life. Instead of finding his lands in ruins, someone had already rebuilt the estate from the ashes.

They passed the fields of grain, and he saw a few familiar faces mingled with others he did not know. Most of the serfs paid them no heed. One man glanced up for a moment, but he immediately returned to his work. No one spoke—there was only the endless silence of labour.

That was what bothered him most—the lack of conversation among them. Something was wrong, but he didn't know what it was.

No one reacted to their presence. He fully expected them to recognise Morwenna, but if they did find her familiar, no one acknowledged her.

'We should go towards the castle to find our answers now,' Morwenna murmured. 'I don't think they're going to tell us anything here.'

He agreed with her and took her hand. They joined behind a large cart entering the gates, following the others before Robert pulled her back into the shadows. He didn't want anyone noticing them, and since it was a sennight before Midsummer, their presence would only draw attention. Morwenna stepped back to hide behind a wooden support beam beneath a parapet, while he studied their surroundings.

The new Earl of Penrith clearly had wealth and power. There was prosperity here, and the sight of it unravelled Robert's plans. He wasn't certain his people would welcome his return— they already had a leader. He turned to Morwenna, wondering what she thought of all this.

But she continued to stare, and he turned to see what she was looking at.

A noblewoman was walking down the stairs of the keep. She wore a grey gown, and her hair was the colour of sunlight. A golden circlet rested upon her brow, and she smiled at something her female companion said. It had to be the earl's daughter.

Robert studied her for a time, trying to determine what sort of person she was. He couldn't deny her beauty, but he noticed that Morwenna had shrunk down even lower. The two women could not be more different—the noblewoman had an innocent beauty and grace, whereas Morwenna's features were rough and raw. But he'd always admired her spirit and the way she was a survivor.

You have to marry the earl's daughter, he reminded himself. He couldn't let himself get distracted by Morwenna, no matter the reason. He studied the woman on the stairs, noticing the way her gaze fixed upon the horizon with a dreamy expression. Did she want to be married? Was this competition her idea or her father's?

'You should go and meet her,' Morwenna muttered. 'I'll go back and find Brian.'

Before he could ask her to wait, she had already slipped out of hiding and hurried towards the gates. He'd wanted to argue with her, but there was no point in doing so after she'd made a decision. Morwenna was strong-willed, and he suspected there were other reasons why she'd left.

As for himself, he wanted to watch and wait. He needed to discover who these people were and where their loyalties lay. He'd come here planning to rebuild his lands and petition the king to have his title restored. But now, he wondered if he'd made a mistake. King John had given his lands to someone else—and Penrith was thriving. They didn't need him.

He'd not expected to find it this way, but for a time, he watched the activity within the gates. There was a sense of order and an invisible air of command.

He was about to join Morwenna when a hand clamped down upon his. He spun, reaching for the hilt of his sword, before he recognised Henry the Fletcher. The man had been a trusted hunting friend of his father, and Robert had seen the pair of them drinking together on many occasions.

He was about to greet the man, but Henry shook his head in a silent warning. Then without another word, the man left.

Robert frowned, uncertain as to what was happening. There was no doubt Henry had recognised him, but he was being careful not to expose his identity. It meant that there was danger at the keep, something beneath the surface.

Perhaps things were a little too perfect, too controlled. He gave a slight nod, not knowing whether Henry saw it. Then Robert joined a small group of serfs and left the inner bailey before anyone else noticed him.

I never should have come to Penrith, Morwenna thought to herself.

It was bad enough knowing that Robert meant to court the earl's daughter. But watching his reaction when he saw the woman for the first time had brought back all her feelings of inadequacy.

A fierce jealousy caught her heart, though she knew she had no right to feel that way. He should marry someone like the nobleman's daughter, a beautiful lady who knew what it was to govern a castle. And surely, the young woman would be delighted by how handsome Robert was. If only it didn't hurt so much to see the admiration in his eyes when he'd glimpsed the young lady. Never had he looked at her in that way.

In one hand Morwenna carried a bundle that she'd retrieved from the old mill. She had returned to their former dwelling, hoping to find a shelter for her and Brian. Instead, there had only been the burned ruins of their home, and another mill had been constructed nearby. A heaviness centred within her chest at the knowledge that she could no longer go back. But then, Morwenna had suddenly remembered her mother's things that her father had hidden away. It had surprised her to find the bundle unharmed, tucked beneath a charred floorboard. She didn't know how it had escaped the fires that night, but she was glad to have it back.

Morwenna walked back to their camp and saw her brother napping against a tree. 'Brian.'

He jerked awake at the sound of her voice and scrambled to his feet. 'What's happened? Where is Robert?'

'He is back at the castle.' Her face reddened at the memory. 'I left him with the heiress.' She went over to stroke the horse, trying to act as if nothing was wrong. But she could feel the rise of humiliation in her face.

Her brother was watching her with suspicion. His gaze fixed upon the bundle she had brought from the mill. 'Did you go back home?'

She nodded. 'Father gave this to me not long ago. It belonged to our mother, and I didn't want to leave it behind.'

'Do you want to return to the mill tonight?' he offered.

Morwenna shook her head. 'There's not much

left of it. It wasn't rebuilt after the fire.' She had no wish to stay in a place that evoked such terrible memories. 'We'll remain here instead.'

Though she continued to pet the horse, rubbing his ears, her brother hadn't missed her darker mood. 'Something happened,' Brian predicted. 'Why are you so upset?'

She didn't answer, and he caught her hand, forcing her to look at him. His steady blue eyes made her realise that she was panicking like a coward. She took a deep breath, then another.

'I'm sorry,' she murmured. 'It's just... I thought I would be fine. But then, I realised Robert doesn't need us any more.'

She had wanted to believe that she could distance herself and help him achieve his goals. Instead, her hopes had been shattered by the sight of the beautiful noblewoman. The woman had been poised and lovely—everything Morwenna could only dream of becoming. And Robert had been caught up by the woman's appearance as if she'd cast her spell upon him. Humiliation had washed over her, and she'd wanted nothing more than to leave.

Brian took the reins of the horse from her. 'You shouldn't have raised up your hopes, Morwenna.'

She closed her eyes, wishing they had never

come. 'I know you're right.' She shook her head. 'I knew that when we came here, but I still wanted to be at his side.'

At that, her younger brother's eyes turned knowing. He reached for her hand again and held it. 'Morwenna…' There was a wealth of sympathy and warning in the single word. He knew, as she did, that the chances of Robert falling in love with her were almost impossible.

'I know,' she answered softly. But then again, she'd never openly admitted her feelings or tried to win Robert's interest. She'd dreamed that she could be part of his life somehow, and she had treasured each day with him. But the moment she'd seen him looking at another woman, she'd behaved like a coward, running away.

Yet she understood her brother's silent message. Now was not the time to turn around and give up. Robert still needed their help.

Brian pointed to the bundle. 'You never showed me what was inside.'

'It's just a gown,' she answered. 'Nothing much.'

Her brother didn't ask anything more, for he had little interest in clothing. 'What do you think Robert will do now?'

'He said he wanted to find out what was happening at Penrith. I think he plans to stay there and gather information. Or perhaps he'll try to court the heiress in secret.' She pushed back the rising jealousy, for it was likely they would have to join him.

'Then we need to go back,' Brian said. 'We have to find out what happened since we left Penrith.'

'Not yet,' she answered. 'It will only draw too much attention with three of us trying to blend in. You should go and hunt for our meal tonight. I'll stay here with the horse until you return.' She needed a few moments to herself, to tamp down her feelings. 'Robert will join us later and tell us what he's learned.'

'I don't want to leave you alone,' Brian protested.

At that, she smiled and rested her hand upon the hilt of her blade. 'Believe me when I say, no one will harm me. Anyone who tries will lose his hand.' At least she had the utmost confidence in her fighting abilities, thanks to their training.

'All right. But as soon as I've found food, I'll return.' Her brother turned to leave, and she held the horse's reins. Morwenna waited until he was gone and then walked towards a nearby pond. She splashed water to her face, clearing her thoughts.

She had spent the past two years training, in

order to transform herself. Her body was lean and muscled now, and she knew how to defend herself against any attacker. She would never be weak again.

But she now questioned the wisdom of that. It seemed that she had mistakenly led Robert to believe that fighting was what she wanted in life. That wasn't the truth at all. What she wanted was *him*. She had trained at his side, wanting to be noticed—craving his attention. And instead of seeing her as a woman, he saw her as a fellow soldier.

Morwenna leaned her forehead against a nearby tree, feeling utterly lost. She reached beneath her shift and withdrew the golden chain and pendant she'd retrieved from the mill. Although her mother had died years ago, her father had given it to her , along with the gown, saying that Morwenna was meant to have them.

It surprised her that her father Geoffrey had kept something so fine without selling it. Still, it was all she had left of Eldreth. She was glad she'd retrieved her mother's belongings for it gave her a tangible piece of her to keep.

Geoffrey had never spoken of Eldreth's past. Morwenna traced the engraving, wishing her mother had told stories about her family. From the fine material of the silk gown and the gold, she believed that Eldreth must have come from the nobility. She wished she had asked her mother questions about her past while she was still alive. But even if she had, Eldreth had never spoken much. They had never been close, though Morwenna had tried to be a good daughter to her. And now, she had no answers at all.

A dull ache caught in her throat. The last time she'd seen her father, their home had been on fire. He'd been trapped inside, and she'd heard his screams before the silence. There had been nothing more horrifying than to hear him die and be unable to stop it from happening. Even now, she could remember the choking smoke and the way she'd fought the rough hands of the soldiers as they'd dragged her away. Brian had tried to save her, only to be captured himself. She'd never understood why the soldiers had taken them prisoner instead of killing them outright. Perhaps they'd intended to make an example of their deaths or use them to coax others to do their bidding. Only Robert had helped them escape.

She tucked the pendant below her shift, feeling the warmth of the gold against her skin. She owed him everything. And until they knew he was safe, they ought to stay hidden. But eventually, she intended to disguise herself among the women, keeping her weapon close at hand, and guarding Robert as best she could.

It was all she could do for him.

Chapter Two

Robert followed Henry to the fields. His friend picked up a scythe, and he did the same, rolling back the sleeves of his tunic. The late-summer sun was warmer than usual, and he was surprised at the early harvest. Henry led him to a section of the field, and for a time, they cut grain side by side in silence.

It was unnerving how silent it was. No one spoke, no one sang. There was only the endless labour. Two riders patrolled on either side of the fields, each armed with a bow and quiver, as well as a sword. They were guarding the serfs, he realised. But why? Did the people not farm the land for a share in their own food and a place to live? There was no reason for guards.

He thought about speaking to Henry in a low voice but decided against it. If no one was speaking, there was a reason. The last thing he wanted was to draw attention to himself. He continued working, wondering where Morwenna and Brian had gone. At the time, he hadn't wanted her to leave, but now it seemed like the wisest course of action.

Morwenna wasn't the sort of woman who would remain quiet and obedient. She would demand answers and woe betide any man who tried to stop her. He hid a smile, thinking of her bold ways.

He wondered what the earl's daughter was like. From his brief glimpse of her, she seemed beautiful and kind, a good choice for a wife. Though, in truth, what did he really know about courting women? Morwenna was right. He did need to win the lady's consent, and he wasn't certain if winning the competitions would be enough.

He'd lived behind castle walls all his life with little interaction with women. Even the serving maids hadn't spoken to him much at all. He'd never really considered his ignorance of women to be a problem until now.

But then again, he was good at solving problems. All he had to do was take it apart into its simplest form. When a metal gear or a pulley was not oiled or cared for, it could break. Whenever he had taken something apart to learn why it was broken, inevitably one of the pieces had not been cared for. A woman ought to be the same, he decided. Like a hinge that needed to be oiled, he simply had to learn how to give her what she needed.

Robert decided he would ask Morwenna about it tonight. At least with her, he could speak freely, and she would answer with honesty.

He continued labouring alongside Henry for another hour, and after the sun grew hot, Robert motioned that he wanted a drink of water. His friend shook his head.

No water? What about food? He moved beside Henry and motioned about that, too. Again, the man silently refused.

Things were indeed worse than he'd imagined. Why would the people endure such an existence? His question was answered a moment later after an older man stumbled when he was reaching for a stalk of grain. The moment he hit the ground, one of the guards fired an arrow directly at him. The shaft embedded in the dirt, but not before the old man scrambled to his feet and lifted the scythe again.

Robert stared at the guard in shock. The old man had done nothing wrong, and he'd nearly been killed for it. These people were no better than slaves, held captive for their labour. He made a promise to himself that once he married the heiress, he would find a way to set them free from this misery. As for Morwenna or Brian, he intended to keep them both far away from this place. It wasn't safe.

After the day's work ended and the sun began to set, the people formed a single line. They were each given one drink of water from a wooden cup and one fist-sized serving of bread. There was no meat, no fish, nothing else to offer.

Why were the people not returning to their homes and enjoying their own meals? Why were they waiting in line for food? He couldn't understand it.

Robert drank the cup of water with his head lowered, not knowing if anyone would recognise him. If they did, they said nothing. He declined the food, intending to hunt later that night after he joined Morwenna and Brian. But first, he wanted to speak with Henry.

He followed the man back to his small roundhouse where his wife awaited him. Henry tore his bread in half and gave a portion to her. Robert wished he'd kept his portion, if for no other reason than to offer them more.

Only when Henry closed the door behind him did he speak in a low voice. 'You're alive.'

Robert nodded. 'I went into hiding after the

attack.' He didn't miss the glimpse of frustration on Henry's face, but there was nothing he could have done differently. 'Tell me what has happened here,' he urged. 'And why no one speaks.'

Henry glanced at his wife. 'King John sent Alfred of Tilmain to become Lord Penrith. At first, we were grateful. We thought he would help us.' With a shrug, he added, ''Twas winter, and when we needed shelter, Lord Penrith divided us among the remaining houses. He sent soldiers to help us rebuild, and we were grateful. In turn, we rebuilt the castle, and all of us laboured to restore it.

'We thought he'd be a good lord at first. But then, come the spring, the he started making changes to the way we planted our fields. He made us plant earlier, and we lost some of the seed to frost. One of the men—Justin the Cooper—defied Lord Penrith and argued with him in front of everyone. And he paid the price.'

'What kind of price?' Robert asked, though he suspected the worst.

'Lord Penrith brought Justin's family before him—his wife and four children. We weren't certain why, but I thought it was to bear witness. We thought Justin would be flogged for what he'd said. They had already bound his hands behind his back, and I saw one of the soldiers holding the whip. Then my lord said, "The actions of one man affect everyone. Rebellion is a poison that must be removed so it does not spread."' Henry grimaced and added, 'Then Lord Penrith took Justin's eldest son and had him flogged in front of everyone. The boy had done nothing wrong.'

Robert could hardly speak from the anger that flooded through him. 'And what did the people do after they saw it? What did Justin do?'

Henry made the sign of the cross. 'The new earl gave a signal, and the boy was released. After that, they slit Justin's throat. It was to remind us who was master of Penrith. We were not to question our lord's methods. Any hint of rebellion—any disobedience—would be punished with death.' His tone remained grim. 'And those of us with children would watch them suffer as well.'

Robert couldn't bring himself to speak. His skin had grown so cold with horror, for a moment he wondered what he'd done by returning. His people were held prisoner by a lord so vicious, he'd never imagined such retribution.

'What of your son? Is he—?'

'I sent him south to my brother, in secret,' Henry answered. 'I told him not to return. It was better that way. I don't know if he arrived there or not. But better to take the risk than stay here.'

His wife began weeping silent tears. Robert didn't know what to say to her, for even if he did win the lady's hand in marriage, he didn't know if he could overthrow the new Lord Penrith. Especially if the people were too frightened of the man.

'What did the king say when he learned of this?'

Henry shook his head. 'The king doesn't care what happens to serfs, my lord. No one does.'

Robert wanted to argue, *I care*, but the words meant nothing. Until he saved his people from this tyrant and cast him out, they were naught more than words.

'Lord Penrith is favoured by King John,' Henry said. 'We've seen him sending gifts to maintain his standing. Sheep, cattle, sometimes costly silks or jewels.'

'And where did he get these silks and jewels?'

'Possibly stolen from raids,' Henry admitted. 'He sends out groups of men every few weeks for supplies. We don't know for certain. But what we do know is that he demands obedience. If we do as he asks without question, and if we never bring our troubles to him, we live in peace.'

'What do you know of his daughter?'

'He keeps Lady Gwendoline away from us,' Henry answered. 'I don't believe she knows what's happening. Or if she does, she can do nothing to stop her father.'

'I came here to win her hand in marriage,' Robert said. 'I understand there will be competitions at Midsummer.'

'Aye, Lord Penrith plans to find a match for his daughter. But you've quite a task ahead of you, my lord. Penrith has invited suitors from all over. He has demanded a high bride price for Lady Gwendoline. I don't know how you'll pay it.'

'I thought the winner of the competitions would gain her hand.'

Henry slowly shook his head. 'Her father is using her to gain power in the north. These competitions are only for entertainment. Her true suitor must be a man of wealth and standing.'

The warning wasn't a surprise to Robert. 'I hope to regain my father's lands and bring everyone here under my protection. But no one can know who I am.'

Henry appeared uncertain. 'I will tell the others and ask them to say nothing.'

Robert gave a single nod, considering what Henry had said. He needed to speak with Morwenna and Brian to tell them what he'd learned. But more than all else, he needed them to stay away. If Morwenna dared to return, he had no doubt that her outspoken ways could put her in grave danger.

'Thank you for telling me all this,' Robert said quietly. 'I still hope to win the lady's hand. After that, I will do everything I can to free you.'

Henry's expression remained weary and full of doubts. 'I would like to believe that it's possible. But we've lived like this for nearly a year. It's not going to change.' He walked to the door with Robert. 'You'll have to get past his guards to reach the forest. I bid you good fortune, Robert of Penrith.'

It seemed he would need it.

Later that night, Morwenna had followed her brother to make camp beneath a stone overhang. Although it was a fair distance from Penrith, it provided shelter from the evening rain. Morwenna had cleaned and cooked the rabbits Brian had snared, and she'd saved a portion of the meat for Robert.

But as the hours went on, she sat beside the fire, keeping her knees drawn up. She didn't know if he would find them or even if he would want to return. Her mind conjured up images of him feasting with the new lord while his beautiful daughter gazed at Robert with adoration. The stone of jealousy weighed heavily in her gut, but she reminded herself that he didn't see her as a woman. Even if she told him of her feelings, it would make no difference. He was here to win the heiress, nothing more.

Brian had already gone to sleep, but Morwenna poked at the fire with a stick, unable to rest. The rain continued to spatter against the stone overhang, but at least the shelter kept the fire from going out. She stared at the flames until at long last, she saw Robert approaching.

Heedless of the rain, she ran to him. A hundred things crowded her mind. She wanted to know if he was all right, she wanted to apologise for leaving, and she wanted to know what he'd learned. In the end, all she could blurt out was, 'You found us.' Then she closed her eyes, cursing herself for behaving like an idiot. 'I mean, I'm glad you're here. Are you hungry?'

'Starved.' Robert smiled warmly at her, and his presence made her heart quicken. His hair was wet from the rain, along with his clothing. She made space for him by the fire and tried not to stare at the way his wet tunic clung to his muscles.

'Sit and warm yourself,' she said. 'I saved you some rabbit.'

'I could kiss you right now for that,' he teased.

His voice was deep, and it warmed her in spite of the rain.

I wish you would.

But she dismissed the thought, knowing it was too soon for that. Instead, she sat near him and asked, 'What did you learn at Penrith?'

He sobered while eating, as if trying to decide what to say. Then he admitted, 'You were right to leave earlier. It's not safe for either of you.'

'But why?' The castle keep had appeared in good condition after being rebuilt. She'd noticed that the homes of the serfs were also new, with freshly thatched roofs. The fields were golden with grain. Why would he say it wasn't safe? If anything, the lands appeared more prosperous than ever.

'Because the new Lord Penrith is a man who holds his serfs under an iron rule. They are all but slaves under his dominion. And I don't know how I can free them.' He told her a story about a man named Justin who had tried to protest and had lost his life because of it.

His voice held resignation and doubt, and Morwenna didn't know what answers to offer him. Instead, she murmured, 'I'm sorry to hear it.'

Robert finished the rabbit and afterwards held his hands out in front of the fire. He turned quiet, and she realised that he was still sitting in wet clothing. She went to the back of the shelter and retrieved a fur from their belongings. 'Here,' she offered. 'You may want to dry off and get warm.'

He thanked her and stripped off the soaked tunic. She caught a glimpse of skin and sinewy muscle that made her heartbeat quicken. He pulled the fur across his shoulders, and when he saw her staring, she turned away.

'What will you do?' she asked.

'I haven't decided yet. I should probably stay so I can gain more knowledge about the earl's defences and his soldiers. But he cannot know who I am, and I fear others might recognise me. I spoke with Henry the Fletcher, and he will try to silence them. But I don't know what will happen if the earl learns the truth about who I am.'

'I lived at Penrith for a year, and I only saw you twice from a distance, in all that time,' she said. 'There's a strong chance they won't recognise you.'

Robert's expression turned grim. 'It shouldn't be that way. Sometimes I wish my father hadn't allowed me to stay indoors, surrounding myself with books. He should have forced me to train with his men.'

Morwenna agreed with him but didn't voice the words. Instead, she said, 'It may be an advantage to you now. They won't suspect you've returned.'

'I don't see how it could be an advantage. Especially after we fled.'

'I disagree,' she said. 'Let the people believe you are there to find a way to free them. They won't betray you if they think you are their salvation. They may even find a way to help you during the competitions.'

He picked up a piece of firewood from beneath the overhang and tossed it on the flames. 'I'm no one's salvation, Morwenna. If anything, I'm a coward who deserves to lose everything. It's the people who didn't deserve this.'

She saw the bitterness in his gaze, the hollow sense of guilt. 'Then do something about it. Put your doubts aside and help them.'

He stared at the flames for a time, gripping the edges of the fur. 'I want to, believe me. But I don't know where to start.'

'Gather information in secret,' she suggested. 'I can do the same, and so can Brian.'

'No. I don't want either of you in danger. You'll stay here, and I'll return to you at nightfall.'

Though she knew his command was voiced out of concern, it conjured up her own sense of rebellion. Did he expect her to wait here, day after day, until he returned? That wasn't at all what she wanted.

'So, you'd rather be a martyr and leave us wondering what's happened to you?' She shook her head. 'No. I'm not going to wait here. We go together or not at all.'

His gaze darkened, and he took her hand in his. The touch startled her, and he squeezed her palm. 'While I admire your courage, this isn't wise.'

'What *you're* doing isn't wise,' she murmured. 'You could be captured again if the earl learns who you are.'

'But he won't. I'll make certain of that.' He reached for his tunic and laid it out beside the fire to dry.

Morwenna watched him again, distracted by the way his skin gleamed in the firelight against the flames. For a man who had been so isolated all his life, she couldn't help but admire the way he'd transformed himself.

She reached out to warm her own hands by the fire. Robert moved closer beside her and dropped the other end of the fur over her shoulders. Her thoughts grew scattered at his nearness.

'There's something I've been wanting to ask you,' he said. 'About women.'

It was the last thing she'd expected him to say. 'Wh-what do you want to know?'

'I've been thinking about what you said. About winning the heart of Lady Gwendoline.'

She hardly knew what to say. His bare shoulder was touching hers, and she could feel his body warmth beside her.

'I need to know what a woman truly wants.' He started talking about tools and how to care for them. Something about hinges and oil and God knew what else. She was too distracted by his skin, the masculine scent that made her want to press her lips to his shoulder.

'Morwenna?' he asked. 'If I'm to court the Lady Gwendoline, I need to understand what she needs.'

Her face burned hot, but she answered honestly. 'A woman needs love. She needs to know that a man has feelings for her, that he cares what happens to her.'

Against the firelight, she saw him frown. 'I don't even know the lady. I can protect her, but I'm not certain I can pretend to love someone I've only just met.'

'No, but you should get to know her,' Morwenna suggested.

'How?' He stared at the crackling flames and added, 'I'm not sure I believe the minstrels who sing love songs about shepherdesses. And I can't exactly tell the lady that I love her when it's not true.'

Morwenna held her silence, for she didn't want to help him at all. Not in this.

'I could tell her she's beautiful, for that's true enough,' Robert mused. 'Do you think that would work?'

She shrugged.

Keep your mouth shut, she warned herself.

'Morwenna?' he prompted.

'I don't know, Robert. You'll have to find that out for yourself.'

He appeared lost in thought, his brow furrowed. And then, against her better judgment, Morwenna blurted out, 'What does she enjoy doing for amusement?' At his blank look, she nudged, 'Perhaps she likes to sew. Or she may enjoy riding.'

He seemed to consider her words. 'The way you like to fight.'

'No. I don't enjoy fighting at all.'

At that, he gaped at her. 'But you trained with us for two years.'

'Only because I wanted to defend myself. Not because I liked it.'

He appeared utterly confused by her words. 'But the shield…'

She'd left it behind but chose her answer carefully, not wanting to hurt his feelings. 'I know you wanted to give me a gift, but Brian could use it more than me. I appreciated the thought. You meant well.'

Robert let out a sigh. 'I suppose I'll have to give the lady a gift. And a shield won't be appropriate.' He stared into the flames. 'I don't have silver, so I suppose I'll have to think of something else. Perhaps flowers.'

'You could,' she agreed. 'Or perhaps a food she likes. Or an animal to love, like a kitten.' Her face softened at the thought.

'Was that what you wanted?' he asked quietly. The yearning in her heart rose up so strong, it took effort to push back the feelings. He was asking her for the sake of someone else.

'It doesn't matter what I wanted,' she answered. 'I'm not the woman you are courting.' The words were bitter, but she needed to push him away.

'No, you're right.' Robert reached for her hand, absently caressing her palm with his thumb. 'I suppose I should study Lady Gwendoline during the next few days. That would give me an advantage over the others.'

He seemed unaware of the effect he had on

her. The gesture nearly undid her senses, though she knew it was foolish to imagine more.

'Robert, don't,' she warned, pulling her hand from his. To him, the caress was only a gesture of friendship. But to her, it crossed a boundary, making her dream of more. She didn't want to be an afterthought, a woman in the shadows while he dreamed of courting someone else.

'Sorry.' He laid the fur across her shoulders and stood. Then he stared off into the distance, lost in thought. Against the firelight, she saw the gleam of his muscled chest, the strength of his arms. Her attraction was so strong, she wondered what would it be like to lie beside him at night, to feel those arms around her? The longing caught in her heart while he chose a different blanket from his own belongings. She imagined the two of them sheltered together, skin to skin with the furs surrounding both of them. Her heart pounded while she watched him in silence.

Though she wanted to believe that she meant something to him, she was not the woman he needed. She had nothing at all to offer. At least, not yet. But inwardly, she made a silent promise of her own. If he needed information, she could gather it in a different way.

He wanted her to remain hidden and stay out

of danger. But he was about to learn that she could easily disguise herself and become who she needed to be.

During the next two days, Robert worked among the men, listening for whatever he could learn. Henry had given him a place to sleep on a pallet, and he'd tried to make himself invisible among the others, so as not to attract notice. On occasion, he saw a nod from one of the serfs, but no one gave his presence away. He wondered if Henry had spoken to them or if they suspected why he'd returned to Penrith. For now, he was grateful for their silence.

Thus far in his quest for information about Lady Gwendoline, he'd learned that she enjoyed the outdoors. Each day, she would walk along the parapets, staring off into the distance and lifting her face to the sun.

Still, it wasn't enough. He needed to get closer to her, to meet her in secret if possible. But she remained heavily guarded inside the castle keep. He planned to speak to Henry about her that night, to see if it was worth an attempt to slip inside the castle walls.

It was already late in the day, and soon enough, it would be time to stop labouring in the fields. But Robert grew distracted by the sound of approaching horses. He turned and saw a cloaked woman accompanied by a single guard. He couldn't quite tell who it was, but the soldiers opened the gates without question.

He sent Henry a questioning look, but the man could only shrug. Robert's instincts went on alert at the sight of them. He joined the line of men for water and bread, using it as the chance to take a closer look.

One of the soldiers helped the woman down, and he led her towards the inner bailey. At that moment, she lowered her hood. Robert froze when he realised who it was.

Somehow, Morwenna had managed to buy a green gown. She had tamed her shoulder-length dark hair into a simple arrangement, and around her throat, she wore a golden chain and pendant.

For a moment, he could only stare at her. He'd never seen Morwenna like this, and it felt as if he'd been struck by a longstaff. He'd grown accustomed to her hiding her body within trews or a tunic. He'd never realised it, but the gown revealed her slender form and generous curves he'd never suspected she had.

A forbidden longing tightened within him, the unexpected heat of desire he was trying to suppress. He wanted to rest his hands around that waist and explore her softness. It was as if she'd tamed her wild beauty to captivate him, tempting him with a glimpse of bare skin at her throat. He imagined pressing his mouth to that skin, wondering how she would react.

Had she always looked like this? Or had he been too blind to see it? As she turned back, there was a deceptive vulnerability about her. She appeared shy and demure, like a woman in need of protecting. But he knew well enough that she could defend herself.

'Who is the woman?' he asked the soldier distributing the bread. Though he knew the answer well enough, he wanted to know what story she was telling the others.

'We found her on the road just now,' the man answered. 'She said that she and her escorts were attacked and robbed.'

Robert nodded in reply and took the bread while he walked towards the gates. He finished the food and then followed a group of men inside. Anyone would believe that Morwenna was a noblewoman, from her appearance. She carried herself with her shoulders back, her chin raised up. Brian had disguised himself as her personal guard. They started to ascend the stairs, but within moments, Lady Gwendoline led her inside the castle keep.

What was Morwenna doing? She'd somehow

infiltrated the most dangerous place of all. It was both reckless and brilliant. She would be privy to the information he needed, but what would happen if someone recognised her as the miller's daughter? She could be harmed by the new lord or his guards, and Robert would be powerless to stop them.

Unless he followed her inside the keep.

It was a terrible risk, but one he had to take. For a moment, he questioned whether to reveal himself as a suitor. But no, it was too early for that. Better to wait until the other men arrived. Instead, he planned to slip inside the castle to try to learn more about the lady.

Robert studied the movement of the people within the castle and saw several servants carrying platters of food towards the keep. If he kept his head down, there was a chance he could go unnoticed. He waited until a small group of serfs approached the keep, and he lifted his hood to hide his face. When he reached the entrance near the guards, he lowered his head and followed the men inside.

The men began to disperse, and Robert continued towards the kitchens. It was the best way to get inside the keep, for he could carry food to the lord's table. He needed to know what Morwenna was doing, but more than that, he wanted to ensure that he could protect her. She had no idea of the danger she could face. And though her brother was with her, if they caught her in the lies... God help them both.

Robert had nearly reached the entrance of the kitchens when suddenly a hand clamped down on his shoulder and someone stripped the hood away. He spun with his fists raised...only to see the cook.

When the man caught sight of him, he stared at Robert. Years ago, Wilfred had slipped him occasional honey cakes, and Robert had given the cook a few silver coins in return. There was no doubt he'd been recognised.

Robert gave the cook a slight nod of acknowledgement before he picked up one of the food platters. Then he turned and held Wilfred's gaze for a long time, silently questioning whether the man would give away his presence. Instead, the cook turned away.

Robert followed the men into the keep towards the Great Hall. He carried a platter of roasted capon, and the scent made his mouth water. Like the other servants, he brought the food to the new Lord Penrith, who was seated upon the dais. Lady Gwendoline had offered Morwenna a seat beside her, while a servant had taken her cloak. Robert approached the earl and offered a portion of the capon. The man sliced off a wing and then served his daughter Gwendoline without sparing Robert a single glance.

But when Robert reached Morwenna, her eating knife clattered upon the table, her eyes widening. Then she covered her reaction by saying to Lady Gwendoline, 'Forgive me. I fear that my weariness has caught up with me.'

'I understand,' the lady soothed. 'I will find a place for you to sleep, and you may stay with us until your father arrives.'

Morwenna gave the woman a nod, and Robert had no choice but to continue serving the other high-ranking members of the lord's retinue. It seemed that her lie had worked. But before he departed, he met her gaze once more. He needed to speak with her, but it was too dangerous here. He glanced over at the door, hoping she would meet with him outside the keep tonight.

She gave no indication that she understood his message, but instead turned back to Lady Gwendoline and conversed with her.

Robert followed the other men back to the kitchens, sneaking a bite of the remaining capon as he did. He'd underestimated Morwenna. Though she'd been born a serf, he was startled to see how easily she fit in. Her talent for imitating the nobility made it clear that she could easily take a lady's place here. He'd never known she was so observant. He'd been accustomed to the fierce warrior she'd become, not the guise of the gentle lady. Now he was wondering how well he knew her at all.

Where had she found the dress and the pendant? Her transformation unsettled him, for the new image was now branded in his mind. The green silk bliaud had clung to her slender form, the voluminous sleeves blending in with the long skirts. The colour had only accentuated her dark hair, and he'd never truly imagined she could be so desirable.

When he returned to the kitchens, Wilfred dismissed the others but ordered Robert to stay behind, claiming that he would have to help with cleaning. He obeyed, dipping one of the knives in water and scouring it with sand until the men and maids were gone.

Only after they were alone did Wilfred address him. 'I cannot believe you're alive, my lord.'

'Do not call me that here,' Robert warned. 'I've asked the others not to acknowledge me. It's better to pretend I'm a stranger, for if Lord Penrith learns who I am...'

'He'll have you killed,' Wilfred finished. 'Aye, it's not safe.'

And the more people who recognised him, the greater the risk. 'I intend to court his daughter and gain her hand in marriage without the earl knowing who I am.'

The cook's expression turned grim. 'And when the king finds out what you've done?'

He didn't understand what Wilfred was inferring. 'I've done nothing wrong.'

'Your father was executed for treason. He refused to pay the higher taxes King John demanded and was accused of conspiring against him. If you try to claim Penrith, both the king and the earl might try to implicate you in your father's misdeeds,' Wilfred warned.

Robert sobered. Though he had never been close to his father, he hadn't understood why the king's men had attacked that night. His uncle had never told him the reasons, probably to protect him. It bothered him even more to realise that the king's men had taken him and Piers, intending to use them as leverage.

'After you escaped captivity, they searched everywhere for you,' the cook continued. 'I heard the soldiers that night. It's by God's grace that you escaped, my lord.'

Though he'd known they were in danger, he'd never really understood how grave it was. 'What of my father's wife?' Robert asked. 'Does she live?'

Wilfred shook his head. 'She was killed the night we were attacked.'

A pang caught Robert, for although Clarine was not his mother, his father's wife had always been kind to him. She'd never had any children of her own, but she had treated him as if he were her own.

Robert added, 'I want to watch over Morwenna and Brian. They are staying in the castle tonight.' Although they had made the decision to come here, he felt responsible for them.

The cook opened a small storage pantry with herbs and braided onions hanging from the rafter. There were several sacks of grain stacked against one wall. Wilfred added, 'You can sleep here, my lord. It's not much, but no one will find you.'

'Thank you. It will only be for a little while until after I've joined the other suitors. I won't forget your kindness.' He was grateful to have an ally in the castle, someone who could help him find out more about Lady Gwendoline.

And he needed to be nearby to ensure that Morwenna was safe.

It was late at night when Morwenna left her bed. Lady Gwendoline had offered her a place to sleep in her own chamber, and she had readily agreed, for she'd never seen anything so fine. The sheets were soft, and the brazier of burning peat kept it warm within the room. Not like the hayloft she'd slept in so many nights during her childhood. She longed to stay and sleep, but she also knew that Robert wanted to see her. The look of shock on his face when he'd served her at table had warmed her with pride, for he'd not known she could blend in so seamlessly.

She had mimicked Lady Gwendoline's manners, and they had believed her tale of being attacked on the main road and robbed. Lord Penrith had promised to send word to her father— but of course, no one would be able to find him, for he was dead.

Brian had dined with the other soldiers, keeping to himself. His height disguised his age of fifteen years, but she wondered if the other soldiers suspected anything. Her brother had a way of blending in while others conversed around him. It seemed that she had done the same, for no one recognised her. Her mood dimmed at the realisation that she truly had made no friends among the villagers. She was more alone than she'd thought.

She needed to speak with Robert, but she had to wear the old clothing she'd brought with her.

It would be easier to avoid questions if she disguised herself as a boy. Morwenna tucked her hair beneath a cap and tiptoed outside the chamber and down the stairs. She continued around the sleeping men and women in the Great Hall until she managed to slip outside. She didn't know where to find Robert, but she intended to start near the kitchen since he'd brought food to the table. It was dangerous, but Morwenna had to take the risk.

As she walked through the darkness, the chill in the air seemed to sink into her bones. She had shared a table with the earl and Lady Gwendoline, and outwardly, they had seemed like good people. Robert's earlier claim, that the serfs were being treated like slaves, seemed like an exaggeration. But the silence of the people made her question what was real and what was not.

When she reached the kitchens, she paused at the doorway, studying her surroundings. The men guarding the keep would only see a boy in search of food, if they cared to look. She moved inside the doorway and nearly screamed when a hand clamped over her mouth.

'Don't speak,' Robert murmured. 'Come with me.'

She nearly sagged with relief but obeyed. He led her into a smaller storage pantry and closed the door behind him. It was so dark she couldn't quite see him.

'I'm glad you're all right, Morwenna,' he said, keeping his hands upon her shoulders. 'But I cannot believe you took the risk of entering the keep tonight. You could have been killed. Or worse.'

She was taken aback by his words and his overbearing tone. 'You really don't have faith in me, do you?'

In answer, he pulled her into a hard embrace, and her cap fell off. He rested his face against her hair, and she fought the rise of her own emotions. In one move, he'd disarmed her completely.

For a moment, she savoured the unexpected affection, even as she warned herself, *It means nothing. Do not let yourself believe it's more.*

He pulled away at last and brought her to sit on a large sack of grain. 'Tell me what you've learned.'

She knew this wasn't about gossip, but instead answered, 'The earl keeps twenty soldiers in the keep and another two dozen around the inner bailey. Six more are on horseback guarding the fields. They have a few archers among them, but most are swordsmen.'

'Why so many?'

She shook her head. 'I don't think all of them are his own men. I think at least half may be the king's soldiers, but I don't know why they're here.'

He sat back, thinking in silence. She knew he was trying to make decisions, but she didn't know what he would do now.

'What of his daughter?' he asked. 'What have you learned about her?'

'Lady Gwendoline knows very little about what is happening among the people. She is uneasy about the Midsummer competitions and her father's plans to arrange her betrothal.'

He seemed to think it over. 'Has she said anything about it? Will her father truly allow her to make the choice?'

She gave a shrug. 'Neither of us knows. She has said that there are very few men who meet her father's standards.'

Robert leaned back against the sack of grain, and as they spoke in the darkness, she felt a sense of intimacy between them. 'What do you think of her?'

She answered honestly. 'I like her. She's kind, and it seems as if Gwen tries to see the best in everyone.'

He seemed to think it over. 'She's his only heir, isn't she?'

'She is.' Morwenna closed her eyes, for the thought of him courting Lady Gwendoline was a blade in her heart. She knew this was why he'd come back to Penrith. And she'd known that she had no chance of winning Robert's affections.

Life was unfair in so many ways. If she had been born to nobility instead of to a miller, *she* could have been wed to a man like Robert. She wanted to curse her low birth, for it had destined her to a life of poverty. In the darkness, she reached for the gold pendant, wishing she'd known the name of her mother's family. Her mother had never spoken of them, and whenever Morwenna had asked questions, Eldreth had ignored them. Even her father had told her nothing when he'd given her the gown and pendant. So many secrets…and now she would never have her answers.

'I need to meet Lady Gwendoline,' Robert said at last. 'Can you arrange it?'

His question caught her off-guard, and she answered, 'Possibly. But what if she learns who you really are?'

'It's a risk,' Robert agreed. 'But Lord Penrith doesn't know I am here.'

She tightened the iron grip around her feelings. 'You cannot hide who you are for ever. If they find out the truth…'

'They won't. I've asked the others not to reveal my identity. I might even use another name during the competitions.'

'I don't like it,' she confessed. 'It's dangerous.'

But more than that, she was afraid he would succeed in winning Gwendoline's hand in marriage. Against her will, the emotions rose up within her, her heart aching in her chest.

You knew this was why he came to Penrith.

But he did not share her feelings. It would only embarrass both of them if she revealed the truth.

'Are you certain this is what you want?' she managed to ask. 'To marry her?'

'What I want is to restore Penrith and help my people. I intend to become the earl I was supposed to be. And if wedding the lady is the means to that end, so be it.'

Morwenna didn't know how to respond to that. Though it was tearing her feelings apart, she forced herself to close them off. 'All right.'

'I need your help, Morwenna,' Robert admitted. 'I haven't been around women often, except you. I don't know how to court Lady Gwendoline.'

A hard lump caught in her throat, though she'd known he would need her help. 'Just be kind to her.'

'Ah, Morwenna,' he sighed. 'Would that it

were so easy.' He reached out and took her hand. 'I don't know what to say or how to behave.'

The touch of his hand on hers only heightened her misery. She both welcomed his touch and wanted to tear her hand away. It weighed upon her, and she wished she could simply blurt out the truth. But then, he might pity her for feelings he didn't return. Instead, she squeezed his hand, enjoying the slight attention even if it meant nothing to him.

He paused a moment and asked, 'Where *did* you get that gown and the pendant?'

'They were hidden back at the mill,' she answered. 'They're all I have left of my mother.'

His thumb traced a circle over her palm. 'Were they hers?'

She understood his unspoken question about Eldreth's past and nodded. 'I suppose she was a woman of wealth who fell in love with the wrong man.' The words held a heavier cast to them, for she felt the sting of them. She knew exactly why her mother might have left everything behind—Morwenna would have done the same for Robert—and Eldreth had likely surrendered everything for her marriage. Her family, her riches…all of it.

Yet, somehow Morwenna suspected there was more to the story. Her father had always appeared so ordinary. Geoffrey had never appeared to be the sort of man who would inspire a deep and abiding love. And while her mother had kept the house, cooked the meals, and had taken care of her and her brother, her parents' marriage had not seemed as strong as it could be.

'Do you remember her?' Robert asked.

Morwenna nodded. 'I was twelve when she died. It was after a winter illness. She hardly ever spoke to us, and we weren't close. Sometimes I wonder if she missed her family. It often seemed like she didn't care very much.'

'I'm surprised your father brought you to Penrith. Most folk don't leave their villages or their families.'

She wasn't at all surprised. Her father had never stayed in one place for long. 'He wasn't always a miller. I remember him trying many different things. He laboured in the fields one summer. The next year, he tried learning how to brew ale. One year, he even sold ribbons at a fair.' She leaned back against the sack of grain. 'He always seemed rather lost. And after my mother died, perhaps it was true.'

'Did your father die on the night of the attack?' Robert asked.

'Yes. And I don't want to speak of it.' She never wanted to remember the sound of him dying, and she let go of Robert's hand. 'It's late. I should go back.'

He stood beside her and offered, 'I'll speak with Brian tomorrow and find out what he's learned from the men. Find out if there's a way for me to meet with the lady and let me know. I am staying in the kitchens.'

'I'll try.' She paused at the doorway, wishing she could say the words buried inside. But what good would it do? He had never seen her as a woman he could love. Better to put those useless thoughts aside.

And as she turned away, she cursed herself for her cowardice.

Chapter Three

Morwenna awakened to the sound of Lady Gwendoline speaking in hushed tones to her maid. She rose from the bed she'd shared last night and stretched. It seemed strange to enjoy a feather mattress after she'd grown accustomed to sleeping on the floor.

'I am sorry if I woke you,' Gwendoline apologised. 'We tried to be quiet.'

'I did not mean to lie abed for so long.' Morwenna reached for her mother's gown, but before she could put it on, the maid took it from her.

'I will help you dress, my lady.'

She thanked her, and the maid helped her lace up the back of the gown. Gwendoline turned a critical eye. 'Is that the only gown you have to wear?'

Morwenna nodded, feeling the invisible criticism. 'I know it's not what the other ladies are wearing, but my belongings were stolen.'

'Hmm.' Gwendoline studied her closely. 'I think I have something that might fit you. The hem will need to be let down, but Aelish could do it for you.'

'I couldn't possibly ask that of you,' Morwenna argued.

'Don't be foolish. I have dozens of gowns. Whenever my father travels on the king's business, he brings back something new for me.' Gwendoline smiled brightly as if it meant nothing at all.

Inwardly, Morwenna wondered if her father had been looting castles and bringing back the spoils of battle. But she said nothing about it.

'Aelish, go and fetch the crimson bliaud. I think that would suit Morwenna's dark hair very well.' After the maid departed, Gwendoline lowered her voice. 'I know you said you were set upon by thieves on your journey home. But there's more to this, isn't there?'

The woman's voice was calm, offering a listening ear. It was almost tempting to lay the truth before her, but there was no reason to take such a risk.

Yet, at the same time, Morwenna saw an opportunity. Perhaps a version of the truth might help.

She hesitated and nodded at last. 'Some of what I told you was true. I was attacked.' She shuddered at the memory of the king's soldier who had torn her gown two years ago. 'But my father is dead. He was killed in a raid and... I don't know where I can go now. Our lands were taken from us.' She reached for Gwendoline's hands. 'Please don't tell anyone. I just need some time to decide where I can go that would be safe.'

'What about your mother's kin?' the lady suggested.

'I thought of that, but I don't know where to begin.' Morwenna released her hands and admitted, 'My mother died a few years ago. She never spoke of her family and she...married below her rank. I suspect her family cast her off.' Morwenna held out the necklace. 'This was hers.'

'Then we have a mystery to solve,' Gwendoline said, her eyes gleaming with interest. 'And until we find your mother's family, you will stay with me as one of my ladies.'

'Won't your father command me to leave?' She couldn't imagine that the Earl of Penrith would want to take in a stranger.

'I will tell him that we must also send word to your mother's family. It will be safer for you to remain here until your escort arrives.'

'I don't want you to lie on my behalf,' Morwenna said. 'I really don't know where to find them.'

'But we will find out,' Gwendoline promised. 'I would be glad to help you.'

'I am grateful.' Although she wasn't certain it was wise, Morwenna asked, 'And what of you, Lady Gwendoline? I overheard that your father is hosting a feast at Midsummer to help you find a husband.' With a light smile, she enquired, 'Is there anyone who has caught your attention?'

The lady's expression grew wistful as if she wanted to say something but then changed her mind. 'Not yet, though my father keeps suggesting different alliances. I told him that I will gladly wed, but only a man of honour. So many of them tell lies that they think I will not see through.'

The maid returned with the crimson gown, and Morwenna marvelled at its beauty. She had never worn anything so fine in all her life. Although she had done well at mimicking the behaviour of the nobles, this gown surely cost more than her father had earned in a year. It only reminded her of how she did not fit in among these people.

'I like this colour on you,' Gwen said while Aelish helped her to change. 'And while we are talking of husbands, what of you? Did your father have the chance to arrange your own betrothal before he died?'

Morwenna shook her head, though she felt a warmth in her cheeks. 'No, he did not.'

'But there *was* someone, wasn't there?' Gwendoline predicted. 'I can see it in your eyes. Do tell me about him.' Her eyes sparkled. 'Is he handsome?'

Morwenna sighed. 'I have never seen a more handsome man. But he does not know of my feelings.'

'You should tell him,' Gwen suggested. 'Let him know what is in your heart.'

'I cannot,' she protested. 'He doesn't seem to notice me. And if he did know of my feelings, and I wasn't enough, it would…hurt too much.' It startled her that it was so easy to talk to Gwendoline.

The lady smiled. 'Then we will have to change that, won't we? I think you should join me at the competitions, and we will invite the man who has captured your heart.'

'He is already intending to come,' she admitted. 'And that is part of the reason why he does not hold affection towards me. He plans to court you instead.'

Gwendoline turned serious. 'If you tell me who he is, I will not choose him. I promise you.'

Morwenna didn't know what to say, for Robert's only reason for coming to Penrith was to wed the lady.

Gwendoline saved her from answering by continuing, 'Then we will make you so gloriously beautiful, he will fall on his knees to have you.' The lady put her arm around her and led her to sit upon a chair. 'Aelish will fix your hair. Were you ill last year? It looks as if someone cut it.'

'I had a fever,' Morwenna lied. 'It has taken time to grow back.'

'Well, she can pin it up for you, and with the right veil and jewels, no one will know.' She reached back and pulled Morwenna's hair up. For a moment she grew quiet and then said, 'Do you know how long it's been since I've had a friend to talk to? I've missed it so much.' She let Morwenna's hair fall and said, 'Ever since we came here, it's felt like an exile.'

There was an opportunity here to ask questions. Morwenna ventured, 'It does seem a little strange at Penrith. The people don't talk as much as I'm used to.'

The expression on Gwen's face grew grim. 'A month after we arrived, there was a man who was causing trouble. Justin was his name. He kept defying orders, and one night, he tried to murder my father. He nearly succeeded in stabbing him in his sleep.'

'I'm so sorry,' Morwenna said. This wasn't at all what she'd heard from Robert, and it made her wonder what the truth was.

'My father hid his wounds from the people. He didn't want to look weak in front of them, but he had no choice but to have Justin executed for his crimes. Ever since then, it's been different.'

'I think the people are afraid,' Morwenna suggested.

Gwen nodded. 'But what choice did Father have? He couldn't allow someone to stab him and let that go unpunished.'

Morwenna nodded in agreement, but it still seemed as if the earl had told his daughter a different version of the truth. She decided not to say anything.

'But let's not talk of that any more,' Gwen said. 'I want you to tell me about the man you are hoping to wed. And then, on the morrow when we go hunting, I will speak to my father about it.'

It was just the sort of opening Robert would want. Not only the chance to court Lady Gwendoline as a suitor, but during the hunt, he might have the chance to meet her privately.

'I will ask Father to let you choose from among the remaining men,' Gwendoline continued. 'I must choose first, of course, but you may have second choice if you wish. And I promise I will not choose your man, if he comes to compete.'

'Do you think your father will agree to this?'

Gwen linked her arm with Morwenna's. 'Of course, he will. Now tell me of your perfect husband.'

Robert wandered through the cellar, running his hands along the cool stones that lined the walls. Wilfred had sent him to find a cask of wine, but as he walked through the familiar area, he stopped in front of a small passageway that led uphill.

A forgotten memory crept into his mind of the years he'd fought off death. The illness had held him captive within these walls, and he'd never really known what it was or why he'd been so sick. Or even more, why he'd started healing for no apparent reason.

One memory, in particular, stood out in his mind. He'd been violently ill for most of the day, only to see a tapestry rippling on the opposite wall. Moments later, he saw a young boy watching him.

The boy's face held concern. 'You're very sick, aren't you? I thought they were lying to me.'

'Who are you?' he managed to ask, his voice

hoarse. When he tried to sit up, dizziness washed over him, and he sank back on the bed.

'Piers,' *the boy* answered.

From his ragged clothing and tangled hair, Robert guessed he was one of the stable boys or the son of a serf. But the boy walked past the tapestry, staring at Robert's bedchamber.

Then he came *closer and touched the bed coverlet.* 'This is yours?'

He nodded. Another wave of illness washed over him, and he tried to hold back the nausea. 'Please go.' *He* didn't *want the boy to be there while he heaved out his guts.*

But the boy never *moved.* 'You don't understand.'

'What?' *he gritted out, clenching the sheets.*

'I'm your brother,' *the boy said.* 'I found out from the cook. I thought we could—'

'Get out!' *Robert ordered. He reached beneath the bed for the pot, and barely made it before he vomited. The humiliation and wrenching pain made his eyes water.*

The boy retreated, staring at him. 'But...'

'Just leave me.' *His voice broke in a whisper, for he believed he* would *die in a few days. The pain never ended, and he was weary from lack of food or sleep.* 'I don't want to be your brother,' *he whispered.* 'Or your friend.'

The words were cruel, but better that than to become attached to anyone. The only person he ever saw was his father's wife Clarine. His own mother had been dead for years.

Piers's expression turned stony. And then he disappeared behind the tapestry, closing the hidden door behind him.

The memory of that day had crept in without warning. But it had been the start of his brother's hatred. By the time Robert regained his strength, Piers treated him like a despised enemy. His half-brother constantly played tricks on him, stealing his medicine or food. Clarine found out and sent the boy away to live in the stables.

Piers's mother had died a year later and after that, Robert rarely saw his half-brother. His father had ignored his bastard son completely, which wasn't right. But despite Robert's desire to end the animosity with his brother, there was no opportunity. Piers had begun working alongside the other serfs, accepting the life he'd been given. It was only after they'd spent two years together, after their escape, that they had begun to mend the rift between them. And mostly it was because he'd given Piers someone to fight. Many were the nights when both of them were bruised and bleeding after a long day of sparring.

It was strange to realise that he missed his brother.

Robert rested his hand upon a wooden barrel, wondering what had become of Piers. It had felt wrong to leave him behind, but his stubborn half-brother had refused to join them. He could only hope that Piers would somehow earn his fortune and find the happiness he wanted.

Robert found the cask of wine and brought it back to the kitchen. Wilfred had already gone to bed, so he returned to the small pantry space. He lit an oil lamp and then heard the sound of footsteps approaching.

The door opened, and he saw that once again, Morwenna had dressed as a boy to escape notice. She closed the door behind her and said, 'Lord Penrith is taking us hunting tomorrow. I think that may be your chance to meet with Lady Gwendoline.'

'It's a good idea,' he agreed. 'Thank you for telling me.'

She sat upon one of the sacks of grain and pulled off her cap. Dark hair spilled out, and he detected a faint floral aroma. He inhaled deeply but couldn't quite place the scent. It was a scent that reminded him of something from long ago. But what was it? He came closer and drew a lock of her hair to his nose.

'Robert, what are you doing?' Morwenna looked aghast. 'Are you smelling my hair?'

He was but saw no harm in it. 'Is it rose petals?'

'Lilac,' she corrected.

That was it. It reminded him of the herbs his mother had used in her bath. At night when he'd been a young child, she had embraced him before he'd gone to sleep, and he remembered that scent.

Morwenna snatched her hair from his grasp, and he felt the urge to tease her. 'You put dried lilac in your bath, didn't you?' He could smell the fragrance on her skin as well. The scent was faint but alluring.

Her face turned fiery red, and she crossed her arms. 'What business is it of yours if I did? Can't I bathe if I want to?'

For a moment, he imagined her naked in a wooden tub, surrounded by the dried flowers. The steam would rise to her face, dampening tendrils of her hair. And the sudden image of bare female skin and droplets of water spilling over the curve of her breasts brought an unexpected jolt of response. He'd never thought of her in that way before, and he forced the vision back, wondering why his brain had conjured such an image.

'I'm glad you did,' he answered, keeping his

tone even. But when he saw the furious look on her face, he realised that somehow, he'd offended her. He'd meant to tell her that she smelled nice, but he had a feeling that if he did, it would only provoke her more.

'You could do with a bath yourself,' she pointed out.

At that, he gave a laugh. 'I'll admit, that's something I do miss. Hot water for bathing.' More often than not, he washed in an icy stream.

'You have a hearth fire and a pot of water. Use it.' She appeared so indignant he couldn't stop his smile.

'Perhaps I will. I suppose I'll need to prepare for the contests. I asked Wilfred to help me find some of my father's old clothes.'

'You'll need them,' she agreed. To divert the subject, she said, 'Especially if you intend to court Lady Gwendoline.'

'What sort of man does she want?'

Morwenna's face turned pensive, almost as if she was reluctant to speak. 'She likes honesty. When men lie to her or tell her what they think she wants to hear, she finds it false.'

He was intrigued to hear it. A woman who valued honesty was intelligent, too. 'What should I say to her when I meet her for the first time?'

Morwenna rolled her eyes at him. 'You could bid her a good morning.'

'But what name should I give her? I cannot give my own.'

She thought a moment. 'I would tell her the truth, Robert. If you lie to her and she finds out who you really are, you'll lose her.'

He disagreed with that. 'If I tell her that I'm the true Earl of Penrith, her father will have me hanged within hours.' No, that could never happen. 'I suppose I could tell her a piece of the truth. That I was driven from my lands. I could give her my middle name, Anthony.'

She appeared uncertain about that, and he was starting to agree. There were too many folk who knew him by the name Robert. If anyone asked, he could make up a different name to describe where he was from.

'If you give her a false name, when she finds out who you really are, why should she ever trust you again?'

'I hope by then, she will have feelings for me.' He believed that if he said the right words and if his actions were kind, she might understand his reasons. Surely courting a woman could not be all that different from learning a new skill. If he paid attention to her and became the man she wanted him to be, it ought to be enough.

'Starting with lies is not the way to win her affections,' Morwenna cautioned. 'If anything, it will drive her away.'

He understood what she meant, but in this situation, he saw no alternative. 'I will try to tell her what truths I can.' It was the best he could offer. She let out a sigh, and he added, 'I know you're only trying to help, Morwenna.'

She met his gaze squarely in the dim lamp light. 'I am, though you'll need more help than I can give.'

'I am grateful to you.' Robert reached out and squeezed her hand. 'When this is all over, I will be in your debt. And whatever you want, if it's in my power to grant it, I will do so.'

Her eyes seemed to hold a pain he didn't understand, but she gave a nod. 'In the morning, find a horse and go to the forest. Follow our trail and I'll try to separate Lady Gwendoline from the others. Do you know where the stream passes by that large oak tree?'

'I do, aye.'

'Then I will bring her there. Be waiting, and for the love of the saints, do not try to smell her hair.'

Robert only smiled.

It was just past dawn when they joined the hunt. Morwenna rode alongside Lady Gwendoline while three soldiers accompanied them. Lord Penrith had been kind enough to let her join in the hunt, but his gaze continually searched the horizon as they searched for deer. Sometimes she wondered whether he was looking for something else…or someone. He had a quiver of arrows on his back while they rode deeper into the forest. Gwendoline also had her own bow, which surprised her. She hadn't known the lady could shoot.

When they neared the stream, the earl raised his hand in a signal to stop. Then the hunting party dismounted to walk. For a time, they remained by the stream, waiting. Morwenna knew Robert would be on the far end of the stream by the oak tree. Now all she had to do was arrange for them to meet—and that meant separating from the others.

She caught the attention of Lord Penrith and motioned to herself and Lady Gwendoline. Then she nodded towards the other end of the stream, asking permission silently. She added a squirm to make it seem as if she needed to relieve herself. Thankfully, the earl inclined his head, and Morwenna took Gwendoline by the hand, leading her along the stream.

'Where are we going?' she whispered.

'Somewhere we can talk,' Morwenna answered. 'Don't you find the waiting dull?'

At that, Gwendoline beamed. 'I knew I liked you.'

They continued through the forest, following the stream. When they were within a short distance of the oak, Morwenna excused herself. 'I need a moment. You can keep walking, and I'll catch up. Meet me by that large tree ahead.'

'I can wait for you,' Gwendoline offered.

'No, I'd rather have…privacy,' Morwenna countered. 'I'll be there soon.'

The lady seemed to accept her excuse, and after a moment, Morwenna disappeared into the underbrush. She knew this part of the forest well, for it was only a short walk to their camp. Part of her felt guilty, but she watched as Gwendoline continued along the edge of the stream. Perfect. Morwenna could claim that she'd walked in the wrong direction and had got lost. If all went to plan, Robert would have his chance to meet the heiress.

The burning flare of jealousy caught up in her stomach, making her feel like a fool. Gwendoline was her friend now, and she didn't want to imagine the young woman falling in love with Robert. But she hadn't wanted to refuse his request, despite how much it bothered her.

Morwenna crouched low as she continued her way deeper into the woods. She saw a set of footprints beside the stream, and most likely they belonged to Robert. Although the fire had burned out in the camp hearth long ago, she struck flint and coaxed it back to life with some kindling.

Then she closed her eyes, resting her face in her hands. For a moment, she indulged in self-pity. She'd all but led Robert into Gwendoline's arms. Why? She never should have agreed to it. Already he found the lady beautiful, and it wouldn't take long for him to gain her attention.

Enough, she told herself. There was no sense in feeling sorry for herself. She'd done as Robert had asked, telling him what the lady wanted. With any luck, Gwendoline would choose a different suitor. It was the best Morwenna could hope for since the last thing she wanted to see was Robert with someone else. But even if he failed in his quest, he wouldn't want her. Better to distance herself from the feelings that would only cause her heartache.

She decided to wait a little longer, and in the meantime, she busied herself around camp. It was then that she noticed something was different. Something was out of place, but she couldn't quite decide what it was. Then again, she hadn't slept here in two nights. Robert or Brian might have returned to the camp.

Her gaze narrowed upon a small bundle. It wasn't Brian's, and she didn't recall seeing it earlier. Where had it come from?

She was about to untie it when she heard footsteps approaching. The dry leaves rustled, and she turned to see her brother. Relief flooded through her, and she smiled, turning to greet Brian.

'Are you all right?' he asked.

'Yes, of course.' She explained how she'd arranged a meeting between Robert and Lady Gwendoline. 'I'm just waiting to give them some time together.'

Her brother's expression tightened. For a long moment he stared at her, and she wondered what was wrong. 'Why did you leave Penrith? I know you weren't among the soldiers escorting us on the hunt. Did something happen?'

He gave a single nod but didn't elaborate. She waited for him to speak, but a myriad of emotions crossed over his face—apprehension, anger, and possibly fear.

'Brian, tell me,' she urged. 'Whatever it is, we'll solve the problem.'

'The earl is watching you,' he said. 'He knows

something about your past. I heard some of the soldiers talking.'

She shook her head, not understanding. 'What do you mean? Our father moved from place to place, and we went with him. What else is there to know?'

'Morwenna, where do you think Geoffrey got that gown? And that pendant?' Her brother's expression turned grim. 'I think our father was a thief. And we kept moving from place to place so he wouldn't get caught.'

A sour fear clenched her stomach. 'A thief? No, that's not possible.' Their father had been the most ordinary man she'd ever known. He'd rarely spoken more than a few words, and she couldn't imagine him being capable of stealing.

'We need to leave,' her brother said. 'I don't like the way the earl is asking questions about us. If they find out we're the miller's children, disguising ourselves to be inside the keep, we could be in trouble. And worse, I think Father was hiding secrets. He knew nothing about grinding grain.'

That was true enough. 'But he tried many ways to earn a living. How would he know how to grind wheat if he'd never done it before?' she pointed out. 'That doesn't make him a thief. And why would he give the gown and pendant to me? He said it belonged to our mother.'

'Did it? Do you think he was telling the truth?' Her brother shook his head. 'Morwenna, something was wrong. I've been trying to find out more, but there aren't enough answers.'

'What do you mean?'

'Why did they take us that night?'

She didn't understand what he was implying. 'We were taken because they were raiding. We were hostages.'

'Then why didn't they take anyone else?' He came closer, and in his eyes, she saw an intensity that bothered her. 'Morwenna, I would swear they were hunting us. They knew where to look.' He closed his eyes, his voice filled with pain. 'I don't think it was an accident that we were taken.'

She felt a chill even before he spoke again, a sense that he might be right. Brian reached for her and gripped her hand. 'I don't have the answers, and I'm not even certain we'll find them here. But you must be careful. I think we should leave as soon as we can.'

'We can't leave yet. Robert is competing in the contests,' she said dully. 'If he marries Lady Gwendoline, he'll get Penrith back.'

'The new lord won't allow that. He has his own plans for an alliance.'

'I suppose, but if she loves him—'

'It doesn't matter what she wants. She's her father's pawn, and he'll use her to get what he wants.' Her brother squeezed her hand. 'I have to go back now. But Morwenna, promise me you'll be careful. Do nothing that will draw attention to yourself. And warn Robert not to pursue the heiress. Lord Penrith will only have him killed if he dares to court her.'

She didn't want to believe him, but her brother was not one to lie. He'd risked a great deal to warn her, and she needed to tell Robert. But even so, she suspected he wouldn't believe Brian.

'I should go and find Gwendoline,' Morwenna said. 'They'll come searching for me otherwise.' She gave her brother a quick embrace and said, 'I promise I'll behave like a lady. Or at least, I'll try to.'

But as she went back to find Gwendoline, she wondered if Brian was right. Had their father buried secrets in the past? And was there a reason why they'd been captured on the night of the attack?

She walked back to the stream and hurried towards the oak tree. Though she didn't want to see Gwendoline and Robert together, she had to return. Once she reached the oak tree, there was no one there. She walked farther towards the opposite end of the stream, but there was no sign of Gwendoline.

Morwenna followed the stream in the direction they'd travelled earlier and picked up her skirts as she ran. Still no one. Her fear quickened as she wondered what the earl would say if she had to confess that she'd misplaced his daughter.

She breathed a sigh of relief when she saw Gwendoline standing near the horses. The men had shot a deer, and two of the soldiers were busy cleaning the carcass.

'Where have you been?' Gwendoline asked. 'What happened?'

'I went the wrong way down the stream,' she lied. 'By the time I realised it, you had gone the other direction. I'm so sorry. I should have been more careful.'

Gwendoline linked her arm in Morwenna's, and it was then that she noticed the flush on the young woman's face. 'There's something I need to tell you.' She led her away from the men to stand a short distance from them. In a whisper she confessed, 'I—I met someone in the forest.'

Morwenna tried to feign surprise. 'Who was it?'

Gwendoline's smile broke through, and she

blushed. 'I shouldn't tell you this. But I think he's one of my suitors. And he's so handsome.' She let out a sigh. 'He offered to help me search for you, but then we started talking and I...got carried away.'

Morwenna glanced at Lord Penrith, who was still occupied with his men. 'What do you mean you "got carried away"?'

Gwendoline's smile turned blinding. 'He kissed me.' She hugged herself, leaning back against a tree. 'It was simply wonderful. Everything I imagined it would be.'

Morwenna couldn't bring herself to return the smile, but Gwendoline didn't seem to notice. 'Do you know his name?'

She nodded but didn't say it. 'He promised to come to the feast tomorrow night. He's going to compete against the others.' Gwendoline let out a sigh. 'I cannot wait to see him again.'

Before Morwenna could ask another question, Lord Penrith summoned them to return. She and Gwendoline mounted their horses and began the ride back to the castle keep.

'I'll tell you everything when we're alone,' Gwen promised. 'You simply won't believe what happened.'

It was a strain to keep a smile on her face, but Morwenna answered, 'I want to hear all about it.'

Chapter Four

The following day, Robert spent all morning and afternoon within the castle in an effort to gain more information. He'd hoped Morwenna would come to him last night, but she had remained in the castle keep. His mood was frustrated, and he'd hardly slept after waiting for her. Nothing had gone as he'd expected yesterday morning, and Morwenna had answers that he needed about Lady Gwendoline.

But he was done with waiting. Tonight, he intended to join the other suitors and compete for Lady Gwendoline's hand. Wilfred had brought him an old trunk of his father's clothing that one of the servants had hidden away—probably in the hopes of selling them at a later time. But for now, Robert would use the clothes to begin his own transformation.

He made his excuses to Wilfred and went

into the small pantry to change his attire. It felt strange wearing Degal's belongings, but the long dark blue tunic fit him perfectly. Only two years had passed, yet it seemed like a lifetime ago.

Once he was ready, his thoughts drifted back to Morwenna. She, too, had revealed her hidden beauty. Her green eyes captivated him, and with her hair pulled back, it accentuated the soft curve of her face. She'd claimed that she intended to find her own husband here, and Robert had no doubt she would succeed. But a sudden twinge darkened his mood at the thought of some love-sick swain courting Morwenna. His protective instincts rose up, for he didn't want another man trying to steal a kiss or worse. A possessive flare came over him at the memory of the soldier who had torn her gown. If any man ever dared to hurt her, Robert would kill him. She deserved better.

But no matter what he thought of Morwenna's marital prospects, he had to keep his attention on Lady Gwendoline. Although he'd attempted to see the young woman, she had not left the castle keep, and he'd been unable to slip inside.

Tonight would be different, he vowed, as he walked outside. Torches were lit at intervals, and he joined a group of young men dressed in similar finery. There would be contests of strength and speed, followed by a feast and recognition of the winners. Robert had confidence in his archery and in his speed, but he questioned whether he'd learned enough about swordplay. It was one matter to train with Piers and Brian—quite another to fight against experienced swordsmen.

Morwenna stood beside Gwendoline, wearing a crimson bliaud trimmed with gold. Her dark curls were caught up in a pearl-studded veil, and in the late afternoon sun, her brown hair gleamed with a reddish tint. Gwendoline wore a gown of white, with silver embroidery and a silver torque at her throat. When she smiled, her face shone with happiness. The pair reminded him of fire and ice.

Though he kept his gaze fixed upon Lady Gwendoline, he was fully aware of Morwenna. She appeared uncomfortable being surrounded by so many men. He hoped Brian was standing nearby since Robert could not get closer to them.

When they gathered at the bottom of the stairs, Lord Penrith spoke. 'Tonight, we begin a series of contests. Those of you who choose to join will compete for my daughter's hand in marriage. There will be games of skill and prizes for the winners, but it is your chance to show her your strength and abilities. By tomorrow, she has promised that she will choose a husband from among you.'

He turned then to Morwenna. 'And if you are not chosen, there is another lady who wishes to marry. You might consider the Lady Morwenna after Gwendoline has made her choice.'

Robert stiffened at the mention of Morwenna, though she'd said before that she intended to marry. But he noticed more than one man glancing at her with admiration. She kept her gaze fixed upon the gates, her chin held high.

Someone bumped against him, and he turned to see her brother Brian. His expression was grim. 'Did you know about this? Does she really mean to choose a husband?'

Robert shrugged. 'She said she would consider it.' His gaze centred on her once again, but Morwenna wasn't looking at him. 'It might be her way of getting you both out of here.'

'I'm responsible for myself, Robert.'

'Aye. But if you want to stay at Penrith, you don't have to leave. If it's in my power to do so, I'll find a place for you.'

Brian's gaze shifted over to the men who were setting up a game of quoits. The target lay a good distance away, and the first competitor picked up a horseshoe to throw. 'I need my sister to be safe first. Then I'll go my own way.'

His loyalty to her was unwavering. And truthfully, Robert knew it might be good for Morwenna to marry a nobleman who didn't ask too many questions. She could make another life for herself and live as a lady. But none of these men was worthy of Morwenna, much less Lady Gwendoline.

Robert saw another group of men preparing for a wrestling match, and the thought of pouring his frustration into physical strength was a welcome respite. He wanted to win, to prove that he was stronger than any of them.

He waited his turn among the competitors, and when it was time for his first match, he noticed that Morwenna had brought Lady Gwendoline closer. He stripped off his tunic so that he was wearing only his hose. His opponent did the same. The man was slightly shorter, but there was no denying his strength. He eyed Robert as if questioning who he was.

'I've not seen you before,' the man said, as they circled each other.

Robert didn't bother to address the remark. Instead, he studied his opponent's physical form. He would need to move swiftly and force the man off balance.

From the side, he noticed Morwenna and Gwendoline moving in closer to watch. He lunged, shoving just below the man's waist. His opponent managed to keep from falling, but before he could gain the advantage, Robert locked his arm around the man's neck and flipped him to the ground. He'd wrestled enough with Piers to know how to make his opponent helpless. It took only moments to wrench the suitor's arm behind his back. He held the man motionless and gained the win.

Lady Gwendoline smiled and clapped, along with the others. He met her gaze and answered the smile before he noticed Morwenna's worried expression. She masked it quickly and ventured a faint smile after Robert released his opponent and claimed the victory.

He won the second match and the third, but by then, Lady Gwendoline had gone to observe some of the other competitions. Eventually Robert was named the winner, and it eased his confidence. Morwenna handed him a linen cloth that he used to dry off, and he leaned in to talk to her. She seemed nervous, and her cheeks flushed when he murmured, 'What happened the day of the hunt?'

At that, her face turned brighter. 'I think you know the answer to that better than me.' She started to turn away, but he caught her arm.

'I waited for hours by the oak tree.'

She stopped and faced him. 'What do you mean? I sent her to you.'

'I waited, but she never came. And when I went to look for her, I could only find her father and the other men. I had to remain in hiding.'

She paled and then bit her lower lip. 'So…you never met Lady Gwendoline yesterday morning?' It looked as if she wanted to say something else but stopped herself. He couldn't guess what she was thinking.

'No. I assumed she went back to her father.'

'Or got lost,' Morwenna mused. 'I should have walked with her. But I wanted it to seem like an accidental meeting.' Her expression grew troubled. 'I should return. But stay in the competitions, and if I have the chance, I will introduce her to you.'

She started to turn away, but he called out, 'Wait.' At her questioning look, he asked, 'I want to know if this is what you truly want, Morwenna. To find a husband?'

She appeared disconcerted by his words. 'What other choice do I have?'

He didn't quite know how to answer her. 'You and Brian could—'

'Could what? Continue wandering all over England, searching for a place to live?'

'I was going to say you will always have a home here.' He didn't want her to feel abandoned. And though he had no doubt she could easily find a man to wed, it should be her choice, not a move made out of desperation.

'Do you think I'd really want to live here and watch you with her?' she blurted out. Then she turned and departed, leaving him to wonder what had just happened.

He couldn't quite grasp what she'd said. Her words held more than wounded feelings—there'd been a trace of jealousy. He didn't know what to say or do now, and it felt as if the ground had been knocked out from under him.

He had come to Penrith to win Lady Gwendoline's hand, but it had always been out of duty. He wanted his family's lands back, and marrying her was necessary to regain them. It had nothing to do with emotions.

He'd thought Morwenna understood that. But her words made him think of what it would be like to watch her smile at another man or worse, let him touch her. His fist clenched at the thought. The irrational jealousy made no sense. He'd lived with Morwenna for two years, and there was nothing between them. Why should it matter if she chose a husband? He had no claim to her. Right now, he needed to keep his focus on regaining Penrith and marrying Lady Gwendoline.

But even so, he couldn't quite push aside his dark mood or his worry.

As a distraction, he joined with the other suitors, preparing for the foot race. But even as he waited, his mind was caught up in thoughts of Morwenna. She truly was a beautiful woman with a fiery personality.

He stared at her across the inner bailey and saw her face soften with a smile. Against the setting sun, her brown hair gleamed with gold, and the sight of her struck him senseless.

Do you think I'd really want to live here and watch you with her?

Her words were like a physical blow. She cared about him in a way he'd never expected. And now that he knew the truth, it made him entertain thoughts he shouldn't. He remembered her lithe body and the way she'd moved with the blade he'd given her. He'd held her hands, guiding her in each movement.

And those green eyes had stared back at him with a longing he'd been too blind to see. During the past two years, Morwenna had become such a part of his life, he didn't know what he would do after she was gone.

And that posed a problem.

Morwenna's thoughts were spinning out of control. She hadn't meant to spill her feelings to

Robert, and from the stunned look on his face, he'd never realised her hidden jealousy.

Humiliation burned her cheeks, and she wanted to retreat to Gwendoline's chamber and bury herself beneath a coverlet. Why had she said anything at all? There had been no reason to tell him, and now, he likely pitied her.

Morwenna forced herself to return to the others, inwardly shutting down her embarrassment. She couldn't wallow in self-pity when there was a bigger problem—Gwendoline's mysterious suitor. She'd mistakenly believed that her friend had spent time with Robert yesterday, but now she realised it had been someone else. One of the noblemen must have arrived early, but who? Gwendoline had confessed that she'd kissed the man and had been giddy with joy. It didn't bode well at all for Robert's chances.

She shouldn't be happy about that. Not at all.

Morwenna pushed back the inappropriate feelings and hurried over towards the archery contest to join her friend. She managed a smile and asked, 'Have you found your suitor from the forest yet?'

'No, not yet,' Gwendoline answered. 'But he will come. I'm certain of it.' She was watching the men draw back their bow strings, taking careful aim. Although most of them struck the straw targets, none of the arrows embedded in the centre.

'I could shoot better than that,' Gwen mumbled beneath her breath. Morwenna hid her smile. Although she'd never seen her friend shoot a bow, she suspected that Gwendoline was strong enough.

'So, it was none of those men,' Morwenna said. 'For a moment, I thought it might be the man who won the wrestling matches.'

'No, it wasn't him.' But Gwendoline's expression turned sly. 'I saw the way you were watching him though…and the way he was looking at you. He *is* a handsome one. And so strong.'

'Do you want to meet him?' Morwenna asked. 'I could arrange it.'

'No.' The young woman's voice turned dreamy. 'I'm waiting on the man from the forest. And besides, I wouldn't want to interfere with your happiness.' With a knowing look, she added, 'He's the one, isn't he? The one you wanted.'

Another blush warmed Morwenna's cheeks. 'It doesn't matter what I want. You have the first choice.'

But Gwen was already shaking her head. 'I won't interfere. If he is the one you love, then you may have him.'

'He's not,' she forced herself to say, though the

words were bitter in her mouth. And though it pained her to say it, she added, 'But I have seen him before, and others have spoken well of him. You should truly consider him for a suitor.'

They walked closer to the archers, but her thoughts remained in turmoil. She needed to find out who the man from the forest was. As she studied each of the archers, none appeared familiar to her. Gwendoline paused to study each of the men, but it was clear that she had interest in only one person—and he wasn't here.

On the opposite side of the bailey, the sword competition had begun. Morwenna asked the lady, 'Will you tell me when you see him?'

'Of course. And I'll need your help so my father will let me choose him.' They walked towards the fighting, and she saw Robert donning chainmail armour for his match. He'd brought his sword from the abbey, and as he awaited his turn, he studied the movements of the other competitors. She did the same, and for a time, they simply watched the fighting.

From across the dirt, Robert caught her gaze, and she saw the concern in his eyes. He'd never fought men like these, seasoned warriors who had faced true battle. One of the fighters had an unusual sword that had undoubtedly been made in the East. Likely a Crusader.

Although these were only games, she understood Robert's unspoken apprehension. Did he have the skill to fight these men? She wasn't certain, and from the look of it, neither was he.

'Do you want to watch them?' Gwendoline asked, and Morwenna nodded.

They stood close by, and Robert prepared for his first fight. His opponent had his back to them, and he wore a hood so they could not see his face. He chose his own armour and selected a sword from among the weapons.

But when he made his way to the fighting circle, Morwenna glimpsed his face in the chainmail cowl. And she caught her breath.

'It's him,' Gwen breathed. 'The man from the forest.'

Morwenna saw the sudden shock on Robert's face, but he masked it quickly with grim determination. She knew that this battle would be fierce, one that went beyond friendly competition.

For his opponent was his half-brother Piers.

Robert circled Piers, who had a faint smile on his face. 'What are you doing here?'

His half-brother answered the question by slicing his sword towards Robert's neck. Robert blocked the blow and Piers leaned in. In a low voice, he said, 'I thought I'd court the Lady Gwendoline. She is a beauty, is she not?'

Robert shoved him back, letting the fury pour through him. Piers knew what this competition meant to him. Why would he join in? Was he trying to claim Penrith for himself?

Robert had mistakenly thought that they had come to a truce during the past years of hiding. It seemed he'd been wrong. 'Stay away from her,' he growled. 'She's a high-born lady.'

'So she is,' Piers answered. 'And I've a right to be here, the same as you.' He cut off any further conversation by renewing his attack. Their swords struck hard, the iron ringing within the bailey. His brother seemed to be fighting his own battle against the injustice of being born a bastard. But Robert could not allow him to threaten Penrith. These were his lands, claimed by an earl who was terrorising the serfs. He had to win Lady Gwendoline's affections, for it was his only chance to help the people.

His brother's sword slipped past and nicked Robert on his chin. He felt the warmth of blood and renewed his own attack, lunging forward. All around him, he could hear the shouting of the crowd, and he glimpsed Morwenna and Gwendoline watching. There was no choice but to defeat Piers. He struck as hard as he could, circling his half-brother and attacking.

He knew he was approaching this fight the wrong way. He ought to strategise, to use Piers's weaknesses against him. But the sight of the man had brought back all the anger and frustration he'd suppressed. He gave in to the raw emotions, hacking his sword as he fought.

Piers parried his blows, using his own strength to push back. Robert nearly lost his balance but regained it before he swung at his brother's head.

The fight seemed endless, and beneath the weight of the chainmail he wondered how much longer they could endure. Sweat ran down Piers's face, and his own arm burned with fatigue.

But then he heard a woman call out, 'Stop! This match is over.' He turned towards the sound and barely avoided another strike from his brother's weapon.

Lady Gwendoline hurried towards them, followed by Morwenna. 'I declare this match a draw.' The worry on her face revealed that she knew it had been more than a competition. 'You will both dine with me and the Lady Morwenna.'

Robert sheathed his sword, and Piers handed his weapon to one of the other fighters. They removed their armour and joined the women. But he didn't miss his brother's triumphant smile when Lady Gwendoline took his arm and walked with him towards the castle keep.

Damn him for this.

Morwenna came to him and murmured, 'We need to talk.'

'Why is Piers here? And what does he want?'

She tightened her grip on his arm. 'I think you already know the answer to that.'

Her reply only heightened his annoyance, for he did know. No matter how much time had passed, his brother always seemed to covet what Robert wanted. And now he'd set his sights on Lady Gwendoline and Penrith.

'I won't let him do this.' There was too much at stake. He needed to regain command of Penrith for the sake of the people. This wasn't only a competition for Lady Gwendoline's hand in marriage—it was a contest to win the land. And his half-brother knew nothing about running an estate.

Morwenna stopped walking and faced him. She smiled warmly for the benefit of the onlookers, but her words were like stone. 'If you want to replace Piers in Gwendoline's affections, then you must rise above your anger and treat her with kindness. Be the better man.'

Her words made him realise that he was falling into his brother's trap. Piers wanted him to be angry and fight back, for then it would make Robert appear frustrated and impatient.

'You're right,' he admitted.

'You've been given an opportunity,' she said quietly. 'You can join Lady Gwendoline at table and speak with her then.' But as she walked alongside him towards the stairs of the keep, he noticed the weariness in her eyes. She was trying to keep a smile on her face, but it appeared strained.

'Morwenna,' he said quietly, slowing his steps. 'What you said earlier…'

She wouldn't meet his gaze and cut him off. 'It doesn't matter. I've always known you were going to return here. And marrying Gwendoline *is* the best way for you to help Penrith.'

He wanted to find the words to make this right, for he didn't want to hurt her. But what could he say? He'd never allowed himself to think beyond reclaiming his estate. He'd never considered what would happen afterwards.

When she'd told him that she didn't want to stay and watch him with Lady Gwendoline, it had bothered him to think of hurting her. Morwenna was right. After he married the heiress, it would be cruel to invite her to stay.

She slowed her steps to wait on him. 'I will find someone to wed, Robert. And once I have chosen a husband, I'll leave Penrith and make a new life somewhere else.'

He gave a nod of agreement. 'Choose someone who deserves you, Morwenna. Someone who won't try to force you into a life you don't want.' He'd known her for the past two years, and he couldn't deny his own overprotective feelings towards her. Though he knew it was practical for her to marry, his mood darkened at the thought.

She turned back to him, and for a moment, her green eyes met his. In them he saw sadness, mingled with a hint of longing. It struck him to the core, for he couldn't deny his own response. It had always been there, just beneath the surface. For a moment, he dared to imagine what it would be like if circumstances were different.

He remembered the scent of her skin, the softness of her hand in his. And a heaviness sank into him, the mirrored frustration of having to watch her with someone else.

They entered the keep, not looking at one another. A long table was set upon a dais, and several servants waited against the walls with pitchers of ale. Lady Gwendoline and her father led them inside the keep, but soon it became apparent that the earl was not going to allow his daughter to be seated between two suitors.

Instead, he kept Gwendoline on his right, followed by Piers. He placed Morwenna on his left, and Robert took the seat beside her. It seemed that there would be no means of him speaking to Lady Gwendoline during the meal. But at least Piers would have to face the earl's direct questioning.

Lady Gwendoline introduced his half-brother as Piers of Grevershire. And when she turned to him, Robert answered, 'I am Robert of Inglewood.' He'd decided it was better to keep his first name, in case anyone called him that. When the earl gave no reaction, he decided it was safe enough.

As they were seated, the earl turned to Morwenna. 'Are you enjoying your stay with us?'

'I am grateful for your hospitality, my lord,' she answered. But even as she accepted portions of roasted venison, salmon, and bread, Robert didn't miss the way she tensed. She risked a glance at Gwendoline, but the young woman appeared captivated by Piers.

'There has been no news from your family thus far,' Lord Penrith continued. 'And while I am content to indulge Gwendoline in this competition evening, and I do not mind if you find a suitor of your own, it is not my place to arrange a betrothal for you. If you find a man who suits you, tell him to speak with your father.'

Robert could see that Morwenna had gone pale under the earl's scrutiny. 'Do not concern yourself with me, my lord.'

Though her words should have eased the earl's concern, Robert noticed that the man's gaze was fixed upon Morwenna's throat. 'I noticed you wearing that pendant when you first arrived. May I take a closer look?'

She started to remove it, but the earl reached out and his knuckles grazed her bodice as he lifted it. Morwenna flinched, and Robert barely suppressed the rise of his own fury. He wanted to shove the earl back and demand that he take his hands off her. And yet, he could not say a word.

'Such a unique design,' the earl remarked. 'I believe I have seen this emblem before, though I cannot remember. Where did you get it?'

'It belonged to my mother,' she answered. 'My father gave it to me only a few years ago, but she died when I was twelve.'

The earl's expression narrowed. 'I know I've seen this before. I won't stop thinking of it until I remember where.' He let the chain fall back and then turned to his daughter. Beneath the table, Robert reached for Morwenna's hand and squeezed it hard. When she met his gaze, he saw the terror in her eyes. Though he didn't fully understand what had just happened, he wanted her to know that he was here.

Across the table, he saw Piers watching Lady Gwendoline. He appeared uncomfortable, and though Robert couldn't hear the conversation between him and the young woman, he suspected that his half-brother would face an inquisition by her father.

In a whisper, Morwenna said, 'I need to leave, Robert. Can you find a way to help me out of here?'

'It's too early for that,' he warned. 'I can try to give you a moment, but we have to return.'

'I can't breathe.' Upon her face he saw panic, and her complexion had turned to snow. 'I just need a moment. There are so many people, and they're all staring at me.'

'All right.'

Robert cleared his throat, interrupting the earl's conversation. When he had the man's attention, he said, 'My lord, forgive me, but the lady is feeling unwell. May I have permission to escort her outside for a few moments? Some air might help her.'

'You look well enough to me.' The earl eyed Morwenna with irritation.

'It's so warm, I am feeling faint,' she replied.

'Could you grant me a few moments, I beg of you?'

The earl appeared annoyed, but he waved his hand in permission. Robert offered his arm, and she took it gratefully. They wove in between the guests, and once they passed the doorway to go outside, she inhaled a deep breath. Even so, it wasn't enough. Something had frightened her, and he wanted to let her speak freely.

Since most of the guests were inside, he led her towards the barbican gate. There was a small guard's entrance, and a staircase that led to the battlements. Morwenna followed him to the top, and for a moment, she stopped to stare out at the darkening landscape. The sun rimmed the horizon, and the wind whipped at her cheeks.

Robert didn't ask if she was all right, for he knew the answer already. The earl's sudden interest had frightened her when she'd not been able to pull away from his unwanted touch. 'I shouldn't have come here,' she murmured. 'I thought I could wear her gown and a golden chain and pretend to be a lady for a few nights. But I don't belong in the keep. It's not who I am.'

She closed her eyes, taking a deep breath. For a long moment she remained silent before she stared out at the horizon. 'The earl knows I'm lying. And he's playing a game of cat and mouse that I'm going to lose.'

'You could go with Brian and leave tonight,' Robert offered. 'Return to the abbey, and they could give you sanctuary.'

She didn't answer, and he turned her to face him. 'Or if you stay, I will protect you Morwenna, just as I've always done. You needn't fear.'

'But you cannot protect me for ever. And this is not a battle fought with swords.'

He knew she was right about that. He was fighting for his lands and his people. But, more than that, he was fighting the invisible battle for his own self-respect. He'd failed them before—and it would never happen again.

'I may not always be there,' he conceded. 'But once I'm wedded to Lady Gwendoline and have command of Penrith, I will help you,' he swore. 'Whatever you need.'

But his promise seemed to only deepen her misery. 'I'm not your responsibility any more.'

He was trying to reassure her, Morwenna could tell. But the truth was, she'd lived in fear during every hour she'd spent in the castle keep. The earl was enjoying his game. She had no doubt he knew of her lies, but he was waiting for them to unravel. The only question was what he wanted from her.

Although Robert claimed that he would keep her safe, he could do nothing without threatening his position with Gwendoline. And then there was Piers, who was trying to stake his own claim.

'I'll find my own way out of this,' she told him. 'It's my fault that I even came here. You were right about the danger.'

In his eyes, she saw concern for her welfare. He would try to protect her, certainly, but not at the cost of Penrith. 'Are you all right now? Do you want to return to the keep?'

She didn't answer at first. Then he rested his hand against her cheek, and his touch was like fire. Did he think he was comforting her? She caught his hand and held it there, both to cling to his touch and warn him to stop.

'I'll be fine,' she said.

But he didn't pull his palm away. Instead, he continued to study her. 'If I didn't know better, I would believe that you're a high-born lady. You've done well with this illusion, Morwenna. If you want to find a husband, I have no doubt you could choose any man you desire.'

Any man except him.

She took a step back. Why couldn't he ever

see her as a woman? The words hurt, for she wondered if he understood the depths of her feelings. She wished she'd never told him the truth. He was probably only offering consolation, for he didn't return her feelings and never would.

I wish I could choose any man I desire, she thought, but didn't say it.

Then she turned around and started walking down the stairs. Robert walked behind her, keeping guard as they continued towards the keep. When she reached the entrance, she heard a voice call out, 'Lady Morwenna.'

She turned and saw that it was one of the men who had competed in the contests earlier. He was thin and wiry, and she recalled that he had won second place in the archery competition.

As a courtesy, she nodded to him but did not speak. The last thing she wanted right now was to be involved with someone else.

Robert had fallen farther behind and was speaking to one of the servants. She continued into the Great Hall and walked past the trestle tables until she reached the dais. Thankfully, Lord Penrith was questioning Piers, and Morwenna sent Gwendoline a slight smile as she took her place at the table. Her friend appeared uncertain, but there was no means of escaping. Robert entered the keep at the far end, and several of the servants stopped to speak with him.

They recognise him, she realised.

But not her. She felt like a stranger here, as if the fine clothing had transformed her into someone else. Yet it was naught but an illusion. She knew better than to believe she could ever be lady of a castle.

She took a sip of wine, watching Robert, and suddenly she realised that she was hiding from her life, just as he had. He'd spent years behind castle walls, disconnected from the outside world. Her own life had been similar, for she'd travelled constantly with her father and brother, never making a place for herself. Never having any true friends.

Morwenna risked a look at the people, and it was as if she were watching as an outsider. Lady Gwendoline had all eyes upon her, the men transfixed by her beauty. Lord Penrith reigned over his conquered castle, enjoying his high rank. Even Robert was speaking to the people, trying to find a way to regain what was lost.

And what was she doing? Letting him believe that he could win Lady Gwendoline when she knew the lady had kissed Piers. His chances of winning the noblewoman's heart were fading fast, and Morwenna had said nothing.

She'd been living her life in the shadows, caught in a trap of her own making. And she didn't care for it at all.

It had to stop. No longer could she hide behind her invisible shield, waiting for the scraps of his affection. Robert had made his decision to court Lady Gwendoline, and despite her feelings for him, it was time to stop living her life based on his.

He finally joined her at the table, apologising for his delay. 'It's all right,' she said. Then, before she lost her nerve, she asked, 'Could we talk again later tonight, alone? I think there is something you could help me with.' She decided to tell him the truth and make her plans to leave. And then she would gather the courage to say farewell…even when it broke her heart.

He was already nodding. 'If you wish.' He dropped his voice lower and added, 'Come to the kitchens. It will be safer there.'

She gave a nod, trying to push back the rise of her own nerves. But it was time to face him and be truthful, whatever the cost.

When the feasting ended, Lord Penrith called on the winners to come forward and be recognised. He presented each contest winner to his daughter, including Robert and Piers. Lady Gwendoline was gracious to each man, but Morwenna saw that her gaze lingered upon Piers. Her friend was still fascinated by the man, likely because she'd kissed him in the forest.

'My daughter has chosen five men who will remain at Penrith,' the earl said. 'She will choose an appropriate husband from among them, with my permission.' Then one by one, he named the men. Robert and Piers were both chosen, along with the archer Morwenna had seen earlier. Then there were two others—one who had won the footrace and another who had won the spear-casting competition.

Morwenna noticed that the earl had said nothing about her, which was a relief. If he was too concentrated on Gwendoline to pay her any heed, so much the better.

The earl ordered music and dancing to begin, and the pipers played a lively tune. 'Come, and let us dance,' Gwendoline said to Piers. She nodded to Morwenna and Robert. 'Join us, won't you?'

The men pushed the trestle tables back to make space, and it wasn't long before there were many partners. There were more men than women, and Morwenna found herself joining hands with suitor after suitor, whirling and spinning while the musicians played. She grew dizzy, but it was fun to be part of the merriment, even if it felt bittersweet.

When Robert danced with her, she was conscious of his palm upon her spine and the warmth in his eyes. Her traitorous heart welled up with longing that could not be forsaken.

Don't believe it's real, she reminded herself.

He only saw her as a friend. Lady Gwendoline was a means towards an end, a way for him to peacefully reclaim Penrith. But when his gaze drifted over to Gwendoline, something inside Morwenna went cold.

She excused herself during the next dance, pretending that she needed a cup of ale. She returned to the table and picked up her half-empty cup, holding it as she watched the dancers.

'Lady Morwenna.'

She saw the archer approaching her once again, but this time, she decided to give him a chance. 'Yes?'

'I am Gareth of Watcomb. I've been hoping for a chance to speak with you.' He appeared slightly awkward as he chose his words. 'You really are quite lovely. Forgive me, but I...have little experience with women. I don't know quite what to say.'

His attempt at being charming made her sympathetic, so she decided to give him the chance he wanted. 'It's all right. I am glad to meet you.'

'I know the heat was bothering you earlier,' he said. 'Would you like to walk outside for some fresh air?'

She hesitated but then realised it was perfectly safe with so many guards surrounding the inner bailey. 'All right.'

Gareth offered his arm, and she took it, allowing him to lead her past the dancers and the crowd until they reached the doors.

Outside the moon had risen high, illuminating the shadows. She took a deep breath of fresh air, enjoying the scent of the night. Beside her, Gareth remained quiet at first. Then he asked, 'What are you hoping to find in a husband, if I might ask?'

No one had ever asked her that before. And while her first thoughts were of Robert, she stopped herself to think of an answer. 'Someone kind,' she said at last. 'Someone who I want to be around, who makes me smile.'

She hadn't had much of a reason to smile lately. After her father had died, her life had been one disaster after another. But perhaps it was time to move on and begin again. She ventured a smile at Gareth, and he returned it.

'May I tell you a secret, my lady?'

'If you wish.' She took a sip from her cup, waiting for him to speak.

'I am hoping that Lady Gwendoline does not choose me. I'd rather be your choice instead.'

Her cheeks flushed at his words, and she didn't quite know what to say. 'Thank you,' was all she could manage. It was bewildering being the centre of a man's attention, and she felt shy beneath his gaze.

Or perhaps it was her own feeling of awkwardness. He started to say something else, but Morwenna grew distracted when she caught sight of a woman she'd not seen in two years. The woman was older, her brown hair carelessly bound in a braid. Shock filled her at the sight of the woman. It was her father's lover, Lena. Morwenna had mistakenly believed she was dead.

Clearly, she'd been wrong. Brian had said nothing about the woman, so he likely hadn't known she was here.

Her father had dallied with Lena after his wife had died, but he'd never married her. The woman knew exactly who Morwenna was, however—nothing but the miller's daughter. A knowing smile came over Lena's face before she turned to walk inside the keep.

Was she planning to tell the earl? Panic rose up, for Morwenna knew her entire deception could come crashing down within a matter of moments.

Then again, had she really believed it could last? She had gone along with Gwendoline's wishes, not truly expecting anything at all.

'My lady?' Gareth was asking.

She forced her attention back to the noble-man, realising she'd heard nothing else of what he'd said. 'Forgive me. I thought I saw someone I recognised. But of course, that's impossible.'

Brian's earlier warning sharpened in her mind. He wanted her to leave Penrith, and she was starting to believe he was right. But not before she spoke with Robert. The thought only stirred up her nerves again.

'I was asking about your home,' Gareth con-tinued. 'Do you live far from here?'

'Not so very far,' she hedged. 'But sometimes it seems that way.'

'Do you have any older brothers or sisters?' Though the question appeared ordinary, she sus-pected his true question was whether or not she was an heiress. Or whether there was a brother who had already inherited the lands.

'I have a younger brother,' she answered. 'And you?'

'I have four older brothers.'

Which meant that he would inherit next to

nothing. It was no wonder he was paying court to Lady Gwendoline and herself, in the hopes of gaining his own property.

'Would you care to walk through the inner bailey?' Gareth was asking.

'No, I think I'll go inside, thank you.' She allowed him to lead her back and, once inside, she saw Lena pouring the earl a cup of wine. Morwenna didn't know whether the woman had said anything to Lord Penrith, but she had to be prepared for the worst.

She took her place, and Gwendoline slid over to sit beside her. 'You don't look as if you're enjoying yourself, Morwenna.'

She forced a smile. 'It's just a little overwhelming. I've never seen so many suitors.'

'Have you met Piers of Grevershire before?' Gwendoline asked. 'He's quite handsome, but… I know little about him.'

He's Robert's bastard brother, Morwenna wanted to say, but didn't.

It occurred to her that she could intervene and be truthful with Gwendoline. She'd been wanting to confront Piers anyway, and this was her chance. 'Do you want me to find out?'

'Please. Come, and I'll arrange it.' She led Morwenna over to Piers, who was drinking a cup of wine. When he glanced up at her, his blue eyes turned wary.

'This is Lady Morwenna.' Gwendoline introduced her. 'And this is Piers of Grevershire.'

Morwenna kept her gaze fixed upon him, but she inclined her head. 'I am glad to meet you… my lord.' She paused on the last two words, for neither of them was nobility.

'Morwenna would like to dance,' Gwendoline said.

Piers inclined his head and held out his hand. It would give them a chance to speak privately. But then she saw Robert staring at her nearby, and he appeared furious that she was with Piers. She ignored him and Piers took her hand, leading her out among the dancers.

'It seems I'm not the only one disguising myself,' he said. 'But you look well, Morwenna.'

'Thank you.' It surprised her that he was being polite, so she did the same. 'As do you.'

He was a better dancer than she realised, and she wondered where he'd learned. She, herself, was terrible and half of her movement was stumbling around, trying to copy the others. 'What are you doing here, Piers?'

He smiled then, but it was the cut-throat smile of a mercenary. 'What do you think I'm doing?'

'Causing trouble,' she answered. 'Just as you like to do.'

He spun her in a circle. 'That's true enough. It was your idea to dance, wasn't it?'

Morwenna nodded. 'I told her I would find out everything about you.'

At that, he laughed. 'I've always liked your honesty, Morwenna. What will you tell her?'

'It depends on what you want me to say. I hope I can tell her the truth. So, what *are* your plans? Were you hoping to marry the heiress and claim Penrith, as you've always wanted?'

His smile grew strained. 'If I can, aye.'

At least he was being forthright. Though she ought to be annoyed with him, his honesty held a wicked charm. 'Why do you even want these lands, Piers? Why not claim your own somewhere else?'

'Because I was born here. And Lord Penrith forced me to live in this castle, surrounded by the things I would never have.' It was then that she heard a faint edge of anger in his voice. 'It was a mockery, and Degal knew it. So, there's nothing I want more than to claim what should have been mine,' he insisted. 'And I will have my vengeance for what he did to my mother.'

'What did he do?' She'd never heard this tale.

'She died because of him.' There was pain in his words.

'You cannot take vengeance on a dead man,' she said gently. 'It won't change anything.'

'Claiming Penrith would change my life,' he admitted. He took her hand as they moved to join the others in the dance. 'And if I have a beautiful woman as part of it, I'll not complain.'

'Lady Gwendoline is a kind person,' she insisted. 'Don't make her part of your revenge.'

'She's not.' He moved her in a circle, and she saw that Robert was already approaching. He looked ready to start a fight with Piers.

She would have to intervene between them, but before that, she asked, 'What do you want me to tell Gwendoline?'

'Nothing at all,' he answered. 'Stay out of it.'

'Do not break her heart,' she insisted. 'You know this cannot end in a betrothal. She's high-born…not like us. And if you're not going to treat her with kindness, then end it.'

'So fierce,' he remarked, touching her chin. 'But you're wrong. I intend to get what I want this time. All of it.'

It was then that Robert interrupted. Morwenna stopped him from causing a scene by taking both his hands. She pulled him back and put his hands on her waist, pretending she was switching partners. 'If you start a fight, you won't help your chances with Lady Gwendoline.' She led him away and added, 'I've spoken with Piers already.'

'I know my brother,' Robert insisted. 'He cares naught for words, and I won't let him overturn my plans.'

She faltered, wondering what he meant by that. 'I need to return to Gwendoline,' she said. 'I will meet with you later tonight.'

She started to turn away and nearly bumped into Lord Penrith. Immediately, she dropped into a curtsy. 'My lord.'

He offered his arm. 'Walk with me a moment, won't you, Lady Morwenna?'

She recognised the command and obeyed. Her heart was pounding in her chest, but she smiled as if all was well. The earl led her along the hall and remarked, 'It seems you've made quite an impression upon the men I invited to Penrith. I suppose that must be…very different from what you're used to.'

He knows.

Her fears multiplied at the unspoken warning not to overstep her place. But she answered, 'I am grateful to you for a place to stay until I can return home again. And certainly, we both hope that Lady Gwendoline will find a suitor whom she will marry.'

I understand my place and will do nothing to threaten her chances.

He nodded at that. 'I remembered where I saw that pendant before. It's curious that someone like you would possess it.'

She didn't understand what he meant. 'As I said before, it was my mother's. I don't know where she got it. Possibly from her family.'

The earl's expression turned smug. 'I highly doubt that. Considering that this pendant once belonged to Queen Eleanor.'

Chapter Five

Robert waited for Morwenna in the kitchens for hours, but there was no sign of her. But to his surprise, Henry the Fletcher returned, along with two other villagers. His expression was grim as they closed the door behind them.

'What is it?' Robert asked.

'We need your help,' a fair-haired man said.

Henry gestured for him to sit, but Robert refused. He waited for the man to continue, and then the third companion, a tall, bearded man, spoke. 'We know you're here to win the hand of Lady Gwendoline. And if you wed her, you'll become the Earl of Penrith once again.'

Robert nodded. 'I intend to gain her hand in marriage, aye.'

'You must win,' Henry insisted. 'Even if it means defeating your own brother.' He glanced at the fair-haired man. 'We need your help, Robert. Penrith's men are getting worse.' Before he could ask what the man meant, Henry added, 'Bertrand's daughter was…hurt by Lord Penrith's soldiers.'

'They took her,' Bertrand said dully. 'And she was given no choice. I know the men defiled her.'

A tightness caught in Robert's gut. 'Is she a prisoner?'

Bertrand shook his head. 'They sent her back early this morning. She hasn't stopped weeping.' His expression grew murderous. 'I want to bury every last one of them.' Then he nodded towards the bearded man. 'Landon lost his son last year. He was killed by one of the guards.'

'I'm sorry,' Robert said quietly.

'You fled,' Landon accused. 'And we need you back. You have to take command of Penrith.' He stepped forward, closing the distance with his fists clenched. 'We've done our part, hiding you from the earl. But I swear to God above, if you turn coward again—'

'I won't fail you,' he promised. 'I swear it on my father's life. I will do everything in my power to set you free.'

Henry exchanged a look with the other men. 'Alfred has to die, Robert. And whether you take Penrith through marriage or conquest, we care not.'

Their pain and loss were tangible, and Robert would not rest until he'd taken the lands again. 'I will keep my vow,' he said. And inwardly, he hoped he could somehow avenge Bertrand's daughter.

The men turned to depart, but Henry held back a moment. 'Have a care, Robert. How can you win the heart of Lady Gwendoline if all your time is spent at Morwenna's side?'

'Morwenna is helping me,' he insisted. But still, he understood the man's warning. 'And we are only friends.'

From the look in Henry's eyes, he wasn't certain of that. 'I want to believe you,' the man said, 'but know this. If you do not stand by us, we will start our own rebellion. If you don't succeed by the end of harvest...there will be bloodshed. And it will be on your hands.'

A coldness suddenly gripped him, and Robert stiffened. 'No. If you start your own battle, the blood is on your hands, not mine.' He stared back at the men and took a step forward. 'I am doing everything in my power to take back these lands. But I take orders from no one. Not even you.'

With that, Henry turned his back and walked away. He passed Morwenna, who was still dressed in her evening finery, as if she no longer wanted to disguise herself. Robert grew wary, wondering if she no longer cared about the danger. But he didn't miss the look of warning from Henry.

He knew the man was right. He needed to set aside his attraction and pursue Gwendoline as if he truly wanted *her* and not the land. It felt as if invisible chains bound him to responsibilities he didn't want, but he had no choice. His people were suffering, and he had to distance himself from Morwenna.

She walked alongside him, not speaking at first. When she was safely inside the pantry, she appeared flustered, but there was also a trace of fear. 'It took me a while before I could slip away. I had to talk to Gwendoline.'

'Because of Piers,' he guessed.

She nodded. 'She likes him and was asking what I'd learned about him.'

'And what did you tell her?' Though he kept his tone even, it bothered him that Piers had somehow managed to unravel his plans.

'I told her the truth. That I believe he does care for her.'

'How could you think that?' Robert didn't agree with her opinion at all. 'Piers only cares about claiming Penrith by any means possible. He doesn't care for Gwendoline at all.'

'You're wrong,' Morwenna said. 'He has spent

all his time at her side. He listens to her, and I've seen the look in his eyes.'

'So, you're taking his side now, are you? Why did I think you were going to help me instead?' he muttered.

'I'm not taking anyone's side,' she answered. 'But you're no different from him. You both want the land, and you're willing to do anything to get it. The only difference is that Gwendoline likes Piers better.'

He couldn't believe she was comparing them. His intentions were centred upon reclaiming Penrith and helping the people while Piers was trying to claim land that wasn't his. 'She only likes Piers because she met him first.'

'No, that isn't the only reason. You've made no effort to know her. Piers has done everything to see her.'

'I waited in the forest for hours,' he argued. 'And I competed among the other suitors for a chance at winning her hand in marriage.'

'But aside from that, you've spent very little time with her. Admiring her from afar will do nothing at all. Gwendoline has spoken with Piers on more than one occasion.'

Robert couldn't understand why she was defending him. 'It would be a disaster if Piers won her hand in marriage. He has no idea how to govern an estate. Nor does he have a birthright or any claim to Penrith.'

She studied him for a moment, her face growing sad. 'No more than I have the right to be a lady, Robert. I'm nothing but a serf. I have no right to be sharing a chamber with Lady Gwendoline.'

Her gentle chiding made him realise what he'd said. 'But you're not trying to claim something that doesn't belong to you.'

'Aren't I? If I decide to wed one of the suitors, am I not trying to claim the position of lady of his household?'

Yet Morwenna looked nothing like a servant, especially in the green silk gown. Her eyes were luminous against her skin, her dark hair framing her soft features. It struck him that he'd never really admitted to himself how beautiful she was. She had easily passed herself off as a noblewoman. She would have no difficulty at all in finding a husband.

But the blade of jealousy cut deeper. He knew he could not claim Morwenna—but neither did he want her to marry someone else. His honour was hanging by a thread, and no matter how he tried to push back the irrational anger, he couldn't stop the emotions from rising hotter.

Henry's accusation rose up between them, that

he was spending too much time with Morwenna.
Robert knew it was true. And though he told
himself that they were only friends, he could not
deny that there could be more between them. She
captivated him, making him aware of the way
she moved, the softness of her lips.

With reluctance, he forced an invisible distance between them. He had no right to desire
more. Or to forget why he'd come to Penrith.
'You should have been born a lady, Morwenna.'

She traced the gold chain around her neck, the
one that had belonged to the mother she'd lost. 'It
would have made no difference. I am who I am.'

He didn't know what she meant by that. 'You
deserve a better life than the one you had. I hope
you find that with someone.' The words burned
in his mouth, for he didn't mean them any more.

'And which man would you choose for me?'
she asked. There was an underlying tone beneath
her words, one he didn't quite understand.

'I don't know,' he answered honestly. 'Only
you can decide that.'

She stood up from the sack of grain, drawing
closer to him. He saw the sadness in her eyes and
wondered what had caused it. 'Do you know why
I asked to meet with you tonight?'

Her words were vulnerable, holding him spellbound. He didn't know what to say or do, but

when she rested her hands on his shoulders, he knew. All along, he had trained beside this woman, watching her grow lean and strong. She had followed him here, though it was not her battle to face. She faced him, and in those eyes, he saw a yearning that reached down past his goals, past his sense of reason, and kept him fixed upon her.

Morwenna was beautiful in a wild, untamed way. And he could not deny the rise of interest he shouldn't feel. She wasn't his, and he had no right to lay claim to her.

'Why?' he asked.

'Because I'm going to leave and not see you again. And I wanted to tell you farewell.' She reached for his hands and gave them a tight squeeze.

In that moment, something shifted inside him. Robert didn't know what it meant, but it seemed as if every thought abandoned his brain. All he knew was that he couldn't let her go. Not yet. He knew there was no future for them, but despite what Henry and the others had said, she meant a great deal to him.

Morwenna started to pull away, but he held her hands in his. He studied her features, not knowing when he would see her again. Although he had no choice in the woman he had to marry, he had this last stolen moment with Morwenna.

'Robert,' she murmured.

'Don't say it.' He reached for her and pulled her into a kiss. He tasted the soft sweetness of her lips, and it ignited a desire he'd only imagined. Mayhap it had always been there, but he had never allowed himself to consider it. Now, he unleashed the fire that had been banked inside him during the past two years. He allowed his instincts to take hold, and he pressed her up against the wall.

Morwenna wrapped her arms around his neck, and when she clung to him, he felt her hips press against him. His body responded to her, though he had no right to touch her. And yet, he was caught in the storm of need, where all logic abandoned him. He had never been with a woman before—not like this.

She let out a gasp, and he drew his mouth against her throat, tasting the softness there. His own arousal was so intense, he was drowning in her, unable to get enough. His brain warned him that this was wrong. He had an obligation to court Lady Gwendoline.

And yet, he could not deny his attraction to Morwenna. He kissed her again, his tongue sliding against hers. She shuddered, and he wanted to bring her the same aching pleasure that roared through him. He gave in to instinct, and his hands moved up her waist against the silk of her gown. His fingers grazed against the side of her breasts, and she responded by gripping his hair.

He caressed her gently, though he didn't know what to do. He had never touched Morwenna like this, and he didn't want to harm her out of ignorance. With both hands, he explored her softness, watching the way she responded to him. When she didn't pull away, he cupped her breast, stroking it with his thumb. Her nipple grew erect, and a moan escaped her as he caressed it. Her eyes were closed, her face revealing an intimate response.

God above, he wanted to feel her bare skin against him, to take her nipple into his mouth and taste her. He lifted her up, laying her back against a sack of grain.

'Robert, wait.'

Morwenna's body was alive with need. She'd never expected this from Robert. Shock had coursed through her when he'd stolen the kiss, awakening a response she'd never imagined. It terrified her, for she wondered whether she'd misjudged him. Did he have feelings for her at all?

Her emotions were overwhelming, her body craving something it could not name. And so she'd begged him to stop.

He pulled back from her immediately. 'Forgive me, Morwenna. I didn't mean to hurt you.'

He had, though not in the way he suspected. It wasn't his touch or the heated kiss. It was the warmth in his voice and the passion that were enough to crack her heart into pieces. The tears broke through, but it was because he'd given her a gift she'd never anticipated—the gift of hope.

'It's all right.' She straightened her gown, though beneath it her breasts still felt the echo of his touch. 'I just...never thought you would kiss me.' She closed her eyes, the fear of rejection threatening to overwhelm her. 'Robert, why did you?'

An awkwardness descended between them, and he stared at her as if unable to find the right words. 'I don't know,' he admitted honestly. 'I just didn't want you to leave without...' His voice trailed off as if he didn't have the words to finish the sentence.

'Is there anything between us at all?' She hated the aching uncertainty of the question and how pitiful it made her feel. But she had to know the truth and whether she should abandon him and choose a different path.

His expression turned serious. 'We are friends, Morwenna. And always will be, I hope.'

'But you cannot ever wed a miller's daughter, can you?' The words felt heavy, but she had to speak them.

He closed his eyes and sat down beside her. 'My choices don't belong to me, Morwenna. The people of Penrith are suffering because of Lord Alfred. I owe it to them to save them. Don't ask me to choose. Not after I failed them once before.'

The answer weighed down upon her, and she knew he'd spoken the truth. 'And what if Gwendoline marries Piers instead?'

'The people will tell her father the truth about him soon enough,' he said. 'The only reason they haven't told Alfred about me is because they know I intend to help them. In time, the rumours will take care of Piers.'

She took a deep breath. 'I saw my father's… woman Lena today.' She hesitated before admitting, 'I think she told Lord Penrith about me.' Although from their earlier conversations, she suspected the earl already knew of her past. 'It's why I have to leave before I'm forced out.' She no longer believed she had the option of marrying one of the suitors, especially now. Nor did she want to wed any more. It wouldn't be fair to a prospective bridegroom, for she would always compare him to Robert.

'Where will you go?'

She shrugged. 'Brian will find a place for us. We'll wander until we do.'

Robert's expression grew concerned. 'I don't like the thought of you both going off alone. It's not safe.'

'It's not safe here either,' she answered. She thought about telling Robert what Lord Penrith had said about the pendant, but something held her back. What did it matter where the chain had come from? Her mother wasn't alive to tell the tale, so Morwenna would never know for certain.

'Farewell, Robert. I hope Gwendoline brings you happiness.' The words were a physical pain, but now that he'd vowed he would not abandon Penrith, there was no future for them. She had to give up on him.

Her emotions were raw, her gut tightening at the realisation that she had let herself fall into the trap of wanting more. 'Goodbye,' she murmured. She started to turn back, but he caught her hand and pulled her back.

He slid one hand around her waist, the other threading through her hair as he dragged her into one last kiss. His mouth captured hers in a heated storm of regret. She clung to him, heedless of the tears, and kissed him hard. His tongue slid inside her mouth, and the sensation overwhelmed her. Her body craved his touch, and she arched as he kissed her throat, his hands holding her close.

'I don't want you to go,' he murmured against her mouth.

Her heart was pounding, mingled with desire and need. 'Then come with me.'

He closed his eyes, but she already knew his answer. She couldn't stay here, and she would not ask him to give up on his people.

With a sigh, she answered, 'So be it.' She leaned in and brushed her mouth against his, one last time. 'Don't come to see me again.'

Her heart was breaking as she left the pantry, and it was only when she reached the outside that her sobs broke forth. She didn't bother trying to suppress them any longer. Instead, she let the tears flow, weeping for what would never be.

As she made her way towards the keep, she heard footsteps approaching beside her. It was Gareth the archer. She swiped her tears away and slowed her pace. Likely he was waiting to join her as an escort. But to her surprise, his expression appeared angry against the dim torch lights. His mouth was set in a tight line, and instinctively, she took a step away. Something was wrong.

'You were playing us for fools, weren't you, *Lady* Morwenna?'

Before she could move, he seized her right arm. She tried to wrench it away, but his strength overpowered hers.

'Leave me alone.' She raised her voice, hoping Robert would overhear and would come to help her. Then she feigned weakness as her left hand closed over her eating knife. She didn't know why Gareth was feeling possessive, but she wasn't about to become his victim.

'You were pretending to be a virtuous lady, and all the while, you were sneaking off to another man,' he spat.

Her anger flared up at his possessive tone. Had she ever believed him to be kind and gentle? Far from it. She realised now that it had all been an act. He'd only said the words he thought she wanted to hear.

'Unhand me, or I'll scream.' Again, she kept her voice loud, but no one seemed to care. She glanced around, but there was still no sign of Robert. Her nerves gathered, and she sensed that she would only have one opportunity to defend herself. But she only wanted to wound Gareth, not kill the man. She didn't know whether a swift cut would give her time to run.

'You won't scream,' he said, reaching to cover

her mouth. In that instant, she swung her blade at his face with her left hand. The knife cut through skin, and he released her, cursing as he reached for his cheek. Morwenna didn't wait but ran towards the soldiers guarding the keep. She breathed a sigh of relief when they closed around her.

Gareth ran forward but stopped at the bottom of the stairs. She sent him a cold look of fury and sheathed her eating knife. Then she went inside the keep, accompanied by the guards. When one closed the doors behind her, she thanked them. 'I'll return to my chamber now.'

The other guard shook his head. 'We were sent to bring you to Lord Penrith. He wants to question you.'

Question her? About what? Morwenna's fears tightened within her stomach, but she obeyed. Right now, she wished she could return to the chamber she shared with Gwendoline. Instead, she followed the guards towards a smaller chamber behind the dais. She passed by Brian, who appeared alarmed. Though she didn't know what this was about, she sent him a silent message for help. He met her gaze before retreating to the shadows. No doubt he would go to Robert.

The earl sat beside a brazier, his feet resting on a foot stool. His expression remained mild, and he gestured for the guards to step back. They closed the door and stood in front of it.

'I thought you would have been sleeping at this hour,' he remarked. 'It's not safe for a woman to be out alone at night.' His gaze shifted to her left hand that bore the blood stains from striking out at Gareth.

'Thank you for sending your guards,' she murmured, though she knew that wasn't what this was about. 'I wanted a few moments outside in the moonlight.'

She sensed that he recognised the lie, but there was nothing else to say. Instead, he rose from his chair and faced her. 'Did you think I wouldn't learn who you really are, Morwenna?' He gave a thin smile. 'You should have stayed away.'

She gave no answer, and understood that Lena had revealed everything. Her cheeks burned with embarrassment and fear about what would happen.

'I intend to leave in the morning,' she said. 'I thank you for giving me shelter, but it's time for me to return to my family.'

'You're not going anywhere,' he answered. 'You'll be staying here until I know why a miller's daughter stole a pendant that belonged to the queen.'

'I didn't steal anything!' Morwenna protested. 'It belonged to my mother.'

'I've sent for the king's men,' he said calmly. 'This is a matter of justice. Our sovereign lord will decide what's to be done about the theft.' He waved a hand, and both guards closed in, each taking an arm.

Horror washed over her at the realisation that they were taking her captive. And she simply didn't know if Brian or Robert could get her out.

Chapter Six

'What are we going to do?' Brian demanded. 'He's taken her prisoner.'

A numbness settled in Robert's gut at those four words. He could hardly believe Morwenna had been taken. Brian had revealed Penrith's accusation about the pendant being stolen.

Robert's first instinct was to go after her and break her out of her imprisonment. For a moment, his mind constructed the image of every room in the castle. He could visualise all the rooms, sorting through them, until he decided where she might be held captive.

But then, helping her escape would be more dangerous and could result in his own captivity. It was better for Brian to infiltrate their defences by remaining with the soldiers.

'We need more information,' he told the young man. 'Find out where she's being held and tell Lady Gwendoline. She may be able to intervene until we can get her out. I'll speak with the others here and find out what I can about that pendant.'

Brian paused a moment. 'Do you think that's why the king's men came for us two years ago? Were they searching for it?'

'I don't know.' But he couldn't deny that it was possible. There had been no other reason to take Brian and Morwenna prisoner unless it was for questioning. Something larger was at stake here, though he couldn't guess what. 'But try to send word to Morwenna that we're going to get her out.'

A dark resolution centred within him. He'd asked Morwenna not to make him choose between Penrith and her. He'd abandoned his people once before, and he'd sworn he would never do it again. And yet, how could he stand aside and let her become a prisoner? No, he would find a way to break her out and get them both to safety.

'I'm going to speak with Henry and find out what I can.' He wasn't certain the man would have any information, especially since the miller had only arrived a few years ago, and his wife was already gone. But it was worth asking.

'I'm going to return to the keep,' Brian said.

'And I'll find a way to bring her food.' He reached for some dried apples and a loaf of bread.

'Good. Let me know how she is.' He followed him outside but turned back towards the gates. The guards likely would not allow him to leave, so he would have to find another means of getting outside. 'Brian, wait. I need you to distract the guards so I can get through the gates.'

The young man seemed to understand. 'I'll go and ask them about Morwenna.' He paused and found a jug of ale. 'This may help loosen their tongues.'

Robert kept a short distance behind Brian and moved towards the inner bailey wall. The young man approached the gates while Robert held back. Though he didn't hear what Brian said to the men, he waited until the guards drew closer to the young man. Then he slipped outside into the darkness.

As he hurried towards Henry's house, he couldn't take his mind off Morwenna's kiss. Though she had intended it as a farewell, it had shaken him to his bones. She had been there for him during the past two years as a friend, a woman he could talk to about anything. He'd taken her for granted without knowing her feelings.

But what shook him the most was the realisation that he did care about her, more than he'd ever known. Somehow, she had crept past his defences until he couldn't imagine the thought of never seeing her again.

He didn't know what the future would hold or if he would ever get Penrith back again. But he would do everything in his power to set Morwenna free.

Morwenna shivered in the darkness of the castle keep. It had been two days since they'd imprisoned her below ground, and she'd been forced to wear only her shift. Lord Penrith had sent Lena to take back Gwendoline's bliaud, and the pendant. They also had not returned her mother's gown to her, which meant she'd lost everything. The smirk upon Lena's face had only deepened her shame.

The walls were made of cold dirt, and Morwenna wore iron manacles upon her wrists and ankles. Despite it being summer, she felt only frigid air underground, and she couldn't seem to get warm. It conjured up the memory of being imprisoned in the wagon with the others only two years ago. She remembered the soldier tearing her gown, his hand reaching for her breast, and she shuddered at the vision.

But if she didn't get out of here, she would be

at the mercy of the earl's soldiers. What would stop them from violating her? Nothing at all.

She couldn't understand why the earl had conjured up so many groundless accusations. Yes, she'd lied about her family, but he could have simply sent her away with the clothes on her back. There was no reason to imprison her for the deception.

A draught of cold air slid through the room, and she drew up her knees, huddling in vain as she sought warmth that wasn't there. But worse was the isolation.

Gwendoline had not come to see her even once. A small part of her had hoped that they had become close enough friends that the lady would at least come and speak with her. But perhaps her father had forbidden it.

Why had the earl implied that the pendant had been stolen from the queen? She couldn't imagine such a thing. More likely it had been a gift to her mother, but how could she prove it? There had to be far more to this story than she knew.

Until her mother's death a few years ago she hadn't even known of the pendant's existence, much less the gown's. And somehow the pieces didn't seem to fit. Though her father had claimed that her mother had been from a noble family, Eldreth's behaviour was nothing like Gwendoline's. She had obeyed her husband without question, seeming almost afraid of him. It was not the behaviour of a woman accustomed to leading others.

Was it possible that her father had lied to her about the pendant and the gown? Had he been a thief? She dismissed the thought for if that were true, he would have sold them years ago.

Morwenna heard footsteps approaching, and she flinched, moving against the wall. The fears multiplied within her, for in the darkness, she could not see who it was. The flare of a torch momentarily blinded her before she saw the earl accompanied by another woman and two soldiers.

It took a little while for her eyes to adjust. Finally, she recognised the midwife Nelda. The older woman's expression held sympathy, but Morwenna had no idea why she was here.

'I spoke with the villagers to learn more about your mother,' the earl began.

Morwenna couldn't understand why he had gone to such trouble. Why would he care about her mother? He had already taken back the gown and the pendant.

'No one remembered her except Nelda,' he continued.

'But we came here after my mother died,'

Morwenna protested. Nelda couldn't have known her, unless…

'I knew Eldreth from my travels, years ago,' Nelda said. 'I've been a midwife for a long time, and I helped her after she lost her first babe.'

Morwenna sobered at that. 'I didn't know.'

The midwife risked a glance at the earl. 'Eldreth nearly died in the birth. I told Geoffrey she shouldn't try to have more children.'

Morwenna didn't understand why Nelda was speaking about the past or why the earl had gone to such lengths to bring the woman here. What was the purpose?

She was about to ask, when Nelda added, 'You can imagine my surprise when I saw her the following year with a three-year-old and an infant.'

'That's not possible,' Morwenna breathed. She knew what the woman was implying, but she couldn't imagine that it was true. It could only mean one thing.

The midwife answered her unspoken thoughts. 'I don't know where Eldreth and Geoffrey found you and your brother, but you were not her children. After the stillborn death, she wasn't capable of it.'

Morwenna stilled, clutching her hand to her

stomach. Denial rushed through her. She simply couldn't grasp what Nelda was saying. 'Then if she wasn't my mother…who was?'

The midwife glanced at the earl. 'My lord, I would swear it upon my life. And while I don't know where that pendant came from, it never belonged to Eldreth. She was a milk maid, nothing more.'

The earl smiled. 'Thank you for telling me of this,' he said to the midwife. 'You may go.'

The woman hurried away, leaving behind the weight of her words .

You were not her children.

Morwenna wanted to deny it, to insist that the woman was lying or that she was wrong. And yet… Eldreth had never been particularly close to her. Aye, she'd taken care of them, but had she ever loved them?

Confusion darkened Morwenna's thoughts for she didn't understand what the earl was implying. Did he believe that she and Brian had been stolen from their parents? Why would he care?

She waited for him to speak. When Lord Penrith simply stared at her, she felt the uncertainty slide beneath her skin. She didn't know if truth would help her cause, but she saw no other choice. 'I do not know what any of this means, my lord. But I am deeply sorry for pretending to be someone I am not. If you let me go, I will never come back to Penrith. You won't see me again, I swear it.'

'Why did you pretend?' He took a step closer, studying her as if trying to memorise her features. It made her uncomfortable, so she looked away. She couldn't tell him about Robert, so she thought of the only reason she could.

'I…wanted to know what it would be like to be a lady,' she lied. 'Just for a little while.'

'You were born a serf, and you will die a serf,' he announced. 'You must know your place and know who your betters are.'

Did he plan to execute her for the deception? She hadn't imagined her crime to be that bad, but would he try to make an example of her? Fear roared through her, and a wave of nausea caught her stomach.

'I beg you for mercy, my lord.' She had no choice but to plead for her life. No one could save her now.

'Your life is in the king's hands,' he said. 'It will be his decision what to do about the theft.'

Relief poured through her that she would not die at the earl's hands. But she needed him to know the truth. 'I never stole anything. I swear it.'

'You wore the pendant,' he stated, 'while pretending to be my daughter's equal.'

'I didn't know where my mother got it,' she protested. 'I thought it belonged to her family.'

'You will be punished for your lies,' the earl continued, 'and for the injury you caused to Gareth of Watcomb.'

She didn't argue that the man had attacked her first. Right now, one wrong word could make matters far worse. Instead, she closed her eyes, numbing herself to the fear. Though she wanted to believe that Robert and Brian could save her, it seemed impossible now. Soldiers patrolled here, day and night. She could not break free of the chains that bound her.

And she knew not what her punishment would be.

It had taken every ounce of control not to reveal himself to Morwenna. Robert had disguised himself as one of the guards, in order to get a closer look at her prison. As he'd hoped, she'd been so distracted by the earl, she'd not even realised he was there.

But now he knew where she was being held and how. He and Brian had begun to form a loose plan of how to get her out, but a thousand things might go wrong. He wanted to ask Lady Gwendoline for her assistance, but he suspected she could do nothing.

Piers could help them. His half-brother could provide a distraction while he and Brian worked to free Morwenna. Yet, he already knew the price Piers would demand—that he abandon his claim to Penrith. And Robert wasn't ready to do that yet.

Instead, he'd studied Morwenna's chains during the conversation she'd had with the earl. It had been startling to learn that she and Brian were not the miller's children, but his greater focus was on how to help her escape. He'd kept his concentration on the manacles and the number of guards and the location of each one. He knew the tools he would need to free her and where he could find them.

Tonight at midnight, he would try to get her out. He suspected the earl would punish her publicly at dawn tomorrow, so his best hope was to slip inside, dressed as one of the guards. If they could escape in secret, that would be the easiest way.

But first, he wanted to talk to Brian. He walked through the stone hallways beneath the castle. He had explored every inch of the keep, and he now knew that the fire had not destroyed the underground tunnels. There was another way out through the wine cellar. He continued walking until he found Brian waiting just outside the stone staircase. 'Walk with me,' he said in a low voice. Both were disguised as soldiers, and he hoped no one would take a closer look.

'She's in chains and the earl intends to punish her. I'm going to break her out before that happens.' He led Brian towards one end of the inner bailey wall. 'I want you to get the keys to the wine cellar from Wilfred tonight. Unlock it and leave it open for us. I'll break Morwenna out.'

'Do you need my help to free her?' Brian asked quietly.

'No, I'll need you to find horses. Tether them just outside the wall. Then take one of them and ride towards the abbey. Tell my uncle we're coming to seek sanctuary.' It would buy them time until he could decide where to take Morwenna.

He knew that by rescuing her, he was hurting his chances of winning Gwendoline's hand in marriage. But he could never abandon Morwenna at a time like this. The thought of her suffering was like a blade in his gut. She didn't deserve to be a prisoner, and he would do anything to get her out.

And then after he helped her get to safety, he would return to Penrith alone. An ache clenched within him, even if he knew it was the right thing to do. He had to lock away whatever forbidden feelings he held and let her go. They had already said their farewells, and he would simply have to do it again.

'I could wait with the horses,' Brian offered. 'In case you need my help.'

'No. It will draw too much attention. I can get her out if we share a horse, but if they see two horses, they may give chase.' It was too grave a risk, and he wasn't about to endanger Morwenna's life.

There was something greater at stake, something about that pendant. But he didn't want to tell Brian what he'd learned from the earl. At least, not yet. Let him believe his past was real, at least until Morwenna could tell him herself.

The young man paused a moment and asked, 'What about Piers?'

Piers was a complication, but Robert wondered if his brother could somehow become an ally in this. 'I don't know yet. If we can manage to get out without his involvement, that would probably be safest for your sister. And for him.'

Brian inclined his head. 'I'll get the keys to the wine cellar now, but I'll wait until dark to get the horse.' He turned to meet Robert's gaze. 'I won't let you down.'

He rested his hand on the young man's shoulder. 'I know you won't.'

For Morwenna's life and safety depended on it.

It was just after nightfall when two soldiers came for her. Morwenna's heart pounded within her chest as they bound her wrists together with leather straps and unfastened the manacles. She wanted to ask where they were taking her, but she already suspected it had to do with her punishment. Terror welled up inside her, and she struggled to keep her fears under control.

Where were Brian and Robert? Or even Piers? Did they even know where she was?

She'd wanted so badly to see any of them, but no one had come. The weight of her seclusion bore down on her, making her feel so alone.

'Where are you taking me?' she asked the men. But they gave no answer. She feared it would be a public punishment in front of everyone, but to her surprise, they led her up the stairs to a smaller chamber at the back of the keep. Had she been wrong? Had Gwendoline intervened on her behalf somehow?

Her hope died when she saw Lord Penrith waiting. A set of manacles was chained to the back wall. Nausea rose up in her throat when she saw a small table with a whip. A flogging, then.

One other guard was waiting, and she felt the weight of his stare. The guards on each side of her pulled her forward, and Morwenna struggled against their grip. Though she knew it was likely in vain, she prayed for some way to escape.

But the soldiers unfastened the manacles and lifted her arms high, chaining her once again. Then they slit the back of her shift with a blade, revealing her back. The garment fell forward, exposing her breasts to their gaze. Her face burned with humiliation, for she could not cover herself.

'Twenty lashes,' the earl proclaimed. 'For her crime of pretending to be a lady. And for cutting Lord Watcomb's face.'

She trembled at the sentence, terrified of the whip. 'Please, my lord,' she begged. 'Grant me mercy. I swear to you, I will leave Penrith and never return.'

He was silent for a moment and then she heard him say, 'You ask for mercy after you shared my daughter's chamber, wore her gowns, and ate at my table?'

'It was a mistake,' she whispered. 'I know I wronged you both.'

'You did,' he agreed. 'But I am a merciful

man, and as such, I will grant you a choice. I will reduce your sentence to ten lashes.'

She didn't trust him, for there seemed to be a condition. Her prediction turned out to be right when he added, 'After your flogging, I will give you to my men to enjoy.' He laughed quietly. 'Or if you do not want their attentions, you can keep your original sentence of twenty lashes.'

She closed her eyes, unable to stop the tears that flowed. 'Twenty,' she whispered. But as she heard the soldier pick up the whip, she suspected it would not matter. Ten or twenty, she would be at their mercy.

And when the lash struck her bare skin, she could not stop the scream that tore from her throat.

'I thought you said her punishment was at dawn,' Brian snarled. 'We have to stop them.'

Morwenna's scream had stopped Robert cold, ripping his carefully laid plans asunder. His instincts raged to go to her, to kill any man who dared to hurt her.

But while he wanted to run with her brother, his brain warned him to stop and think. If he made the wrong decision, it could cost them their lives. And if she died because he'd been too reckless, he would never forgive himself.

For a moment, his mind was frozen, working through the possibilities while Brian was ready to run down the narrow passageway and break down the door.

'Let's go,' her brother urged.

But Robert gripped the young man's arm, blocking him. 'Wait. We have to have a plan.'

'We don't have time for a plan,' Brian shot back. 'He's killing her while you're standing there trying to think of what to do.'

The accusation struck too close to his fears, but he held fast to Brian. 'If you go in there right now, the soldiers will kill you, and it won't stop her flogging. We're outnumbered. We need more men to help us.'

Another scream pierced the air, and her brother glared at him. 'There are two of us, and we can fight. We're strong enough.'

Robert didn't believe that. Brian had sparred against them, but he had never faced men who were trying to kill him. 'Go and get Piers,' he ordered. 'With his help, we can win this.'

'He won't fight for Morwenna,' Brian retorted. 'He cares nothing for her.' Another crack of the whip sounded, and Brian reached for the door.

Robert jerked him backwards and shoved him up against the wall. 'But I *do* care about her.' It was all he could do not to force the door open and stop the flogging. 'And if you open that door now, they'll kill us both.'

'You're nothing but a coward,' Brian spat. 'You already lost Penrith once. I'm not about to let you lose my sister.'

His hand curled in a fist and he struck Robert hard. He hadn't expected the blow, and he stumbled a moment before Brian burst into the room.

God help them. There was no stopping him now.

Brian unsheathed his sword and went after the man wielding the whip. The soldier turned in surprise, but the other two men closed in on him, their weapons drawn. There was no time to reach him before they struck.

They were going to fail. And unless he acted now, all of them were dead.

While the men were distracted with Brian, Robert unsheathed his dagger and went after the earl. In one move, he took the earl hostage and put a blade to his throat. 'Stop your men,' he said quietly.

When Lord Penrith ignored his command, Robert ordered the soldiers, 'Let the boy go!' At first, it didn't seem that the men had heard him. The earl struggled, and Robert let the blade cut into the man's skin. 'I wouldn't move if I were you.' He overpowered the man, holding the dagger steady.

'Enough!' Lord Penrith called out. But the men already had Brian in custody. Two of the soldiers held him, each gripping an arm, while the third soldier held his sword to Brian's throat.

'Tell your men to release the woman and her brother,' Robert said quietly.

The earl remained silent until he pressed the blade again. Then the older man shot back, 'You're nothing but a common bastard, trying to court my daughter. I knew you weren't good enough for her.'

Robert repeated his order quietly. 'I said, let them go.'

But the earl wasn't listening. 'You won't hurt me,' he tried to argue. 'I have fifty men who will gut you and put your head upon a spear as a warning.'

'Why wouldn't I hurt you?' Robert asked smoothly. 'I am the true heir to Penrith. The king's men may have murdered my father, but I am the rightful earl.'

At that, the man stilled. 'You wouldn't dare.'

'Are you willing to take that risk?' Robert glanced at the soldiers, knowing they had witnessed the people's dissatisfaction. 'The serfs don't seem very pleased with your leadership. It wouldn't take much to cause a rebellion.'

'What do you want?' Penrith gritted out.

'I planned to wed your daughter Gwendoline for the sake of regaining my lands. Now, I'm demanding that you free Morwenna and her brother.'

'And the moment I do, my men will slaughter you where you stand,' the earl responded. 'I'll be rid of you. Are *you* willing to take that risk?'

Robert stared at Morwenna's broken body, the blood dripping from her bare back. Her shift hung at her waist, and it infuriated him to see what they'd done to her. Rage blinded him with the vicious desire for vengeance. She didn't deserve any of this. But he could not let emotions overcome him. If he made one wrong move, all of them could die.

'I will take that risk,' he said. 'Unchain Morwenna and give her to her brother.' Beneath his hands, the earl's blood welled up from the pressure of the blade.

At last, the man gritted out, 'You heard him.'

One soldier unfastened the manacles that chained Morwenna's arms above her head. The moment he did, she crumpled to the ground. It was all Robert could do to keep from slicing the earl's throat, for her punishment had been brutal.

'Now release her brother,' he said calmly. 'Brian, take Morwenna out of here.'

'What about you?' The young man stared back at Robert in horror. 'W-we can't go and leave you.'

'You don't have a choice,' Robert answered. 'Take her to safety.' When Brian didn't move, he snapped, 'Don't you dare make this sacrifice in vain. Get her out of here.'

Brian's expression held the weight of defeat, and he closed his eyes, bowing his head. The soldiers stepped back while Brian took off his cloak and covered his sister, lifting her into his arms. He went to the doorway and stopped to look back.

There was raw anguish in Brian's eyes, for he knew Robert could not move the blade from the earl's throat. And the moment he left it would all be over.

'Close the door,' he told Brian, 'and take her away.' He didn't want the soldiers knowing which direction they'd gone. He'd already shown Brian the passageway in the wine cellar that led outside, and he hoped they would reach it before the soldiers could find him.

Time seemed to freeze, and it was strange to be looking death in the face. He'd never imagined being caught in this trap, but now, he had to find a way out.

The chances of his survival were almost none. But he knew this castle keep better than anyone, and that was his only advantage.

The moment Brian shut the door the soldiers charged forward.

Chapter Seven

It had been two days since her father had locked her in her chamber. Alfred wouldn't say why, but Gwendoline was furious at his behaviour. One moment she'd been deciding upon a possible husband, and the next, he'd sent all the suitors away and had confined her to her room. The competition had ended without a winner. Why? She'd done nothing to deserve this.

Morwenna had gone missing, and something was very wrong. When Gwen had questioned the servants who brought her food, they had only shaken their heads.

No one else came to see her. It was infuriating, and she'd spent most of her hours stabbing her embroidery and imagining ways to escape. Although there had once been a secret passage leading from her room, her father had sealed it, and there was no way out except through her door. She'd thought Piers would help her, but he'd gone missing. He'd only spoken to her once, but she'd worried that he would be caught and had sent him away.

But not before he'd slid a ribbon beneath the door. The ribbon she'd lost that night...

Her face flushed at the memory.

But tonight, when it was time for her evening meal, the door swung open, and she saw a familiar face.

'Piers,' she breathed. He had disguised himself as one of the guards, but she would recognise him anywhere.

He closed the door, and she started to run to him before she stopped herself. She had no right to embrace him, no matter that she found him handsome and was grateful for his rescue.

But despite her hesitation, Piers set down the food and pulled her into his arms, holding her tight. For a moment, she clung to him, savouring the forbidden affection.

Colour flooded her cheeks, but she calmed herself and asked, 'What's happening? Why am I being held prisoner by my father?'

His expression turned stony, and she didn't know what that meant. Then he said, 'Your father doesn't want you to know that he took Morwenna prisoner. She was not...who you thought she was.'

'She's the miller's daughter,' Gwendoline admitted. 'I've known that for a few days now.' Piers appeared startled that she was aware of it, but one of the maids had told her. It made sense why Morwenna had always seemed uncertain of herself.

'Were you the one who told the earl?'

She shook her head. 'No, in truth, I like Morwenna. And even if she is a serf, what of it? Does she not deserve the chance to wed a good man? Why should the circumstances of her birth affect her future?'

An unspoken emotion flashed over Piers's face before he masked it. He took her hands in his and asked, 'Do you want to help her?'

She smiled at that. 'Of course, I do.'

'We'll need a horse,' he said. 'Can you make the arrangements?'

'I don't...think I can. I'm supposed to be a prisoner, remember?'

He uttered a low curse, but then thought a moment. 'Did Morwenna leave any of her belongings here? She had some of her brother's older clothes.'

Gwendoline walked over to her trunk and found the bundle. When she unwrapped it, she found the tunic and hose Piers was talking about. 'Should I disguise myself?'

'Tell the stable master that you are bringing a horse to his lordship. He won't question you.' Piers reached for a battered cap and set it upon her head.

She twisted her braids into the cap, hiding her hair. He was staring at her, and she couldn't guess the thoughts in his head. But when he cupped her cheek, his thumb stroked her skin, and the searing touch burned through her. He'd stolen kisses before, and she wanted to feel his mouth upon hers again. She'd never felt anything like the fierce attraction he'd conjured, but something warned her that she might not see him again. He was watching her as if trying to memorise her features.

'Bring the horse to the barbican gate,' he said. 'Try not to let them see you.'

She covered his hand with hers. 'Are you going to get her out?'

His expression grew distant. 'I'll do what I can. Something happened earlier. Soldiers were searching everywhere. I think Robert might have freed her, but from what I've heard, it went wrong.'

She met his gaze with her own stare. 'You'll be careful?' He nodded. But again, something in his expression suggested that he was going to leave her. 'Will you return to me?'

In answer, he crushed her mouth to his, kissing her hard. She returned the kiss, embracing him. There was a wildness about Piers, of a man who never followed the rules. And whatever his plan was, she sensed that it wasn't safe at all.

'I'm going to wait for you in the hallway while you change your clothes,' he said. 'Then I'll lock the door, so no one knows you're gone.'

Her heart was racing when he closed the door behind him, and she tore at the laces of her gown. Whatever happened this night, she sensed that it would be dangerous.

She could hardly wait.

Robert knew he was going to die. He'd fought the three guards, cutting down two of them before the third wounded him. A sword had sliced his left arm, and he'd taken a hard blow to his head. It had only been sheer force of will that had given him the strength to stumble back into the hallway. He'd crawled through the darkness to hide behind a barrel while the men searched. Before they found him, he'd pried at the secret entrance to the tunnel leading outside. He'd used the rest of his strength to slide two more barrels in front of the passageway to seal it closed so no one would know it was there.

He'd lost all track of time as he'd bled, crawling through the tunnels. His head throbbed with pain, and as he neared the exit, he suspected it would make no difference, even if he did get out. He lacked the strength to get very far.

He hoped to God that Brian had managed to get Morwenna away from Penrith. As long as they were safe, that was all that mattered. He imagined them riding into the woods, and with any luck, they would make it to the abbey.

As for himself, he would probably bleed out here, for he lacked the strength to run. He crawled along the ground, forcing himself to keep moving. With every inch, he thought of the mistakes he'd made and the life he would never have. He'd planned to retake Penrith, no matter what the cost. He'd sworn he would help the people regain their freedom. And now, it would never happen.

He thought of Morwenna as he dragged himself forward. The memory of her kiss would haunt him until he died. She had been his friend, his companion, and now she was all he could envision as he crept towards his last moments. He thought of her wild dark hair and those green eyes. She had clung to him, awakening him to what might have been.

After what seemed like an hour, he finally reached the edge of the tunnel and crawled beneath the brambles. The grass was damp beneath him, and he rolled on his back to stare at the night sky. The stars gleamed against the darkness, and for a moment, he lay there, wondering how long it would take for death to claim him.

It was what he deserved. He should have died on the night of the attack two years ago. It was only a mercy that they'd escaped. His only regret was that he'd never realised how Morwenna felt about him…or how he felt about her. He'd centred everything around Penrith, closing out his own desires. And now it was too late.

All around him, he heard the sound of soldiers searching. They would likely find his body in an hour or two. Robert closed his eyes, hearing the hoof beats as they drew closer. He couldn't see what was happening, but when he tried to lift his head and shoulders, he gasped with the effort. There was the mingled noise of voices, and he couldn't distinguish anything. A rushing sound filled his ears as he tried to shrink back into the brambles.

Then he saw the flare of a torch. For a moment, the light blinded him, and weariness claimed his spirit. They had found him after all.

One week later

Morwenna drifted in and out of consciousness. Her back ached with agony, but the greater pain lay in her heart. Robert was dead. He had sacrificed himself to save them, and she would bear the guilt for always.

She never should have tried to be someone she wasn't. It didn't matter who her mother might have been or who her family was. All that mattered was who *she* was. And she was no one at all. She had dared to dream of loving Robert, and now he was gone.

Tears broke through, and she wept. She blamed herself for all of it. She had dared to reach for something that wasn't hers, and now he had paid the price with his life.

She didn't know where she was or what they would do now, but she was drowning in the pain of her heart and her body. All she could do was stare at the stone wall.

'Morwenna.' She didn't turn around at the sound of her brother's voice. It hardly mattered what anyone said any more. It didn't change her circumstances.

When she didn't answer, Brian came closer and knelt beside her pallet. For a moment, she could hardly bear to look at him. In his hand, he held out the golden pendant that had belonged to their mother. 'I stole this back on the night before you were beaten.'

She didn't take it, for the very sight of the thing evoked memories of the earl. Because of this, she had been flogged. This chain of gold had represented the dream of being someone else. She had worn the clothes of a noblewoman and had lived a different life for a week.

Brian let the chain fall upon the blanket, but she didn't touch it. She never wanted to see it again, for it was a symbol of her failure.

Her brother rested his hand upon hers. 'You'll be safe here at the abbey. Brother Douglas said he would bring you to the sisters at the nunnery.'

He was speaking as if he intended to send her away. 'Brian, what do you mean? Why would you send me away?'

Her brother's expression was grim. 'It's better this way.'

Morwenna struggled to rise from the pallet and then remembered that her shift was still split open at the back. Someone had treated her wounds with a poultice that smelled terrible.

'Were you planning to go somewhere?'

'I know you blame me for what happened to Robert.' Her brother laced his hands together, his expression sombre. 'He warned me that we needed more help to free you. He asked me to wait and fetch Piers, but instead, I broke through the door. And now he's dead because I wouldn't listen to him. No matter what I do, I can never atone for it.'

His words were a blade slicing through a heartache that hadn't healed. In spite of herself, she couldn't stop the tears. 'And you think that by leaving, it will make it all better? Why do you think I would forgive you for abandoning me?'

'Morwenna, I can't forgive myself. I intend to go with the Crusaders to the Holy Land. I'll… I'll fight for God and perhaps find absolution when I die.'

She stared back at him. 'If you go, I'll never see you again.'

His expression remained bleak. 'I deserve that, Morwenna.'

'And did I deserve to lose the man I love and now lose my only brother?' she asked. 'If you go, I have no one.' A flood of emotions washed over her, and this time she ignored the poultices and herbs, clutching her shift as she sat up.

'I caused another man to die because I made a

reckless move. I can't live with that, Morwenna. I deserved to die instead of him.'

The guilt of survival bore down on him, and she needed a way to bring him back from the edge. She tried to think of what she could say, how she could break through to him.

'I know you believe you have to die,' she began. 'You don't, Brian. You made a mistake, aye. But there are other ways to atone for it.'

'How? All Robert ever wanted was to restore Penrith and reclaim it.' He shook his head. 'There's nothing I can do to help with that.'

'Penrith was never our true home,' she agreed.

'We never had a home. Father was always moving us from place to place over the years.'

It was then that she seized on something that might distract her brother from his rash plan. 'Brian... I don't think he was our father.'

His brow furrowed at her statement. 'What are you talking about?'

She reached for the fallen pendant and held it out. 'If he was, he would have sold this. And the gown.'

He took it from her, examining the gold. While he did, she continued. 'The earl brought the midwife when he was questioning me. I didn't know why at the time.'

The memory of the beating made her tense,

but she forced herself to continue. 'But the mid-wife said that our mother couldn't bear children. She believes Eldreth stole us from another family.'

'That's not possible,' Brian said.

'Are you certain? She never had any other children.' The more she thought of it, the more sense it made. Despite her mother having been married to their father for years, there had not been any other pregnancies. 'And why else would they keep moving every year or two?'

Since they had never stayed in one place for long, Morwenna had grown so accustomed to losing friends, it was easier to remain isolated and not befriend anyone. She reached for the fallen pendant and held it out. 'The earl said this once belonged to Queen Eleanor, Brian.'

'We aren't of royal blood,' he argued.

'I know. But how did Eldreth get this? Did they steal it?'

He paled at her revelation as if he didn't want to believe any of it. 'I don't know. The earl might be wrong about the pendant. Perhaps it wasn't the queen's.' He laid the chain back upon the pallet. 'It might have been something they found some-where. Or perhaps he bought it.'

'You don't believe that,' she asserted. 'Our father didn't have two coins of his own.'

Brian only shrugged. With a sigh, he acknowledged, 'You're right. Despite where he got it, he kept it for a reason.'

Morwenna didn't know what to believe. Right now, the weariness overtook her, and she hardly cared where the pendant had come from. She laid back upon the pallet. 'Brian, I don't know who we are any more. But if you leave, there's no one left for me. I don't even know who our real family was.' She reached out her hand, and he knelt beside her. Then he clasped it, pressing their clasped hands to his forehead.

'We'll always be family.' He gripped her hand tightly, and she reached out to touch his hair. For a moment, he remained kneeling beside her, as if asking for a silent blessing.

And then he reached out to touch her face. 'Sleep well, Sister.'

'Will I see you in the morning?' she asked.

But his expression remained stoic, and he gave no answer.

Robert awakened to the piercing light of morning. He shielded his eyes and noticed that someone had bound up his left arm. His head still throbbed, but he was alive. He had no memory of how he'd escaped Penrith. Behind him, he heard footsteps, and he turned around to see his half-brother.

'You're awake, I see.' Piers reached for a crust of bread and tossed it to him.

Robert stared at the man in disbelief. Of all the people in his life, he'd never imagined Piers would save his life. His brother could easily have allowed him to die and later claimed Penrith. It was sobering, knowing that he owed everything to Piers.

'I thought you might be in trouble when I saw the soldiers searching.' Piers crouched down to look at him.

'Why did you save me?' Robert couldn't imagine any reason why his brother would help him.

'I probably should have let you bleed to death,' Piers admitted. 'But then I thought it might bring me an advantage later. You owe me a favour, Robert. And one day I'll collect on it.'

Now *that* ruthless tone sounded more like his brother. He struggled to sit up from the pallet. Piers had bound up his arm with linen, and when Robert reached up to his forehead, he felt another bandage there.

There was a fire nearby, and it seemed as if they were inside a cave of sorts. He didn't recognise this place. His stomach roared with hunger, and he reached for the bread Piers had given him.

Memories started to return. Mostly the memory of pain and exhaustion. He vaguely recalled Piers hauling him on horseback, travelling through the night until he'd passed out from the agony.

Robert ate the bread, and his brother held out a flask. He drank, not realising how thirsty he was until he'd drained the ale. 'Where are we?'

'Not far from Colford. I didn't take you there at first because they were searching near the abbey. I think you've healed enough to go now.'

Though his left arm still ached with a fierce pain, the crushing pain from his head had improved. 'How long have we been here?'

'We've been in this cave for two days,' his brother answered. 'But it's been five days since I found you.'

He gaped at Piers in shock. 'What do you mean? How could it be a sennight?' Had he been that weak that he'd lost all track of time?

'We had to keep moving to different places. Lady Gwendoline helped us escape her father.' His brother explained how the lady had been kept prisoner in her room during Morwenna's questioning, which explained why she'd done nothing to help.

Robert didn't miss the tone of his brother's

voice when he spoke of the lady. He'd been defensive, as if trying to protect Gwendoline.

'What about Morwenna and Brian?' Robert asked. 'What happened to them?' The need to ensure their safety overshadowed all else.

'Morwenna is already at Colford Abbey,' Piers said. 'I'll take you to her. I saw Brian travelling south with some of the monks. I don't know where they're going, but I'm certain they all believe you're dead.'

'I'll send word to Brian,' Robert answered. His uncle could help with that. In the meantime, his greater concern was Morwenna. 'Will you take me to the abbey?' He needed to see her, to ensure that she was all right.

'We'll have to wait a little while until it's dark,' his brother warned. 'The earl is still searching for us.'

Robert tried to stand up, but the moment he was on his feet, the ground tipped. He rested his hand against the stone wall to regain his balance. After five days, he'd thought he would be ready to travel—but now he wondered just how wounded he'd been. It sobered him to realise how weak he was.

'You took a hard blow to your head,' Piers said. 'I thought they cracked your skull. And you lost a lot of blood.' He held out a piece of dried meat and another flask, this one filled with water. 'I imagine you're starving. It was hard to force you to eat when you were mostly unconscious.'

Robert ate the meat and the salty taste of the venison made him tear into the food with a hunger he hadn't anticipated. Piers gave him more bread, which he devoured.

'You saved my life,' he acknowledged. 'I'm grateful for it.'

His brother gave a shrug. 'I suppose you'd have done the same for me.'

Robert agreed with a nod. 'I would have, aye. We may have been born from different mothers, but we share blood. That means something.'

Their relationship had never been easy, but he did want to bridge the distance between them. Especially now.

It seemed as if there was more that his brother wanted to say. Robert waited, and finally, Piers added, 'I saved your life, but there's something I want in return.'

Not Penrith, Robert wanted to blurt out, but he held his tongue.

Instead, he met his brother's gaze. 'What is it you want?'

'Lady Gwendoline's hand in marriage,' Piers

answered. 'She's mine. You will never lay claim to her as a bride.'

The hard, possessive tone took Robert by surprise. He'd believed that his brother's fascination with Gwendoline was tied up with Penrith, but there seemed to be more. For a moment, he wondered if Piers had feelings for the lady.

'And what about Penrith?' he asked.

His brother's face turned stony, and he met Robert's gaze with his own. 'I'm not giving her up. Whether the lands are involved or not.'

His mood tightened over that. But he knew he owed Piers everything and that meant choosing his words carefully. Penrith was far more important to him than the Lady Gwendoline. He just didn't know how to regain the estate.

'I won't pursue Lady Gwendoline,' Robert agreed. 'But you'll have to fight that battle with her father.' He already knew there was little chance of Piers winning the lady as a wife.

'Our fight has already begun,' Piers said but didn't explain any further. He began to saddle the horses, preparing for their journey.

Robert took another drink of water. The truth was, he'd only courted Gwendoline in the hope of winning Penrith. His own feelings for the woman had never ventured beyond admiration. Even when he'd competed for her, his thoughts had always been caught up in Morwenna. He'd been aware of her presence, always conscious of her eyes watching him. And he wanted nothing more than to see her this night. It was a fierce need, to see if she had healed from the whipping, to watch over her and protect her.

Piers paused and turned back to him. 'I don't know what will happen with Penrith. But we both know you'd be dead if it weren't for me.'

Robert didn't answer at first, for he wasn't ready to abandon his people or his quest to free them from Alfred's rule. He hadn't forgotten his vow.

At last, he said, 'Neither of us can have the estate unless the king intervenes. I think we should appeal to him and let him make the choice.'

Piers's expression hardened. 'You owe me, Robert.'

The words hung between them like a sword blade. He knew his brother was right, but he couldn't surrender everything. Not yet.

'It's getting dark now,' he said. 'Let's go to Colford and speak of it later.'

He stumbled his way towards the horses, but the moment he tried to mount one, his brother sighed. 'You're not strong enough.' It was humiliating to have Piers help him up, but he knew better than to imagine that he could walk to Colford. His wounds were healing, but the blow he'd taken to the head still ached, even now.

Though it was just past sunset, his brother didn't bother to light a torch. It wasn't needed because the horse knew the trail, and Robert suspected Piers didn't want anyone following them. As they continued through the forest, he couldn't quite read his brother's mood, but there seemed to be a trace of annoyance.

Had Piers expected him to surrender Penrith to him without a fight? He couldn't do it. Not yet. Though his brother might want to claim it, without the king's blessing it would never happen. If Alfred died, King John would only bring in another nobleman. The matter of ruling the estate was far more complex.

But his brother's resentment was brewing, and he sensed that Piers would not rest until he had taken everything.

It was an hour later when they arrived at the abbey. His uncle, Father Oswald, led them to a small cell with two beds. 'You can sleep here for the night.'

'Uncle, I need to see Morwenna,' Robert insisted. He would not rest until he had reassured himself that she was all right.

'You may see her in the morning,' Oswald answered. 'She is asleep.'

'She believes I'm dead. I need her to know that I survived the fight.' But more than that, he wanted to see her with his own eyes. He needed to look upon her and know that she was healing. Even then, it would not assuage his guilt. Brian had been right. He'd spent too long planning instead of acting. And because of it, Morwenna had paid the price.

When his uncle hesitated, Robert added, 'If you do not bring me to her tonight, I will search every cell until I find her.'

His uncle exchanged a glance with Piers as if suddenly realising that Robert meant it. 'I suppose I can take you to her.'

He led them along a narrow cloister walk with a small courtyard in the centre. Robert leaned heavily on a walking staff, though he kept up with his uncle's pace.

Piers followed him to one of the cells on the far end. In a low voice, he told Robert, 'One of the monks tended her wounds, but the abbot wants to send her to a nunnery. He thinks it would be better for her to be cared for by women.'

Robert answered him quietly, 'That's not going to happen. She stays with me.'

As they drew closer, Piers added, 'Is it right to

make that demand? Morwenna has been in love with you for two years, Robert. If you don't care for her in the same way, it's better to let her go.'

His brother's admonition sobered him, for he didn't know what his feelings were. He knew Morwenna cared for him, but he hadn't allowed himself to think of his own desires. He'd been so caught up in his quest to regain Penrith, he'd shut out the rest of the world.

But after he'd nearly died, right now, he needed to see her as much as he needed to breathe.

'I'm not going anywhere,' he told his brother.

'But I am.' Piers reached out and gripped his uninjured arm. 'I'll stay here tonight, but at dawn, I'm leaving to join Gwendoline again.' With a pause, he added, 'Be well, Robert. But stay away from Gwen.' With that, his brother turned back and walked in the opposite direction.

The abbot knocked on one of the doors, but there was only silence. Oswald paused and said, 'She hasn't answered. We may want to leave her alone if she's asleep.'

'I need to speak with her,' Robert told his uncle. 'And I'm not leaving until I know she's all right.'

The abbot's face revealed his disapproval, but he did not refuse the request. 'I will go and fetch Brother Anselm to change her poultice. You may have a few moments, but that is all.' In this, the abbot would not yield. His face held an iron resolve, and finally, Robert relented.

'I won't be long.' He opened the cell door and saw Morwenna huddled on a pallet facing the opposite wall. The wooden shutters were slightly ajar, allowing a little moonlight into the space. From the flare of his uncle's torch, he could see the angry healing skin on her back. The lines crisscrossed in raw patterns that made his jaw tighten. The flogging never should have happened to her.

'I don't need anything,' she murmured, as if she believed one of the brothers had brought her food. 'You can go.'

Robert closed the door behind him and walked closer. He set the walking stick aside and slowly lowered himself to his knees beside her. 'What if I don't want to go?'

She turned around and saw him kneeling beside the pallet. 'Robert?' Her voice held disbelief, and in one swift motion, he pulled her into his arms. She wept against his neck as he held her, careful not to touch her wounds. 'Brian said you were dead.'

'I managed to break free of the guards, but I was wounded.' He didn't want to go into all the details, but he cupped her face in his hands.

'I can't believe you're here.' She was smiling through her tears. 'You're alive.' Despite her ragged appearance, her dark hair curled against her face while her green eyes were bright.

He rested his forehead against hers, wanting to kiss her, and yet he was uncertain whether she would want him to. His brother's claim that Morwenna was in love with him unnerved him. He didn't know what to do or what to say.

Her lips were soft, her eyes gleaming with tears. All he had to do was lean a little closer and his mouth would be upon hers. And yet, something held him back. She was beautiful, staring at him with silent expectations he didn't know he could fulfil.

She clutched the coverlet to her, but he was fully aware of her bare shoulders and spine. Although the wounds were healing well, it still infuriated him that he hadn't been able to stop the whipping. She hadn't deserved any of this.

'I owe my life to Piers,' he admitted. 'He found me just outside the tunnel and brought me into hiding. If it weren't for his rescue, I would have died that night.'

Morwenna met his gaze openly. 'I'm so glad you escaped.' She embraced him again, and he welcomed her arms around his neck. Gently, he held her waist, careful to avoid her wounds.

'But what will happen now?' she asked when she pulled back. 'You…cannot go back to Penrith.' The tone of her voice revealed her doubts.

He kept his hand on her waist. 'I need to appeal to the king now. He is the only one who can help me regain my lands.'

Her expression tightened as if she didn't agree with him. 'That's dangerous, Robert.'

'I don't have a choice. I swore an oath to the people that I would return. I can't turn my back on them again. Dangerous or not, I have to gain an audience.'

But she was already shaking her head. 'Do you think you can bargain with a man who ordered Penrith to be burned to the ground?' she asked quietly. 'The king wanted us dead, Robert. How can you forget?'

'We don't know that,' he argued. 'There might have been another reason for the attack.'

'Kings don't need reasons. They do whatever they want,' she insisted. 'Leave it be, Robert. It's not worth your life.'

But she didn't understand. Frustration swelled up inside him at his own failure. He hadn't even fought that night two years ago. He'd been captured along with the others, and he'd watched the fires burn while his people had died. His father had always been disappointed in him, and Robert knew that his cowardice had cost lives. 'My people asked me to fight for them. They're suffering, and I can't be a coward—not about this.'

'You were never that,' she countered.

'Wasn't I? After we escaped, I remained in hiding for two years. I let no one know that I lived. I'm not going to stay back and deny those who need my help now.'

Morwenna closed her eyes, and he could see the worry from the tension in her face. 'I don't want you to die,' she murmured. 'I can't stand back and let it happen.'

Her words cut into him, and he understood that this wasn't about the king at all. It was because she worried about him. He softened his words and answered, 'Then what do you want me to do, Morwenna?'

Her expression turned pained. 'I want you to wait. If you're trying to prove your loyalty, you cannot go empty-handed to the king. John needs armies to fight in France. Bring him a gift of gold, and he may listen to your plea.'

'I have no gold, Morwenna.' She knew this, as well as he did.

'Then take some time and earn it,' she said. 'Don't you think the king will believe your fealty if you bring him wealth? He might consider it then.'

'I don't know if I can wait that long, Morwenna. The people need my help now.'

She grew quiet, and he reached out to touch her shoulder. He didn't want to fight with her. Not at this moment. He stroked the skin, watching her expression.

'Are you planning to leave me behind when you go?' she asked.

'It's not what I want. I'd rather take you with me, but it's likely safer if you stay.' He wanted her to be well protected, and there was a chance they could be caught by Penrith's men if they travelled together.

She reached for his hand. 'I will go where you go, Robert. For however long that is.'

He squeezed her hand and admitted, 'I don't know how long we'll be travelling or even where to find the king. But we need to leave soon. We have to go farther to avoid Penrith's men. If they catch us…'

'We die,' she finished. 'But how can we travel without being found?'

'I think I know a way we can escape notice,' he said. 'If we dress as monks or Crusaders.' They would be looking for a woman, but if he disguised her well enough, they might escape notice.

'It seems that I am destined to wear men's

clothing.' She gave a rueful smile. 'But aye, that would be best.' She paused and reached within her belongings, retrieving the golden pendant she had worn at the feasting. 'I also want to speak to the king about my mother. I thought this pendant belonged to her…but Lord Penrith said it was once Queen Eleanor's.'

Robert studied it, but there was no way to know if that was true. 'Do you think he was telling the truth?'

She nodded. 'I need to know how Eldreth got this from the queen and who she was.' She lifted her gaze to his. 'Who I really am.'

He realised then, that she didn't know he'd come to see her while she was imprisoned. 'I was there on the day Penrith brought the midwife. I heard what she said about your mother.'

Her brow furrowed. 'I never saw you.'

'I disguised myself among the guards. I was trying to find out where you were, so I could rescue you later that night. I couldn't reveal myself.'

Her expression held a blend of confusion. 'I wish I'd known. I thought no one would come for me.'

Robert reached out to touch her cheek. 'I will always come for you, Morwenna.' Then he leaned in and kissed her. He needed her to know what she meant to him.

When he drew back, he promised, 'We will try to find the answers about the past.' And he wanted his own answers about why his father had been executed. If there was any means of finding the truth, they would pursue it.

When he studied her, her expression turned vulnerable. 'I want to believe that I'm more than the miller's daughter.'

In her green eyes, he saw the blend of fear and anticipation. She was pinning her hopes on an unknown family bloodline, on a possible alliance that could help him win Penrith.

'You've always been more.' He drew closer and reached for her hand. Though he wanted to tell her how he felt, he also knew that he had nothing to offer Morwenna. Not until he'd resolved the matter of Penrith. He'd sworn to Piers that he would leave Gwendoline alone—and he would. But he could not relinquish his vow to help the people.

'We'll travel south as soon as you are well enough.'

She gave a nod and released his palm. For a moment, he studied her, noting her pale complexion and the thin shift. He touched her shoulder and saw the dark bruises and broken skin on her back.

Guilt washed over him at the sight of her

wounds. He should have found a way to rescue her before this. Her brother had behaved in a rash manner, acting without thought. But it *had* stopped her punishment. Robert despised himself for not acting when he'd first found her in chains. His hesitation had nearly caused Morwenna even more pain. These wounds were his fault, as much as the earl's.

'How do you feel?' he asked. It was a foolish question, and yet it was all he could manage.

'Sore,' she admitted, 'but Brother Anselm gave me a poultice that is helping. It's mostly bruises now.'

'Good.' The awkwardness descended between them once more as he struggled to think about what else to say. Apologies weren't enough.

Her hands moved from his neck to his face. 'I'm glad you're here, Robert.'

For a moment, he simply stared at her. He tried to come up with the right words, but there were none. The tenderness in her eyes was his undoing, and no words were needed as he bent to steal another kiss. Her lips were soft against his, sweetly yielding. A rush of desire flooded through him as he claimed her mouth.

This was what he'd wanted. And somehow the kiss expressed all the feelings he couldn't say. Though he didn't know what he was doing, it felt right to hold her. And when she kissed him back, it was as if she'd lit a flame to his senses. They were both alive and they'd somehow survived again.

The need to touch her was overwhelming.

Morwenna wondered if she was dreaming. Robert had come for her, and she was in his arms. Joy and fear mingled within her—happiness that he was alive and worry that their time together was fleeting. She revelled in the kiss, craving his touch even as she knew it could not last. He cradled her face between his hands before they drifted downward. Her shift hung loose upon her since it had been cut open by the soldiers and Brother Anselm had treated her wounds. Though her body ached with the pain, Robert's touch was a welcome distraction.

'Morwenna,' he breathed. 'I want to kill Penrith for hurting you.' He slid his hands lower, his kiss growing more demanding. Her body filled up with yearning, her breasts tightening as he kissed her.

'I blame myself,' he admitted, pulling back. 'I should have stopped it before it began, no matter the risk.'

'It wasn't your fault,' she argued. 'And you did try to stop him.'

His hands moved to her shoulders. With the lightest touch, he slid his fingers down her sides, trying to avoid her back. 'Not soon enough.' In his voice, she heard guilt and frustration. He cupped her face between his hands and admitted, 'I won't make that mistake again.'

She began to tremble with anticipation as his heated breath warmed her throat. She could hardly bear it as his mouth moved lower.

'I don't have much time,' he confessed. 'But I had to see you.' He kissed the space beneath her throat, and it was then that her shift fell from her shoulders, baring her breasts. Though she knew she should cover herself, she ached for him, wanting more.

He hesitated, asking silent permission. When she didn't move, he drew his hands lower, his fingertips grazing against her nipples. A shock of pleasure deepened her needs.

'Touch me more,' she whispered. 'Just for a little while.'

He obeyed, stroking her breasts and cupping them. Her fingers dug into his shoulders, and she moaned as he caressed her nipples. Between her legs she grew wet, and she didn't understand the rising sensations that gripped her. She was kneeling before him, and when he kissed a path lower, he stopped at her breast. Again, he waited, and she drew his mouth to her nipple. His warm mouth circled it, gently suckling, and pleasure tore through her. She clutched his head, barely able to keep a clear thought as his tongue swirled over the erect tip.

'Are you all right?' he murmured upon her skin. 'Should I stop?'

'Don't stop,' she answered. Her body was arching in a gentle rhythm with an ebb and flow. He took the other breast in his mouth while he continued caressing the first, his thumb circling the taut nipple. She was drowning in need, her body aching for more. Though she had never known lovemaking, she wanted Robert to be her first and only. She wanted to feel the hard length of his body covering hers, and she wanted him to fill her until their bodies became one.

'There's not enough time,' he gritted out. 'They're going to return soon.'

She slid her hands beneath his tunic, her palms touching his hard chest. She explored his bare skin, learning the hard curves of his pectoral muscles. And then her hand moved lower, over his ridged stomach.

To her shock, her fingers brushed across the velvet head of his manhood straining against his trews. She was about to apologise, but he brought her hand back to his erection.

'You can touch me any way you want,' he said.

His breathing was as harsh as her own, and when his tongue caressed her nipple again, she curled her palm over his flesh. He guided her, showing her how to move her hand up and down.

While she caressed him, she felt the echoing ache deep inside. Her body was trembling, so close to a peak she didn't understand. But when a hard knock sounded at the door, she jerked away from him and lay face down on the pallet to hide her nakedness.

The door swung open, and the abbot entered, followed by Brother Anselm. 'Morwenna, Brother Anselm is here to change your poultice. Robert, it's time for you to return to your own cell.'

She felt her cheeks burning with embarrassment and wanted to bury herself in the pallet. Did the brethren suspect what they had been doing? She hoped not.

'Goodnight, Morwenna.' Robert's voice was husky, and in his tone, she sensed the physical frustration that echoed her own.

'You may see each other in the morning,' Father Oswald said. 'Afterwards, Sister Bertrice has promised to come. She will bring Morwenna to the nunnery by Saint Michael's Well.'

Morwenna wasn't surprised at his mention of

Sister Bertrice. The abbot had never been comfortable with her presence here, even when she'd been here before.

But Robert appeared irritated by the abbot's statement. 'Morwenna is not leaving,' he told the others. 'Not for the nunnery, at least.'

His answer startled her, for she hadn't expected him to interfere. Given her state of undress, she couldn't sit up to face them.

'She cannot stay here,' the abbot continued. 'I allowed it for a few days, but she must be cared for by women.'

Before Robert could argue, Brother Anselm interrupted. 'I will look at her wounds now. If you will grant us privacy for a few moments, Father.'

The abbot inclined his head. 'We will leave you to it.' To Robert, he added, 'Walk with me.'

Robert held her gaze for a moment before he left with the abbot. In the darkness, her face grew flushed. She had never meant for things to go this far. But the line had been crossed, and she wasn't sure what that meant. She had never really imagined that he might desire her. But now that he did, she had no idea what to do about it.

Brother Anselm drew closer and examined her back. 'The poultice seems to be drawing out the swelling. You will bear the scars all your life, but it should heal.'

He prepared the new poultice with herbs he'd brought. 'Father Oswald is concerned about the danger you both face. Lord Penrith is hunting for you, and we thought you would be safer at the nunnery.'

His quiet explanation soothed her with the re-alisation that they were still trying to help.

'I am grateful for your offer, Brother Anselm,' she said, 'but my wounds have nearly healed enough for me to travel. I need to know what happened to my family. Robert promised to help me find them.' She didn't mention that she had no idea who they were or where to find her true mother and father. Part of her wanted to know if there was any chance that she was not a com-moner. If she had been stolen from another fam-ily, was it possible?

The queen's pendant held the answers, and she intended to find them. She could not remain in hiding for the rest of her life.

'I do not think you should travel alone with a man who is not your husband,' Brother Anselm said softly.

His words could not have been more blunt. Morwenna held her shift to her, and said, 'He is a lord. He would never wed someone like me, and I would not ask that of him.'

'Do you not believe you are worthy of marriage?' he asked.

His kindness dug deeper into her vulnerabilities, causing tears to rise. It was a dream she didn't dare to imagine. 'Not with a man such as Robert. I know my place.'

She sensed that, despite her feelings, if she stayed with Robert there would eventually come a time when he would break her heart. Just because he wanted her now did not mean there wouldn't come a time when he desired another.

But she intended to savour these moments, fleeting though they would be. Her body flushed at the memory of his touch while she tried to suppress her feelings. 'I thank you for tending my wounds, Brother Anselm. But Robert will be my protector from now on.' Even so, she knew that the risk to her heart was grave.

Anselm's mouth tightened with disapproval, but he said nothing more.

Robert followed his uncle into a small cell. The abbot gestured for him to take a seat, and he did. 'I must warn you that you cannot stay here, Robert. The earl and his men have been searching this area for days now. If you're found...'

'I know,' he finished. 'I won't stay long. I intend to leave in the morning with Morwenna.' Although neither of them was fully healed, they were well enough to travel.

His uncle appeared uncertain about his plans, but he did not dispute them. 'What of your arm, Robert? How are your own wounds?'

'The wound is healing,' he answered. 'But I can fight with my right arm.' The pain was a dull ache, but it was also a constant reminder that he'd survived the worst fight of his life. It made him wonder about what would happen to Piers. His brother had spoken of his intent to return to Penrith for Gwendoline—but, if the earl learned that his daughter's suitor was a bastard, he would order Piers to be killed. And Robert didn't like that risk, especially after his brother had saved his life.

'Brother Anselm can look at your arm, if you wish,' his uncle offered. 'He is a good healer.'

Robert was about to agree, but his uncle wasn't finished. 'I don't think it's wise to travel with the woman. As I said before, Sister Bertrice has offered to escort Morwenna to the nunnery. She will be safe there. Her brother Brian joined a group of my men to fight in the Crusades,' the abbot continued. 'Perhaps you might do the same. God could use a sword such as yours.'

Robert had no intention of leaving Morwenna at the nunnery. He had to choose his words carefully, so as not to offend the abbot. 'Morwenna has suffered a great deal at the earl's hands through no fault of her own. I'm not going to abandon her now.'

His uncle Oswald studied him closely. His face held wrinkles and a neatly trimmed white beard. 'You need to think about what your father would have wanted. My brother made many mistakes, but he obeyed his duties.'

'I don't think I can regain Penrith without the help of the king,' Robert admitted. 'I intend to find him.' He knew not what King John would say, but he hoped the monarch would see reason and give him the chance to restore his father's good name.

The abbot let out a sigh. 'He is travelling north towards Scotland, so I've heard.'

'Then we will go south to intercept him,' Robert said.

'I suppose I cannot stop you, though I think it will be futile,' Oswald replied. 'Your father's rebellion was grave enough to cost him his life. I fear for yours.'

'It is my risk to take,' he answered. Though Robert knew it was unwise to bring Morwenna with him, he sensed that he would never see her again if he left her behind. The instinctive need to keep her close was overshadowing his common sense. 'She comes with me.'

The abbot shook his head. 'If you travel with her alone, you could both be caught by the earl and executed.'

Robert knew the risk, but he had a better way of travelling. If they disguised themselves in the right way, no one would find them.

'But there is something else you should consider,' his uncle continued. 'If you…have feelings for this woman, you risk the greater sin of taking her virtue.' The abbot's face reddened, and he said gently, 'Unless you intend to marry her and abandon Penrith, you should not travel alone with her, Robert.'

He knew what his uncle meant, but he could not even contemplate marriage to anyone until he'd made a decision about his estate. Still, he inclined his head and said, 'Morwenna has already agreed to travel with me.' He met his uncle's frank gaze. 'I will protect her life with my own.'

The abbot's disapproval was evident. 'The longer you stay, the greater the risk becomes. They will find you and surround the abbey.'

He ignored his uncle's prediction and said simply, 'We are leaving at dawn.'

Chapter Eight

The following day, Morwenna rode south with Robert at her side. They wore the cowls and un-dyed woollen habits of the Cistercian monks as a disguise. The abbot had sent them with supplies and bags of grain. 'The crops have failed in many estates this year,' he'd warned. 'You may be able to barter for food and shelter with the grain.' Then he'd sent them off with a blessing, warning them to stay away from the main roads as much as possible.

They journeyed for hours, stopping once at noontide by a stream to rest and eat before they continued onward. Morwenna thought of Brian and wondered if she would ever see him again. Though she'd asked Father Oswald to send word to her brother, there was no way of knowing whether their paths would cross.

A comfortable silence descended between

them, and she wondered about Robert's plans. She'd urged him to wait before appealing to the king, but she wasn't certain he would. He had wrapped up all his expectations in Penrith, and she didn't know if he would succeed in his quest.

She glanced behind her, grateful that none of Lord Penrith's men had followed them thus far. Though they were both armed, she knew better than to think they could fight off the soldiers alone.

Her body was sore from travelling, her wounds aching. Brother Anselm had given her the herbs to make another poultice, but she would need Robert's help putting it on. Her back had healed somewhat, though it was still tender from bruising.

'Are you ready to stop for the night?' he asked. 'There's a stone outcropping ahead. We could take shelter there.'

'Do you think it's safe to build a fire?'

He nodded. 'I've been watching, but there's no sign that anyone has followed us.' He led her towards the clearing, and she saw the limestone rock face he'd described. He helped her dismount and took both horses to the stream to drink. She stretched and began to gather sticks and tinder for a fire.

Robert let the horses graze and returned to

her. 'If you'll start the fire, I'll try to get fish for our supper.' He gave her flint, and she bent beside the tinder she'd gathered. It took time for the dried moss to spark a flame, but she eventually managed to feed it twigs and then a log from the forest. It was comforting to sit beside the fire, and she retrieved a small pot from their belongings that the abbot had given her. After filling it with water, she set it near the fire to warm up. She needed to steep the healing herbs for the new poultice.

Robert returned with two fish he'd caught from the stream. He cleaned them and set them up to cook over the fire. They ate, and afterwards, she asked, 'How is your arm? I have some healing herbs from Brother Anselm. I could tend it for you.'

'It's still sore,' he admitted, 'but the pain is bearable.'

She suspected his wounds hurt as much as hers, though he had not said so. Morwenna added the herbs to the hot water and bade him sit down. She knelt beside him while the herbs steeped and began to unwrap the bandage around his left arm.

'What happened after Brian took me from Penrith?' she asked, unwinding the linen. 'We escaped, but I was so afraid you would die. How did Piers save you?'

'I don't really remember all of it,' he confessed. 'I wounded two of the soldiers, but the third gave me this cut. Someone struck me on the head, and I honestly don't know how I managed to get into the tunnels. Piers found me outside and saved my life. We were in hiding for a sennight because Penrith's men were searching for us. I woke up in a cave before he brought me to the abbey.'

Morwenna took a clean piece of linen and dipped it into the warm water. Gently, she cleaned his wound. Although the skin was still red, the ragged edges had knit together. She washed the wound, and he gave a slight shudder.

'Does that hurt?' she asked.

He shook his head. But his brown eyes held her captive, searing her with unspoken desire. As she touched him, she grew conscious of her own heartbeat and the warmth of his skin. She remembered his hands touching her, cupping her breasts and stroking the erect tips. God help her, she wanted this man.

She wrapped a new bandage around his arm and tied it off. His gaze was heated, and he said, 'Your turn.'

Beneath the monk's habit, she wore her torn

shift. She turned her back to him and lifted the habit over her head, baring the shift. The back hung open, exposing her wounds. Though she had received only five lashes, three had broken the skin. The rest of her back was heavily bruised.

Robert was silent for a long time. 'I cannot tell you how sorry I am, Morwenna. This never should have happened to you.'

'I survived,' she answered, 'and so did you.'

He dipped another linen cloth into the warm water and wrung it out. Gently, he washed her back. Gooseflesh rose up over her skin, but it was his touch that undid her senses. Beneath the shift, her breasts tightened, the nipples growing sensitive beneath the fabric. She remembered his mouth upon her breasts and the sensual ache between her legs.

If she turned to him, would he embrace her? They were alone, and she was willing to steal any moment she could to be with him. The flogging had awakened her to the knowledge that life was fleeting. Robert had barely survived that day, and she was so grateful for it.

She took a deep breath, gathering her courage. 'Robert.'

He stilled instantly. 'Forgive me. I should not have touched you.'

That wasn't what she'd meant at all. 'It's all right,' she murmured. A bead of water slid down her bare back, and her breasts ached for his touch. She could feel his silent hunger. His eyes were hooded and dark, his jaw tight with desire. In her own defiance, she straightened, allowing her shift to slide down one shoulder.

When she stared at him, his gaze drifted downward with unmistakable interest. She wanted more, and so did he. At last, they were alone, with no one to interrupt. And yet, he remained hesitant.

'What are you thinking?' she murmured.

'A thousand things.' His voice was hoarse, as if he were holding himself back. She wanted to break through the invisible wall between them and coax him out of his tight control until he was in her arms. 'Things I want to do. Things I shouldn't do.'

Morwenna reached out to his shoulders, wanting his hands and mouth upon her. For so long, she'd dreamed of being with this man. She wanted him desperately, needing his touch. And yet, they both knew the consequences.

'It's all right,' she whispered, praying he would simply close the distance. Right now, she didn't want to think of all the reasons it was wrong.

But Robert set down the damp cloth. 'You're wrong, Morwenna. It would be taking advantage of you. I won't do that.'

She rose up on her knees, not caring that her shift was falling forward. His gaze turned heated again, and she reached to cup his face. With her hand, she smoothed the edge of his jaw. 'Stop talking, Robert, and kiss me.'

Against her lips his voice was rough. 'If I do, I won't stop.'

'Then don't.' She leaned in close, and he responded by claiming her mouth with his own. He threaded his hands in her hair, and his tongue slid against hers. A raw need coursed through her, and she desperately wanted to seize this stolen moment. He kissed her as if he couldn't get enough, his mouth claiming hers. She yielded to him, even though a part of her knew it couldn't last.

'Morwenna, I don't think—'

'You're right,' she answered. 'Don't think at all.' She drew his mouth back to hers and slid her hands beneath his tunic. His pectoral muscles were like iron, ridged with strength. She explored his body, learning the lines of his stomach and chest.

His kiss grew hotter, wicked in intensity. She clung to him, surrendering to the needs rising.

When his mouth drifted to her throat, sensations erupted over her skin. She couldn't stop the moan that broke forth as his lips moved lower. She wanted his mouth on her breast, his hands everywhere.

She'd dreamed of his moment, of lying in his arms while he pressed her down. Morwenna pushed away the thought of him leaving, unable to think of a future when he wasn't hers. Instead, she would indulge in her own fantasies, making a memory that would have to last.

He paused and rested his hands at her waist. She met his gaze, waiting for more. And yet he held steady, watching her. With his hands, he moved her shift to her waist, baring her to the cool night air. Her nipples puckered, and he never took his eyes off her as he slid his fingers down her skin. His knuckles grazed against the cockled tips, and a spearing warmth flooded between her legs.

He sat down and pulled her hips forward, dragging her to his lap. The position brought her body against his hard length, and she was shaken by the fierce desire building higher. He rocked against her, and her breath caught, her hands gripping his shoulders. He held her waist, moving against her. Her mind filled in the missing pieces, and she imagined him sliding deep inside, joining with her. The thought was both erotic and frightening.

If she allowed him to claim her innocence, it would only hurt more when he left her. And then, there was the risk of conceiving a child. God help her, the thought of growing round with his baby was bittersweet. Every time she looked into the eyes of her infant, she would remember Robert.

The thought nearly broke her heart. It made her realise that she had already accepted the loss of him, of being left alone. She wasn't his equal, and her mind warned her not to dream of what could never happen.

And yet…another part of her wasn't so certain. She loved this man, but was it worth fighting for him? Could she ever win his heart?

It was a different sort of battle, and during the past two years, she'd told herself she could never succeed. But then again, she'd never tried to make him love her. Was that even possible?

He kissed her again, and she felt the ridge of him caressing her intimately with only a layer of fabric between them. She grew wet and feverish, and his tongue echoed her deepest desire, sliding in deep and withdrawing. More than anything, she wanted him inside her.

'You take my breath away,' he said against

her lips. With his hands he cupped her breasts, circling the nipples with his thumbs.

She could scarcely breathe, her lungs seizing up as the sensations rippled through her. He took one breast in his mouth, and suddenly, she felt a deep shimmer blooming inside. She trembled with his touch, and when his hard length swelled between her legs, the sensation kindled a fierce response. She moved against him, wishing he would unfasten his trews and claim her.

But her body took command, and although Morwenna didn't know what to do, she surrendered to her instincts. She found her own rhythm, rubbing herself against his erection. She was quaking, her body coming apart in his arms until a shattering wave of pleasure broke over her. She could do nothing except cling to him while she arched against him, her body enraptured by the shimmering sensation.

She gripped his head against her breast, rocking against him. Then, she reached down between their bodies, needing to touch him. The moment her hand touched his trews, he inhaled sharply. Gently, she stroked him through the layer of cloth, learning the length of him. She stroked a few times, and he shuddered, uttering a dark cry as he lost his own control.

For a moment, neither could speak. She could

only rest with her legs straddling him. Her body had gone pliant, and his eyes stared into hers. He held her hips, his hand stroking her backside.

I am going to fight for this man, she vowed silently. *There has to be a way.*

Robert didn't know if there were any words he could say. Although they were both still virgins, he'd been spellbound by the power of pleasuring her. He'd never imagined the intensity of how it would feel to touch Morwenna. She had given him a glimpse of what lovemaking could be like, and the magnitude of it had shaken him to the core.

He had to tread carefully, for the very sight of this woman made him want to lay her down and spend the rest of the night learning what pleased her. It had been an awakening he'd never imagined, even though his future held nothing but uncertainty.

He was about to kiss her again when he heard horses approaching. It was not the sound of travellers, but instead the rhythmic pounding of someone in pursuit.

'Are they looking for us?' Morwenna asked, her eyes wide with fear.

'I don't know.' Quickly, he handed her the monk's habit and donned his own. If it was Lord

Penrith's men hunting them, they had only moments to flee. He used dirt to extinguish the fire, plunging them into darkness. 'We have to leave. Let's go.'

It was likely that their fire had already been noticed in the darkness. They needed to ride hard, to somehow break away from the soldiers and hide.

Morwenna didn't argue, but they readied their horses, and Robert started to lead them up a narrow path, deeper into the woods. It would make it more difficult for the men to follow, not to mention they would have to slow down.

Then abruptly, he realised the soldiers weren't pursuing them at all. He heard the sound of other riders and realised the men had not slowed their pace. They were travelling west towards the clearing. Robert seized Morwenna's reins and drew her horse to a stop. In a low voice he said, 'They're after someone else. Listen.'

They both paused, and Robert watched as the soldiers rode by with torches. He recognised Lord Penrith's men, and he wondered why they were searching. The only explanation was that they had a different target in mind.

'Who are they pursuing?' Morwenna whispered.

He had a suspicion but didn't say it. 'I'm not certain. But we should stay here until it's safe.'

She reached out to take his hand, and he squeezed it. He was fighting against his own instincts to leave, but they were safer here. He continued holding her hand while they waited, but then he heard the sound of a woman's scream.

Morwenna's hand gripped his. 'Robert, we have to help them.'

Though he understood her sympathy, he had no intention of endangering her. 'It's not safe.'

'But what if it's Lady Gwendoline? That sounded like her voice. And why else would she be running away unless she's with Piers?'

He knew she was right, but he hated the thought of risking her safety. 'We need to know for certain if it's them. We'll move in closer. Are you armed?'

'Not really. I have a knife but no sword.'

They were at a disadvantage, and he added, 'If I get a sword from one of the soldiers, can you guard my back?'

'Yes.' She didn't hesitate in her answer.

'We won't do anything until we're sure it's them,' he insisted. 'And then we need to know how many soldiers are in pursuit,' he warned. 'Follow me, and we'll try to catch up to them.'

He redirected their path towards the soldiers.

As they rode, he questioned the wisdom of getting involved. Neither he nor Morwenna were fully healed. And yet, she had no hesitation about fighting for Piers or Gwendoline.

They continued towards the edge of the forest. In the clearing, they saw two people on horseback, pursued by the soldiers. The moon was bright, and it reflected against the silvery ribbon of a stream. Robert nodded towards the right. 'If we go over those hills, we can catch up to them and flank the soldiers.'

She agreed, and they remained within the trees but turned right to go uphill. There was a narrow path leading higher, and Robert kept the horses on the trail until they reached the top. From their vantage point, he could see that the soldiers were closing in. The light of the torches made it evident that it was indeed his brother and the lady.

'Are you ready to fight?' he asked Morwenna.

'I am.'

He started urging his horse downhill, his mind forming a plan. He and Piers could fight off the soldiers while Morwenna protected Gwendoline. If the soldiers outnumbered them, he trusted Morwenna to guard his back. Though he didn't truly want her fighting, if she could hold a shield and a weapon, it would be enough.

He'd counted nine soldiers. It was a risk to fight them, but Morwenna was right. They couldn't abandon Piers and Gwendoline—not after his brother had saved his life the first time. If the pair of them had fled together, then the earl must have refused the match. But did Gwendoline know the truth about Piers? He wasn't so certain.

'I'm going to go after one of the soldiers in the back and get his weapon,' he told Morwenna. 'Stay back with the horses, and I'll toss it to you.'

He dismounted, but before he could go, Morwenna suddenly caught his arm. She took his face between her hands and kissed him. 'Be safe and come back to me.'

The kiss caught him unawares, but it strengthened his resolve. 'I will.' It would be dangerous, aye, but he intended to guard his brother without any of them being harmed.

The soldiers had closed in on Piers and Gwendoline. The lady dismounted and took her bow and a quiver of arrows, along with a small bundle. Then she started to move in front of Piers, as if she could shield him, but he pressed her behind him.

Robert kept moving closer and saw one of the soldiers standing slightly apart from the others. He crept up behind the man, covered his mouth, and slit his throat. Then he let the soldier sink to the ground. Silently, Robert disarmed the man and crept back to the edge of the woods where he left the weapon for Morwenna.

It was then that the other men realised the attack and sounded an alarm. During the distraction, Piers ordered Gwendoline, 'Run!' She took off, fleeing towards the trees.

Robert unsheathed his sword and attacked from the opposite side. He swung the blade at a second soldier and struck him down.

Piers had his own weapon in hand, and they fought back-to-back. 'Good timing, Brother,' he muttered.

'I owed you a favour.'

The soldiers were well trained, and Robert's arm reverberated beneath a solid blow. Although Piers cut down his own opponent, they were still outnumbered. Two more joined in, but Robert fell into a pattern of fighting with his brother. Their movements matched, and time seemed to blur.

But then he saw two of the men breaking away and running towards the woods. Undoubtedly, they would try to take the women hostage.

'Piers,' he warned, just as his sword pierced his opponent's throat.

'I see them.' But there wasn't time to reach

the soldiers, since they had the last three men circling them. 'We have to hurry.'

Robert swung his sword hard, twisting as he dodged a blow and raised his shield. He lunged at the first man and blocked a strike as the second opponent swung at his head. The two of them pressed the advantage, and he found himself fighting for his life as both soldiers attacked.

The other two men had nearly reached the edge of the woods. Although Morwenna was armed, he didn't know if she could defend Gwendoline against two of them.

But then, out of the corner of his eye, he saw one of the soldiers drop to the ground, an arrow buried in his heart. Gwendoline must have shot him.

But her second arrow missed the other man.

Piers defeated his attacker and swung his shield, striking one of the other men in the forehead. The soldier stumbled, and Robert slashed him down, killing him instantly.

'Go after the women,' he ordered. 'Take the horse.'

Piers swung up on his mount and thundered towards the woods. He had his sword in hand while Robert cut down his last opponent. He took another horse and rode hard, the fear coursing through his veins. If they didn't get there in time...

Piers reached the forest first, and Robert saw the last soldier raise his sword just before Morwenna stabbed him in the heart. Her attacker slid to the ground in front of them, and she stepped back, her hand covered in his blood.

Beside her, Gwendoline held a bow, with an arrow nocked to it. Robert ran hard towards the women, and when he reached them, he crushed Morwenna into his arms. 'Are you all right?'

She nodded, holding him close. 'Are they all dead?'

'They are. But we can't stay here. There could be more.'

Gwendoline was already in Piers's embrace, and Robert turned to his half-brother. 'What happened? Why were you running away?'

'My father was trying to stop us from getting married,' Lady Gwendoline confessed. 'He sent soldiers to bring me back and kill Piers.' Then she turned to Morwenna. 'I am so sorry I could not free you when you were his prisoner. He locked me away in my room, and I had no idea that he had you flogged.' Her expression grew pained. 'I blame myself for it.'

'You couldn't have stopped him,' Morwenna answered. She turned back to Robert and said,

'We cannot stay out here in the open. We need to find shelter.'

'It will be dawn soon,' he said. 'But we're not far from Stansbury.' It was the ruined fortress where they had stayed last year. Though it was far from comfortable, at least they could rest for a few hours before they continued their journey.

'I agree,' Piers said. He was studying Gwendoline and added, 'Good shooting. I'm glad you brought your bow.'

'Thank you,' she responded. 'I just…never thought I would have to shoot a man.'

'I'm glad you did,' Piers answered. He put his arm around her waist in silent comfort. To Morwenna, he added, 'And I'm glad you knew how to fight with a sword. Even if you never liked it.' He sent her a wry smile, for he'd known the reason why she'd sparred.

They mounted their horses and Robert led them southwest, towards Stansbury, where they had lived in hiding during the past two years. The familiar crumbling walls held bittersweet memories.

As they entered the ruins, he felt a sense of regret. Nine men had died because of the earl's insistence on stopping his daughter from marrying the man she wanted. Even if Piers did succeed in marrying Gwendoline, Robert sensed that the fight wasn't over.

His half-brother came to ride beside him while the women remained behind, talking in low voices. 'It seems we're even now.'

'We are,' Robert agreed. With a glance behind him, he asked, 'Does she know?'

His brother shook his head, his gaze fixed ahead. The lie of omission would cause a strong rift between them, if Gwendoline found out Piers was a bastard.

'It's a mistake not to tell her,' he warned, even knowing that Piers wouldn't listen. But he had no intention of interfering between them. Whatever choices his brother made, he had to live with the consequences.

Piers only shrugged. 'I'm going to find a priest and wed her. The sooner it's done, the better.'

But Robert wasn't so certain marrying the earl's daughter would help him achieve his goals—it might end them entirely.

'What of you and Morwenna?' Piers asked. 'Will you wed her too?'

The thought sent a rush of warmth within him. To awaken beside Morwenna each day, to live his life with her, evoked an ache of longing he'd never expected.

But he thought again of the men from Penrith

and their pleas for help. He'd already accepted that he would not wed Gwendoline, but it meant that he would have to take Penrith by conquest. And the only way to do that was to appeal to the king.

It was quite possible—probable even—that King John would refuse to support his claim to the land. But if the king somehow agreed, he would want something in return. Robert suspected he'd have to wed an heiress of the king's choosing—especially if that meant John would gain the gold he needed to fight his wars in France.

'We will witness your wedding,' he promised his brother. 'It's too soon for me to wed.'

'You haven't given up on Penrith yet, have you?' Piers said quietly.

Robert shook his head. His brother stared at him in silence, and it was clear that their own battle for the lands was yet to come.

They rode for nearly two hours before they reached Stansbury. By then, it was dawn and Morwenna was exhausted. Gwendoline had turned pensive, for Piers had left to find a priest. She started braiding her hair, tucking it up as best she could.

'Do you want me to help?' Morwenna asked.

'Please.' Gwendoline ventured a smile. 'It's not the sort of wedding I imagined it would be.'

'What did you imagine?' she asked, while she took a comb and began pulling it through Gwen's tangled hair.

'When I was a little girl, I thought my mother would help me choose a gown. She would give me her jewels to wear and flowers to put in my hair.' Gwendoline's mood turned sad. 'She died a few years ago. I miss her terribly.'

Her eyes welled up with tears and she turned to Morwenna. 'Am I doing the right thing? Should I marry Piers?'

Morwenna paused and studied her. 'You haven't known him long. If you're uncertain, it's not surprising. You could ask him to wait.'

'I've never even met his family,' she said. 'He told me his father died two years ago.'

Morwenna nodded. She wasn't certain how much Gwendoline knew, but she was torn between warning the woman and betraying Piers. Regardless of what Robert believed, she did think that Piers cared for Gwendoline. She'd caught him stealing glances at her, and his expression had held a sort of reverence—as if he couldn't believe this beautiful woman could be his.

Although Gwendoline deserved to know the

truth, Morwenna didn't want to be the cause of a rift between them. The young woman was good for Piers. Already she had softened his anger and brought out the better side of him.

But was it right to enter a marriage based on a lie? And even then, what right did she have to interfere? It bothered Morwenna that she was caught in such a position, between truth and lies. The only solution she could see was to tell Gwen the truths she wanted to hear and not offer anything else.

'Only you can make the decision on whether to wed Piers,' Morwenna said at last. 'Don't listen to what others say or even what he tells you. Listen to your heart and how he makes you feel.'

At that, Gwen smiled. 'Then I know the answer. It won't be easy, and we've made an enemy of my father. But I do want to marry Piers. He needs me.' She turned to face Morwenna. 'But what of you and Robert?'

The question caught Morwenna off-guard, though she already knew the answer. 'Robert cares for me, but he cannot marry a miller's daughter, Lady Gwendoline. He is the rightful heir to Penrith.'

'So that's why he wanted to court me,' Gwen said quietly. 'Like the others, he only wanted

Penrith.' With a soft smile, she added, 'But I could see that he only had eyes for you.'

Morwenna released a sigh, remembering Robert's gaze as he'd touched her. Even now, a flush of warmth flooded through her at the memory of his mouth upon her skin.

'It doesn't matter,' she insisted. 'Despite what we might feel for one another, I know my place. I only have this time with him now. Once we meet with the king…' She shook her head, for it would be over.

'Do you really believe that?' Gwen asked softly, reaching for the golden chain Morwenna wore. 'Especially when you have a necklace that once belonged to the queen?'

'How did you know about the necklace?' Morwenna asked.

'I overheard my father talking about it.' Gwendoline studied it a moment and then said, 'Don't you want to find out more?'

'I don't know if there are any answers,' she answered honestly. 'Your father thought it was stolen. I still believe it was a gift, though I don't know why. I hope to find out when Robert petitions the king.'

Gwendoline sobered at that. 'So, he intends to reclaim Penrith and have my father sent away.'

Her face tightened, and Morwenna wished she

had not told her about their plans to appeal to the king. But she softened her voice and reminded her, 'It was always his home. Your father can return to his own estate.'

There was a sudden glimpse of worry on the young woman's face before she hid it. 'I suppose I will have to go with Piers to his family's lands, is that it?'

Guilt washed over Morwenna at the knowledge that they might have nowhere to go until Robert reclaimed Penrith. All she could tell the young woman was, 'You should talk with Piers about his plans.' Yet, a part of her sided with Piers. She knew what it was to be born with nothing and dream of a better life. What right did she have to ruin his happiness?

'He hasn't told me of his plans,' Gwendoline said. 'But I thought we would eventually return to Penrith.' She straightened one of her sleeves, her expression pensive. 'I just don't know what will happen now.'

Morwenna didn't know how to answer her. She knew it was wrong not to tell Gwendoline the truth, especially since the woman had been kind to her. 'You do have a choice. If you want to wait to wed Piers, you can. You need not marry this day if you wish.'

The young woman hesitated. 'I know you're

right. But after everything that's happened, after all we've been through, I don't think there is any other man who would make me feel the way Piers does.' She took a breath. 'I will wed him. I believe that he loves me, even though he's never said it.'

Morwenna reached for the woman's hand, hoping she was right.

It was dark outside by the time Piers returned with the priest. The old man was unlike any priest Morwenna had ever seen. He appeared completely and utterly drunk. He was holding a drinking horn, swaying on his feet after he dismounted from his ancient mare. Morwenna had no idea where Piers had found the priest—he could not be from the abbey—but she supposed it was the best he could do at such short notice.

Gwendoline appeared beautiful, even in her rumpled gown. Her face was shining with happiness, and Piers appeared dumbstruck.

Robert came to stand by Morwenna's side while the priest took another drink. 'Do you think he'll manage to finish the ceremony before he passes out?'

'I doubt it.' She smiled at him, finding the humour in the circumstances. 'But I hope they will find happiness together.' That much was the truth, even if she knew Gwendoline would be angry when she learned Piers was only a bastard.

You should have told her, an inner voice warned.

But then, she wanted her friend to marry the man she loved. In her heart, she believed that somehow they would work it out.

The priest began the ceremony, and although the Latin words were familiar, she was caught up in watching Piers and Gwendoline. Robert took her hand, and the gesture nearly broke her. It was almost a mockery of the dream she wanted so badly. She knew it was impossible, and yet... she wanted Robert as her husband and lover. For two years, she had been his friend, learning to fight alongside him, dreaming of him. Her heart ached with yearning, and she wished so badly that she could simply forget what it was like to be touched by Robert.

He wanted her—of that, there was no doubt. But would he ever marry her? Not unless she had a title and an estate of her own.

A tear slid free, and she tried to mask it with a smile, pretending they were tears of joy instead of regret.

The priest stumbled through the words of the marriage rite and gave a blessing afterwards, though he did not offer a Mass. It almost seemed that he was so drunk he believed he *had* spoken a Mass, but no one corrected him.

Morwenna brought out small flat cakes that she had baked from the grain the monks had given them. There was no honey, but at least they had something to celebrate the wedding.

Robert had caught fish, and he roasted them over a spit. While they cooked, he pulled out a bottle of wine that she was fairly certain Piers had stolen from the cellars at Penrith. Robert poured a generous cup and passed it to his brother. Morwenna retrieved two small drinking horns and another wooden cup, which he filled.

'I wish you both good health and many children.' Robert raised his drinking horn, and both Piers and Gwendoline raised their own cups. The bride was blushing, and after they drank, Robert offered them some of the fish. They both joined in the feasting and, after a little while, Gwendoline said, 'I have something for you, Morwenna.'

She didn't know what it was, but the woman withdrew a bundle she'd brought from Penrith. Gwendoline unwrapped it and held out a green gown. 'This was your mother's, wasn't it? The one you left behind.'

A rush of emotion tightened in her throat, and Morwenna nodded. When she took the gown, her tears returned. 'Thank you for bringing it back to me.'

'I knew you'd want it,' Gwendoline said.

Morwenna embraced the woman, so grateful to have the gown. With a slight laugh, she added, 'I wish you'd given it to me sooner so I wouldn't have worn the monk's habit to your wedding.'

Gwendoline's eyes brightened and she said, 'I should have, but I was distracted by Piers.' Her new husband came to her side, and it wasn't long before Piers excused them.

'I suppose we'll have to finish the rest of our feast alone.' Robert refilled her cup and ate another of the flat cakes she'd made. 'These are good. How did you find the ingredients?'

'I made them with some grain the monks gave us,' she answered.

They ate together in front of the fire. The sun had set, and Morwenna warmed herself by the crackling flames. Robert sent her a sidelong glance. 'What do you suppose they're doing right now?'

Her face reddened, and she gaped until she realised he wasn't serious. 'Going for a walk, I believe.'

'I don't know,' he teased. 'They could be playing dice. Or they might go to sleep. I cannot imagine what else they'd be doing.' His mock innocence made her laugh, and it eased the tension she hadn't known was there.

'Do you want to play dice or go for a walk?' she offered, teasing him back.

Robert lifted an eyebrow as if she'd implied something else. 'Or I might have another idea.' He stood up from the fire and held out his hand.

She wasn't quite certain what he wanted, but she followed. Robert picked up a torch and led her through the ruins and out towards the stables. For a moment, he paused at the entrance, and then said, 'Good. I wanted to be certain Piers and Gwendoline weren't inside.'

'Where did they go?' she wondered aloud.

'Somewhere far enough from here,' he answered, leading her inside. She wasn't certain if he planned to tend the horses, but he stopped in front of one of the stalls. Morwenna waited to see what he was doing, and then he withdrew a battered piece of wood. She recognised it as the shield he'd given her that she'd left behind in the stables on the day they'd gone to Penrith.

'I'd nearly forgotten about this shield,' she said.

'You could have used it earlier today,' he teased. 'It might have been necessary during the battle, had you brought it with you.'

She picked it up and studied it. In all honesty,

she said, 'Robert, I know you meant well, but this was truly a terrible gift to give a woman.'

'I thought you wanted to be a warrior,' he said. 'At the time, at least. You trained all the time.'

'Because I wanted to be near you,' she admitted. 'It had nothing to do with fighting.'

'I didn't realise it then.' He helped her hold the shield, and his nearness heightened the sensitivity of her skin. He was so close, but the shield remained between them. 'I was blind to it.'

Her hand was trembling, and she lowered the wooden shield. 'I wasn't what you wanted.'

'But you are now,' he admitted. He reached out to tuck a lock of her hair behind one ear. 'You'd better keep that shield between us.'

'Or what?' she whispered, setting it aside.

In answer, he leaned in for a kiss. This time, it was slower, a savouring of mouths. She opened to him, feeling the sleek invasion of his tongue. He stole her breath, and she kissed him with all the yearning in her heart.

'Morwenna,' he murmured, sliding his hands into her hair. 'You're tearing me apart.'

She drew back, uncertain what he meant. At her questioning gaze, he added, 'I want nothing more than to lay you down and kiss every inch of your skin. And then I want to be inside you.'

She reached out to touch his cheek. He kissed

the palm of her hand. 'But you're hurt. And it's not fair to ask this of you.'

She understood that it was both a reason and an excuse not to touch her. Becoming lovers would make matters more complicated.

And yet, she wasn't willing to let him go. Not yet. This might be her last chance to claim the man she wanted. Once they reached the king, everything would change.

'Will you light a fire for us?' she asked. 'It's cold.' In the darkness, she could hardly see him at all. And this night, she wanted more than shadows.

He built a small hearth with stones and wood. Then he used flint and straw tinder, to strike a flame. He fed the fire until there was a comfortable blaze. While he was preoccupied, she removed the monk's habit and her shift until she stood naked before him.

His gaze turned hot, his eyes greedy as he studied her. 'I've never seen anyone more beautiful in my life.'

She turned slightly, revealing her back. 'But not this.'

'Those are the marks of bravery and courage,' he said. 'And the wounds are healing well.'

She faced him and said quietly, 'I want to see you, Robert.'

He stood slowly and removed the monk's cowl and habit, baring himself. His body was more heavily muscled than she'd imagined, with ridges along his stomach and chest. Below his waist, his erection hung straight and firm. She remembered how she had pleasured him by her touch. And she wanted to slide her palm over him intimately.

She drew close to him, but shyness suddenly overcame her.

'Morwenna, you don't have to do this.' He took both her hands, and the warmth of his palms was a contrast against her own cold fingers. 'We don't know what will happen when we find your true family. They might try to arrange a marriage for you.'

She understood his unspoken words, that offering her virginity to him might have strong consequences. And yet, there was no one else for her.

'You're the only man I've ever wanted,' she whispered. 'There will never be another for me.'

'I don't know what the future holds,' he admitted. Which was another reminder that he could never marry her.

'I know that I want you,' she murmured. 'There's not much time left. We should make the most of it.'

'If I touch you, I won't stop,' he swore. 'I don't

trust myself right now. I might hurt you, and I can't allow that.'

It was his honour, she realised. In his expression, she could see the intensity of desire that mirrored her own. He was trying to keep her a virgin as a means of protecting her. Neither of them had taken a lover before, and they had only touched each other.

She released his hands and stared at him. His body was beautiful, and she ached to run her hands over his skin. 'What would you do if you could touch me?'

He exhaled sharply. 'I would kneel before you and cup your breasts.'

She stared at him, never taking her eyes from his face as she reached down to cup her own breasts. The weight of the flesh was light, and she used her thumb to circle the nipple. 'Like this?' Instantly, she felt a flare of heat between her thighs. A sigh escaped her, and she closed her eyes at the deep sensation.

'Yes,' he murmured. 'Now put one hand between your legs.'

She obeyed, feeling the slickness beneath her fingers. A shuddering warmth flooded through her. Though she didn't know what would happen between them, she didn't want to do this alone.

'Put your hand upon your own flesh,' she

commanded. 'Imagine that it's my hand, the way I touched you last night.'

He obeyed, and the rigid tension echoed her own tightness. She remembered the feeling of his thick flesh against her, and as she touched herself, she imagined it was him.

'Put one finger inside you,' Robert commanded. She was startled by his demand, but she did so. Her body welcomed the slight intrusion, and she felt the wetness surrounding her.

'Now move it in and out,' he ordered. The shaking pleasure started to take hold but once more, she wanted him to experience the same thing. She bit back a moan, and the sight of him gripping himself while she stroked herself intimately was enough to push her towards the edge.

'I want you to do the same,' she said. 'Stroke yourself. Let me watch.'

He did, and she was fascinated when his hand curled over the hard length. She started moving her finger to the rhythm of his hand, imagining he was inside her. The wetness intensified, and she arched her back, startled when her fingers bumped against a sensitive place.

'I would kiss you if I could,' she whispered. 'And I would lift my leg around your waist and take you inside me.'

His breathing was coming harder, and he

stared at her while he worked his length. 'Put another finger inside yourself,' he ordered. 'Keep sliding them in and out. I want to know what pleasures you.'

His demand was so erotic, she continued to touch herself. The sensitive place was just above her entrance, and she rubbed it gently.

'Does that feel good?' he asked. His voice was rough and strained.

'Yes,' she breathed. 'When I touch it, I feel as if I'm losing control.' She circled the hooded flesh with one finger, and the rush gathered harder inside her. She was rising higher, her body so close…

And then, without warning, Robert took her nipple in his mouth and replaced her hand with his own. The moment his fingers touched her, she shattered. His hand was gentle, driving her over the edge, and he slid his fingers deep inside. She broke apart again, her body seizing up with pleasure as he plunged and withdrew. She reached for his hard length, her fingers closing over him. She stroked his velvet shaft, her thumb caressing the edge, and he groaned.

As she'd promised, she raised her leg over his hip, and he shocked her by lifting her up. She wrapped her legs around him, and his thick erection poised at her entrance.

'Are you certain?' he asked.

'Don't stop.' Her body felt alive, quaking with fire and she welcomed him inside. Though it was not an easy fit, she moaned as he pulled her down, invading her flesh and claiming her virginity.

Her bare breasts pressed against his chest, and he enveloped her in his arms. She could feel his manhood deep inside, and she cradled his face, welcoming him into her body. There had been a sudden pinch, and she felt the soreness, but he didn't move. Not yet.

Instead, he held her waist, careful of her back. She was self-conscious about the weight of her body, but he lifted her slightly and penetrated again. Once more, the flare of heat rekindled. He was gentle, holding her hips as he thrust inside. And she forgot everything else when he kissed her. His tongue moved against hers as he made love to her, and she squeezed his length.

'God above, you feel good,' he growled. 'I don't know if I can last much longer.' He moved back against the horse stall and leaned against the wood, holding her as he started to move in rhythm. She surrendered to him, the feelings rising higher.

He bent down to suckle at her breast, and she

let out a cry, her body growing even wetter. 'I'm sorry,' he groaned against her skin. 'I can't stop.'

He gripped her hips and hastened the rhythm, lifting her and thrusting deep. Although she was sore, she no longer cared. She locked her legs around him, arching as he took her. Another release gathered inside, and she shuddered as it erupted. He plunged and withdrew until he groaned and spilled himself within her body.

Morwenna clung to him, unable to speak or even form a coherent thought. With their bodies still joined, Robert slid down from the wall until he turned to lie on the ground, with her collapsed atop him. She never wanted to move again.

Chapter Nine

After parting ways with Gwendoline and Piers, they continued travelling south for the next sennight. Though Robert knew that becoming lovers had been a grave risk, he could not deny Morwenna. And the nights he spent in her arms only bound him closer to her. Her wounds had healed, except for slight bruising, but despite the way she slept beside him, he could tell that she was starting to distance herself.

Fortune had smiled upon them, and he could see the King John's entourage in the distance. It was late afternoon, and they could take shelter among the king's travelling court. With luck, he could seek the audience he needed to determine his fate.

Morwenna, in turn, intended to ask about the queen's pendant. She had grown quieter as they neared the king's encampment, almost sad.

'Are you nervous?' he asked.

She nodded. This morn, she had donned her mother's gown again, and she'd braided and bound up her hair. Around her throat, she wore the pendant.

Robert slowed the pace of the horses. 'There's more, isn't there?'

This time, she turned to face him. 'I'm afraid that I won't find any answers at all. Or worse, that they won't be the ones I want. What if my mother was a serving maid? What if she had no connection to the queen and the pendant was stolen?'

He reached out to take her hand, squeezing it gently. 'We'll find out the truth, whatever it is.'

She closed her eyes and took a deep breath. 'Most of all, I'm afraid that I won't see you again.'

'What do you mean?' He wasn't intending to abandon her here.

'I mean that we don't know what will happen after we meet with the king.'

'It could be dangerous,' he acknowledged, 'but we've done nothing wrong.'

'We have no gift for him,' she pointed out. 'And he may not agree to listen to us. He's more concerned about his wars in France.' She ventured a faint smile. 'Unless you have an estate in Normandy that you can give to the king?'

He shook his head. 'Unfortunately, no.' But she had a strong point that the king would be more amenable if they had a gift to bring. He knew Morwenna was right, but he couldn't leave his people to suffer any longer than necessary. It was a grave risk, but he hoped the king would listen and somehow intervene.

'Robert,' she murmured. 'Could we stop for a moment?'

He drew his horse's reins. 'Of course. What is it?'

She dismounted and stood upon the hillside, staring down at the tents before them. He sensed her uncertainty, and he wondered how to reassure her.

He moved his arm around her waist, and she suddenly clung to him, burying her face against his tunic. 'Be with me one last time,' she pleaded. 'Because everything will change as soon as we ride among them.'

He understood then that her fears went deeper than apprehensions about the king. It was about the changes that would happen between them.

She lifted her face to him and brought his mouth to hers. The moment she kissed him, he lost himself. Something about this woman went deeper than physical touch. When he was with her, the rest of the world disappeared. She kissed him with desperation, and he met her need with his own heart-racing desire.

Against the fabric of her kirtle, he reached to cup her breast. The fullness rested in his palm, and he stroked her nipple. She bit her lip and sighed as he caressed her. The tight bud was her sensitive place, and he loosened his trews. She curved her hand over his manhood, and he gritted his teeth at the pleasure of her touch. With her thumb, she drew a circle over the damp head of him, and his own breathing grew ragged.

'You're wearing too many clothes,' he gritted out.

She laughed and lifted her skirts to her knees. 'I think you'll find a way around it.'

Her eagerness made him want her more. Only this time, he wanted to caress her until her hands dug into the earth, her back arching as he pleasured her.

There was a large limestone boulder nearby, a flattened stone, similar to an ancient altar. 'Lie down,' he commanded.

She did, lifting her skirts even higher, but he wanted more than a swift coupling. Instead, he knelt before her, sliding her skirts to her waist, baring her body before him. He bent between her legs, his breath against her intimate opening.

Though he had done nothing yet, he saw the way she anticipated his touch. 'Robert,' she murmured. Slowly, she spread her legs for him, but he wasn't going to join with her. At least, not yet.

Instead, he cupped her hips with both hands and lifted her to his mouth. And when he tasted between her folds, she cried out, shuddering against him. She couldn't speak, but he saw the tremor that took hold. He used his tongue to explore her intimately, kissing her deeply. He noticed the way she jolted when he caressed her hooded flesh.

'Robert, I can't bear it,' she moaned.

But he wasn't finished with her yet. He brought her own hands to her breasts and ordered, 'Touch yourself through the silk. I won't stop until I've finished you.'

She did, and he intensified his efforts, gripping her hips as he feasted upon her. And when he worked her with his tongue, he slid a thumb inside her and it drove her over the edge. She gripped his thumb, shattering as she arched hard.

'Take me,' she begged.

He unfastened his trews and drove hard into her slick opening. Her wetness surrounded him, and she gasped as he invaded and withdrew. He could no longer be gentle, for he had lost all control. Her legs wrapped around his waist, and he thrust hard against her.

Morwenna started to pant to the rhythm of his penetrations, but he wanted more. He wanted her writhing against him, and he knew her sensitive places. He slowed his pace and pulled back, feeling the slickness of her body before he thrust again. The anticipation seemed to build higher, and when he pressed his thumb against her hooded flesh again, she gave a soft cry. He took her gently, sliding in deep as he caressed her. She strained against him, trying to pull his body closer. But he tormented her sweetly, loving the way she was squeezing him within her depths. Her breathing had become swifter, and he held her in a firm grasp, lifting her slightly higher.

'Faster,' she pleaded. 'I need more.' She was so wet, and it took every ounce of control not to shout as she started to meet his thrusts with her hips. God above, she knew how to drive him wild. With her legs around her waist, she arched to meet him, and he quickened his pace.

No longer was he gentle, but instead, he thrust hard, gripping her body in a primal rhythm like a conqueror. His arousal was so thick and hard, he could not stop himself from pounding against her. This time, he surrendered to his needs, taking her as he pressed towards the edge of his own release.

He claimed her, and the speed of his penetrations made her tense, trembling hard as she broke apart. She arched against him, gripping his hair as she took him deep. And this time when he entered and withdrew, she moaned, 'Robert, I love you.'

The words washed over him, and he no longer cared about anything else, save her. He needed to show Morwenna how he felt, for there were no words.

She kissed him and climaxed a second time, her body erupting as she milked his length. Her kiss muffled the shout as he emptied himself inside her. Aftershocks claimed them both, and he could not stop himself from kissing her again, tasting her swollen mouth.

For long moments, he lay inside her, her body flat against the stone like an offering. Her hair had come undone from the braids, and her lips were swollen. Never had he seen anyone more beautiful.

'It's going to be all right,' he promised. 'I will take care of you, Morwenna.'

She sat up and embraced him while he remained inside her. And for a moment, they forgot about the rest of the world and what lay ahead.

They reached the top of the hillside and began their descent into the valley leading towards the king's entourage where dozens of tents were set up. The entire encampment was surrounded by soldiers spaced at even intervals. As they drew closer, four guards on horseback approached, armed with spears.

'Who are you, and why have you come?' the captain of the guards asked. Unlike the other soldiers, he was an older man, and his beard held threads of grey.

Robert held out his hands to show he meant no harm. 'I am Robert of Penrith, son of Degal of Penrith. I have come to seek an audience with the king about my lands.'

But the older man's gaze was fixed upon Morwenna. 'And the lady?'

'She is with me,' he answered. Then to protect her honour, he added, 'Lady Morwenna is my betrothed wife.'

The captain studied her and then lifted a hand to ask the other soldiers to fall back into position. 'You may request an audience, but I should warn you, the king may decide not to grant it.'

'I understand.' Robert inclined his head, and

they rode behind the captain who led them to a small enclosure. Two young lads came to take care of the horses, and Robert helped Morwenna dismount. Though she braved a smile, her face was pale with worry.

He offered his arm as they followed the captain, but as they passed the tents, he grew aware of the folk staring at her. Some turned to whisper, but when he met their gaze, they looked away. He wasn't certain why Morwenna's presence had caused such a stir, but he intended to find out.

The captain led him to one of the tents, but it was clear that this one was not a royal dwelling. 'Lady Morwenna, you may join the queen's ladies. Penrith, come with me.'

He hadn't expected to be separated from her, but Robert supposed it would be better this way. 'I will see you later,' he promised, touching his cheek to hers.

She gripped his hand and looked as if she wanted to say something but didn't. 'Later then,' she agreed.

He followed the captain past more rows of tents until he found an open area near a fire where members of the king's travelling court were present. All wore finer clothing than his, with silks, embroidery, and gold. He saw many men standing with gifts of gold and silver, along with elaborate wood carvings.

Robert grew conscious of his simple attire, wondering if his decision to come without a gift was a mistake. He had nothing at all to offer, save his loyalty. And now, he wasn't so certain it would be enough.

As he studied each of the king's subjects, he caught sight of another man standing near the other side of the tent—Lord Alfred of Penrith. Immediately, Robert turned away, hoping the man had not seen him. Rage boiled inside him, for he wanted the earl dead after what he'd done to Morwenna. Robert tried to keep control of the violent emotions. Never had he imagined that Alfred would be here. The man was a clear threat to everything Robert valued—not just Penrith, but Morwenna, too. And from the elaborately carved chest in his arms, Alfred undoubtedly had gold to give to the king. If the earl denied Robert's accusations, the king would believe him.

Worst of all, if Alfred learned of Morwenna's presence, he might threaten her again.

Never in her life had Morwenna felt so out of place. So many of the ladies were staring at her. Though she murmured a greeting, few spoke in return. Were it possible to escape them, she would have tried.

At last, one of the women approached her. 'I am Sarah of Holyrede.' She was an older woman, with grey strands threaded through her dark hair.

'I am Morwenna,' she answered.

The older woman gave a nod. 'And where are you from?'

'My father brought my brother and me to Penrith two years ago. We travelled a lot over the years, so I've lived in many places.'

The woman studied her for a time. Then her gaze fixed upon Morwenna's throat. 'Where did you get that necklace?'

Her heart began pounding, for she sensed that this woman knew already. She decided to be honest, in the hope that Lady Holyrede could reveal the truth.

'It belonged to my mother. My father gave it to me after she died.'

The woman's expression grew wary. 'Did he tell you that, Lady Morwenna?' She shook her head. 'Your mother isn't dead. But be of care. There are many in the king's court who are her enemies.'

'You knew her?' Morwenna gaped. 'But how is that possible? I haven't even told you her name.'

Lady Holyrede sighed. 'You are the very

image of Rochelle. The king, if he decides to grant you an audience, will know exactly who you are.'

So that was why the people had stared at her. And while she had wanted to learn about her past, it was starting to make her uncomfortable. Why had her mother made enemies? Was it somehow connected to the queen?

'I had heard that the queen gave my mother this pendant,' Morwenna ventured, hoping for more answers.

At that, Lady Holyrede snorted. 'Not the current queen, I vow. She is hardly more than a child.' With a shake of her head, she added, 'The pendant belonged to Queen Eleanor at one time. She might have meant for King John to give it to his wife, but of course, he gave it to his mistress. It caused quite an uproar.'

A sudden terror seized her stomach as Morwenna realised what the woman was saying. 'Then my mother...'

'Was the king's mistress, aye,' Lady Holyrede finished. 'You weren't the first royal bastard, and you won't be the last.'

Morwenna felt as if the air had left her lungs. She sank upon a low stool, feeling faint. 'I don't understand.' If she was a bastard daughter of King John, why had she been raised as a miller's daughter? Did he even know of her existence? Somehow, she didn't believe so.

Had Eldreth stolen her as the midwife believed? Or had her true mother given her away?

And what of Brian? Was he truly her brother? All these years, they had protected one another. Were they even related? A thousand questions spun within her mind, blurring her future.

She tried to calm the turmoil of emotions, centring on finding the truth. 'Do you know where my mother is now?'

The older woman paused. 'I suppose she's still at Banmouth, just south of here. Her husband died only a few years ago.'

The thought of meeting her mother both terrified her and filled her with hope. At last, she would have her answers. For if this was true, it meant that she might have the chance to marry Robert.

She couldn't stop the tremulous smile that spread over her face. 'Do you think the king would allow me an audience?'

'It's difficult to say. King John is given to moods, and no one knows what he will decide.' She eyed her closely. 'I would not trust the women here, either. Especially his new queen.' With that, Lady Holyrede inclined her head and left.

Morwenna hardly cared what the other women

thought of her any more. None of it mattered. For the first time in her life, she was starting to believe that she was a woman of worth. She straightened her shoulders and felt a sense of calm descending upon her. It was strange to think that one conversation had held such a strong effect on her.

She stood up from the stool and left the tent. Right now, she wanted to tell Robert what she had learned. She wasn't certain where to find him, but she could ask the guards.

Outside, the sky was growing darker. She walked past the rows of tents, and as she passed by a few groups of men, Morwenna began to realise that it was dangerous to go in search of Robert alone. It would have been wiser to remain with the women. She nearly turned back, but then she saw one of the soldiers walking towards her.

'Can you tell me where I might find—?' Her words broke off when he continued on his way without stopping.

'Who are you looking for?' came a man's voice.

She turned and saw Lord Alfred of Penrith. In an instant, fear turned her skin to ice, and her back ached in memory. The smug expression on his face revealed his satisfaction at her discomfort. Why was he here?

Her first instinct was to flee, but if she did, others might think she had a reason to run. Instead, she forced herself to gather her courage. 'I am looking for Robert.'

'So, he did survive.'

She could almost imagine the words he held back... *I was hoping he hadn't.*

But she answered, 'He did. Now, if you'll excuse me.'

'Not yet.' He came to stand beside her. 'You've saved me the time and inconvenience of my search. I've lost too many men, and both of you are to blame for it.'

She continued walking, ignoring him. When he tried to reach for her arm, she unsheathed her eating knife and held it out. 'You will not touch me.'

'Sheathe your claws, little cat,' he warned. 'If you cooperate willingly, I might overlook those crimes. You know where Gwendoline is, don't you?'

So that was what this was about. Gwendoline's father was still hunting her after she'd escaped with Piers.

Morwenna shook her head. 'I do not know where she is now.' And if she did, she wouldn't tell him that. 'But she left Penrith of her own accord. I believe you locked her away.' She let the words fall, hinting that rebellion had caused Gwendoline's escape. She wanted to believe that her friend had found happiness with Piers, now that they were married. But she had no idea where the pair of them had gone.

A look of irritation flashed over Lord Penrith's face, and he stared at her as if reconsidering his tactics. 'Do you know why I am here?'

'I presume you're trying to find your daughter.'

His face turned sly. 'No, I've brought His Excellency the taxes, tithes, and rents. He will be most pleased.'

'You're bribing him.'

'I am only ensuring his favour,' the earl corrected her. 'But you would do well to remember that I have his ear. After the harvest, there will be more gold. King John knows this.' She didn't lower her blade, and he stared at her. 'Perhaps I'll tell him that you stole the queen's pendant. What do you think he would do to you?'

She gave no reaction to his open threat. 'Take me to him, and we will find out.' Though she kept her words calm, inwardly, she was terrified. Would the king recognise her at all? What if Lady Holyrede was wrong about her mother?

A hundred things could go wrong, and the risk was grave.

Her heart was pounding, as Penrith met her gaze with a thin smile. 'Oh, be assured, I will be speaking about this…situation…with the king. But you won't receive an audience. Why would the king want to speak with someone like you?' His gaze swept over her attire. 'Pretend to wear finery and gold all you like Morwenna. It doesn't change who you are. King John has no use for you.'

With that, he turned his back on her and walked away. Morwenna remained in place, and seconds later, a hand shot out and covered her mouth. In the darkness, she tried to scream, but the sound was muffled as the man dragged her into one of the tents.

'Don't say a word.'

She nearly fainted with relief when she realised it was Robert. He lowered his hand and crushed her into his embrace. 'You cannot walk alone, Morwenna. Not here. It's not safe.'

'I'm sorry. I was trying to find you and… Penrith was suddenly there.' She welcomed his arms around her, and she closed her eyes, resting her face against his chest. 'Did you hear what he said?'

'No. I only just saw him leaving.' His voice turned grim. 'I want him dead for hurting you.'

She clung to him, taking comfort in his embrace. 'He made threats, but he didn't touch me.'

'Had I known he would be here, I never would have brought you.'

Though Morwenna realised he was talking about her safety, a pang caught in her throat. 'Do you think he'll go to the king?'

'You won't be here long enough to find out.' He drew back and framed her face with his hands. 'I'm going to make the arrangements tonight.'

She stepped out of his arms and regarded him. 'You're planning to send me away?'

He nodded. 'It's better this way.'

'And where do you plan for me to go?' She faced him, suddenly wary of his declaration. Why was he suddenly trying to make decisions for her? And why should he get to decide her fate? He was not her husband. This was her life, not his.

'The nuns can give you sanctuary,' he began. 'I can send word to my uncle for an escort to Saint Michael's Well.'

No. Not again. She put her hand to his lips to cut him off. 'Listen to me, Robert. I am not about to go into hiding at the nunnery.' He needed to know what she'd learned about her mother, about being King John's bastard daughter. 'I've just learned from Lady Holyrede that my mother is still alive. If I go anywhere, it will be to find Lady Rochelle of Banmouth,' she insisted. 'I need to know what happened. Why she gave us to Eldreth…if that's the truth.' Part of her wanted to believe that she and Brian had been stolen. Or perhaps someone had tried to search for them. 'And I need to know who my family is.'

Robert appeared uncertain about the information. 'What if Lady Holyrede wasn't telling you the truth about your mother? Or what if you don't like the answers you find?'

Morwenna lifted her chin. 'They were staring at me today, Robert. Because I look like Lady Rochelle. I need to understand who I am.' She took his hand in hers. 'I want to believe that she is my true mother. And that the king is my father.'

He reached out to trace the line of her face but said nothing. She reached out to cover his hand, the ache resonating within her heart. Didn't he understand what this meant to her? 'What if I am, Robert? What happens to us then?'

Her greatest hope was that she could be worthy of marrying Robert. Her heart belonged to him, and when he'd lied to the soldiers, introducing her as his betrothed wife, she had wanted nothing more than it to be true.

'We don't know what the truth is,' he acknowledged, 'but whether or not you're the king's daughter, it's not safe for you here. Not with Lord Penrith.'

She knew that. But if she had even a drop of royal blood, it gave her the advantage she needed. 'I want to see King John,' she insisted. 'He was not yet married when he met my mother. I want to see if he recognises me the way the others do.'

'I'm not certain if he'll agree to see either of us,' Robert admitted. 'Gaining an audience is more challenging than I thought it would be. He refused to see any of us today—even those noblemen who brought gifts.'

'Grant me one more day,' she said. 'If I cannot gain an audience, then I will go to seek the answers from my mother.' Emotion gathered up inside, and she closed her eyes to push back the raw feelings.

'Do you really want to open up the past?' he asked gently. 'What if she's not…who you want her to be?'

Morwenna was afraid to voice the truth, uncertain of what to say. It meant making herself vulnerable, laying her heart bare before him. But if she didn't take the risk, he wouldn't understand her reasons.

She steeled herself and admitted, 'Because if I do have noble blood, it gives us the chance to be together.'

Her words hung between them, suspended by hope and fear. In his eyes, she saw the flare of desire, before it faded to resignation. 'I don't want you to get your hopes up, Morwenna.'

Her cheeks reddened with disappointment. 'What do you mean?'

'I may not be able to regain my lands,' he admitted. 'And if that happens, I may have nothing left to offer you.'

'I don't need wealth or riches or land,' she said. 'The only thing I've ever wanted is you.'

But in his expression, she saw the trace of failure. 'It's not enough for me. I don't want to give up on Penrith or my people. I cannot surrender what was mine and live my life travelling from place to place. It's no life at all.'

'It's the only life I've ever known,' she answered. For a long moment, she stared at him, wondering what sort of future he saw. Were they really such worlds apart? If he didn't regain Penrith, would he be unable to live a life as a commoner? Or what if she learned that Lady Holyrede had lied and there was no royal blood—or even noble blood—in her veins? She was starting to feel as if the ground were shifting beneath her feet.

'Will you try again on the morrow for an audience with the king?' she asked at last.

He nodded. 'But I don't know if he will see me. Some say if you wait long enough, you might be fortunate. But I am not certain I've done enough—especially since I have nothing to offer.' He paused a moment. 'I thought at first that I could plead my case and ask for help. But you were right. Without gold, none of it matters to King John. And where does that leave me? With nothing at all.'

She could feel him slipping away. Anguish rose up within her, for she sensed that if she went to find her family, she would not see him again. If he could not regain his lands, he would likely go to fight in the Crusades like her brother. And then, she would lose both of them.

'You have me,' she said, feeling the heaviness in her voice.

'But I may not be able to provide for you.' He stroked her hair. 'I don't want a life where we wander from place to place, fighting to survive.'

'It's not so terrible.' She met his gaze. 'There's no responsibility for anyone but ourselves. We can go anywhere.'

But from the expression on his face, she could tell that it wasn't enough for him. And it broke her heart to know it.

Chapter Ten

It wasn't fair to crush the hope in her eyes. But pride kept him from offering her promises. Even if she did find out the truth about her family, Robert could not imagine asking her to wed him if they had nowhere to live.

'I'll take you back to the other ladies,' he offered.

The devastated look in her eyes was a silent blade between them. 'Not yet.' Her green eyes met his, and he saw the pain he'd caused her.

'Am I to understand that, unless you regain Penrith, we will never be together?'

He didn't want to tell her yes. But there was no other answer he could give. He didn't deserve a wife or a family if he had nothing to offer in return.

To avoid an answer, he cupped her nape and drew her mouth to his. He kissed her hard, tasting the salt of her tears. When her tongue threaded with his, he went rigid, aching to be inside her. He did care for Morwenna, and if he had Penrith, then he wanted her at his side.

'I don't know what will happen, Morwenna,' he swore, 'but I do know that I would defend your life with my own.'

She wound her arms around his neck, kissing him back. Against his mouth, she pleaded, 'I don't want this to be the end, Robert. Please.'

'I'll find a way to gain the king's favour,' he promised.

'I could come with you,' she offered. 'King John might agree to see both of us.'

He understood that she believed the king was her father. But King John had fathered a number of bastard children and seemed to have little interest in them or their mothers.

'I'm afraid Lord Penrith will try to interfere,' he admitted. 'He has already brought a chest of gold to the king with rents and tithes. And I don't want him near you again.' It was bad enough that the man had threatened her a second time.

Morwenna tucked a strand of her hair back. 'I have to face the king one day, Robert. If he *is* my father.'

He was about to tell her no, but then he caught himself. She'd been right earlier—he could not dictate her actions. She deserved the choice of what to do. But he would not compromise on her safety.

'I could arrange for you to travel to your mother's lands, if that is what you want,' he offered. 'I only ask that you not remain at the king's encampment while Lord Penrith is here.'

Her expression grew uncertain. 'I suppose I should speak with my mother first. But if King John truly is my sire, then I will want an audience.'

Robert inclined his head. He pulled her into his arms once more, resting his mouth against her cheek.

But she suddenly pulled away from him. 'Robert—I will go to my mother's estate for now. But promise me, if you cannot regain Penrith, I want you to come back for me.'

It sounded as if she had no faith and had already given up. He couldn't do that. He'd failed his people once before, and he couldn't imagine walking away from them.

He traced the edge of her cheek, not wanting to answer. 'Don't think of that now.'

'You're not coming back, are you?' she murmured. 'You're going to leave me there.'

He heard the pain in her voice, which was the last thing he wanted for Morwenna. But she also deserved a home of her own and the life of a noblewoman. If he couldn't give that to her, then it was better for her to stay with her mother.

He stared into her eyes, wishing he had another answer for her. But he could only nod. 'If I cannot retake the lands that are my birthright, then I can give you nothing.'

A tear slid down her cheek. 'You're wrong. You could give me love, and it would be enough.'

'Love isn't enough to give us shelter or food,' he argued. 'We lived like that for two years while we were in hiding, and it was miserable.'

'For me it was wonderful.' Her voice was soft. 'I was with you every day.'

He hated hurting her, but she'd asked for his honesty and he'd given it. 'I don't want to be a failure again, Morwenna. If I have no land and no title, what right do I have to a wife or a family? Especially if I cannot provide for you.'

'You've already given up, haven't you?'

'Not yet. I still intend to appeal to King John. It's not over.'

She swiped at her tears, but he could see that she didn't believe him. 'I will leave for Banmouth in the morning. For now, take me back to tent where the ladies are staying.'

There was an imperceptible distance between them, one he didn't know how to bridge. But he wouldn't lie to her or give her false hope. All he could do was try to find a way to regain what was lost.

Morwenna barely slept that night. She'd learned that Lady Sarah of Holyrede was travelling south later in the afternoon, after her husband had finished his business with the king. The lady had agreed to let Morwenna travel with them, since Banmouth was a stopping point on their own journey home.

An uneasy feeling weighed upon Morwenna, for she sensed that Robert would be unsuccessful in his attempt to gain an audience. The waiting was slowly killing her, but she had not heard from him or seen him this day.

But then, a soldier arrived at their tent and interrupted. 'Lady Morwenna, you've been summoned to meet with the king.'

Fear and anticipation rushed through her, and she turned back to Lady Holyrede. 'I have to obey. Lady Holyrede, could someone escort me to the king's tent? And…will you wait to travel until I return?'

The woman nodded. 'I will send one of my men to guard you. But we do want to leave soon. Make haste if you can.'

'I won't be long,' she promised.

Lady Holyrede's guard shadowed her when she left, and they both followed the soldier towards the king's tent. She hoped she would find Robert nearby, for she wanted to see him before she left. Her heart bled at the thought of never seeing him again.

As they drew closer to the king, she saw a gathering of men outside the royal tent. Perhaps they were all waiting for King John, but when they saw Morwenna approaching, the men drew back to let her pass.

'Why are they here? Is something wrong?' she murmured to her escort.

'I do not know, my lady.' But he drew closer to her side. There seemed to be a heightened sense of anticipation.

'Wait here,' the other soldier said before he entered the tent.

Morwenna obeyed, wondering why everyone was gathered around. She couldn't see beyond the crowd of men in front of her, but she thought she heard a sword being unsheathed. Her heart began pounding, and then she saw the king emerge from the tent. He went to sit upon a raised dais, but Morwenna could not yet see who had captured his attention. Instead, she was studying his features, wondering if this man could be her father. She could not tell the colour of his eyes, but his hair was dark blond. He did not look in her direction at all, however.

'Come with me,' the soldier said. He led her through the men to the front of the crowd.

Morwenna covered her mouth to stifle a cry when she saw Robert facing Lord Penrith. They were circling one another, swords drawn.

'What is happening?' she asked one of the bystanders. 'Why are they fighting?'

'Lord Penrith accused this man of arranging his daughter's abduction. The king agreed to let them fight.'

Her heart sank, and she wanted nothing more than to run forward and intervene. This wasn't at all about Gwendoline, she knew. It was about the ownership of Penrith. If Robert died, there was no one except Piers to challenge his right to the land—and the king wouldn't allow it since Piers was a bastard. If Lord Penrith died, Robert could reclaim his lands with the king's permission.

This was the battle that would end the strife, and she suspected it was what Robert wanted. But her gut clenched with fear, for Lord Penrith would not engage in a fair fight. Although he was older and his body was built like a stone wall, he never would have agreed to this fight if he didn't believe he would win.

Robert had told her nothing of this battle. Had he known about it last night?

She moved forward to the edge of the fighters, ignoring her escort, who was caught up behind her in the crowd. The king's soldier who had summoned her and another soldier came to her side, protecting her from the other men who were trying to push their way through. From her position, she caught a glimpse of the king, but he still could not see her at all. It hardly mattered, for her entire concentration was upon Robert and Alfred. The older warrior raised his sword and struck hard. Robert deflected the blow with his shield, and she could see the intense focus in his eyes. He was studying Alfred to find the man's weakness.

The earl offered a thin smile. 'When you're dead, I'm going to take your woman back to Penrith and give her to my men. They deserve the entertainment.'

Robert's expression tightened with rage. She knew the words were another weapon, meant to spur his anger and make him reckless. But he seemed to gather his control, and he swung his sword at the earl's head. The man dodged the blow, and he renewed his own attack.

'You're never going to touch her,' Robert said,

circling his enemy. 'And when you're dead, I will free the people of Penrith from your command.'

With that, Alfred swung his sword with brutal force. Robert staggered back as he caught the blow with his shield. He held his balance and struck back.

'But you're wrong. She came to watch our fight, and my men are with her right now.' Alfred moved to the side, and called out, 'Take her!'

At that moment, the two soldiers on either side of Morwenna seized her arms. Only then did she realise the king's soldier had been lying all along. There had never been a summons. These were men hired by Lord Penrith, and his hunger for vengeance was clear.

'You shouldn't be here during a sword fight, Lady Morwenna,' the soldier said. 'It's no place for a woman.'

'Let me go!' she called out. Her other escort tried to intervene, but the two men surrounded her, dragging her away. She struggled against her captors, but her strength was no match for theirs. She screamed, hoping someone else would intervene, but no one did.

'My men will take her now,' Lord Penrith proclaimed. 'After all, she's only a serf dressed as a noblewoman. She needs to be taught her place.'

'Leave her alone,' Robert snarled.

Morwenna tried to scream for help, but the other men ignored her as she was pulled towards one of the tents. Oh, God, there was no one to save her now. There were three men, and even if Robert somehow managed to win the fight, there was no time for him to rescue her.

She would have to save herself.

No one made any move to stop Penrith's men. Fury blazed within him as Robert faced his opponent. He let the rage tear through him, no longer caring what happened. All that mattered was winning this fight.

He attacked with all the anger, all the pain, pouring the emotions into his sword. He doubled his speed, knowing that his swiftness gave him an advantage. The earl had girth and strength, but Robert could move faster.

'How does it feel, knowing you cannot save her?' the man taunted. 'But then, does it even matter? How many men has she already had?'

The words infuriated him, but he knew the earl was deliberately baiting him, in the hope that he would turn careless. Robert lunged forward with his blade, but before he thrust, he caught the earl's parry with his shield and used his sword to slice at the man's legs.

For a moment, it was as if his mind and his

body were one. He stopped thinking of how to fight or where to strike—this time, he fought on pure instinct. His weapon moved in accord with his thoughts. There was no hesitation, only his will to conquer.

Alfred stumbled, and Robert slashed his blade again, silently taking command of the fight. He needed to gain the advantage, and as he dodged another blow, he thought of a way. He needed to raise the earl's own anger to make him reckless.

'I had nothing to do with Lady Gwendoline's disappearance,' he assured him. 'But I know who did.'

The earl let out a growl as he slashed with his weapon. 'Where is she?'

'She ran away with my half-brother Piers,' he said. 'So, any thoughts you had of an alliance with another family are over. Morwenna and I witnessed their marriage before a priest.'

The earl's face turned purple, and he heaved his sword with all his strength. Robert caught the blade in his shield, and twisted hard, disarming the man. He threw Penrith's weapon to the side and went after the man with his fists.

The earl swung a punch and caught him across the jaw and ear, which caused a ringing in his skull. Robert struck his own blow, and seized Alfred, shoving him to the ground. For a moment, it was as if he were standing outside himself. He remembered Morwenna's whipping, and the suffering she'd endured.

He wrenched the man's arm, twisting it back while he released all the pent-up anger, striking hard against the earl's face and ribs. He fought back against the coward he'd been as a boy, against the helplessness he now felt as he fought for Morwenna.

And when Alfred lay unconscious, Robert unsheathed his dagger and held it at the man's throat. He raised his eyes to the king, waiting for the sovereign's permission.

Everything within him yearned to kill the earl and go after Morwenna. Her time was running out. But he could not insult the king—not when the monarch held the power to grant him Penrith or deny it.

The king slowly shook his head in a silent command for mercy. Robert sheathed his blade and stood up from the earl's unconscious form. Then he bowed to John and backed away until he could go in pursuit of Morwenna. He knew it was a terrible risk to leave the king's side without permission, but he wasn't about to let her be attacked.

Some of the onlookers pointed in the direction the men had taken her, and he hurried that way.

When he reached the tent, he found her escort bleeding outside the entrance. Robert shoved his way inside and saw Morwenna cornered by one man. She held a blade in her hand and another man lay dead at her feet. Robert wrenched the other soldier away and slit the man's throat with one slice of his dagger. Only when she was safe did he breathe again.

'Are you all right?' he asked.

Morwenna ran to him, dropping the blade as she did. Her hands were bloody, and he didn't know if it was her blood or theirs. She clung to him, and he held her tightly, breathing in the scent of her hair. 'Yes.'

'Were there any others?' he asked.

She shook her head. 'My escort protected me, but he was hurt. We should get him help.'

Robert agreed with her. But when he turned back to the tent entrance, he saw two other men helping the escort up. They promised to take the man to a healer, so Robert turned back to Morwenna.

'Is Lord Penrith dead?' she asked. 'What happened?'

'I defeated him, but the king granted him mercy,' Robert answered. 'It's not over yet.' Although he had wanted to kill Penrith, he couldn't risk angering the monarch.

Morwenna grew sombre. 'Lady Holyrede is waiting for me. She promised to take me to my mother's estate since it's on their journey.'

Her words soothed some of his fear, for she could not stay here—not with Penrith still alive. And although Robert had asked for an audience, he was uncertain the king would grant his request. King John had appeared irritated at his victory.

In truth, it wasn't safe for either of them.

'I agree, you should go with them, Morwenna. I can't risk your life again.' He framed her face in his hands, memorising her features.

She embraced him hard, and he stroked her hair back from her face. 'What will become of us, Robert?'

'I don't know. But when I reclaim Penrith—'

'Penrith can burn for all I care,' she responded, drawing back from him. Though she had tears in her eyes, there was no denying her fury. 'You almost died today, Robert. Do you think I care whether you have any land at all?' He didn't know what to say, but tears spilled from her eyes. 'I am tired of fighting over your father's land. I'm tired of men telling me I'm nothing but a serf and unworthy of you.'

She took his hands in hers. 'Either you love me in the same way I love you and we find a way to be together, or we part ways now. Please,' she begged, 'come with me to Banmouth. Let the land go.'

'Morwenna…' He started to speak, but when she waited, he didn't know what to say. The right words abandoned him, and he didn't know how to tell her what he felt. He felt torn between his obligations and his desires. And after what he'd done before, running away from his lands and his people, it felt selfish to claim what he wanted. What kind of man would he be if he turned his back on them to be with her?

The thought of living alone, fighting a battle he might never win, weighed upon him heavily. But it was clear that she'd lost faith in him. She didn't believe he could regain Penrith, and how could he blame her? He'd done nothing but fail.

'You're asking me to abandon them. It's a choice I cannot make,' he said at last.

'Then you've already made it. And you didn't choose me.' She closed her eyes and let go of his hands. Watching her walk away sliced his feelings to the bone. He wanted to go after her, to change his words. But how could he put his own needs above the people's? Lord Penrith was alive by the order of the king. Though he'd won a victory, it was still a failure.

His mood darkened as he questioned what to do next.

Three days later

A rise of nerves gathered in her stomach as they neared Banmouth. Morwenna tried to calm her fears, but there had been no time to send word to her mother. Rochelle might not even be there.

She rode alongside Lady Holyrede, staring at the horizon. Inside, she felt as if her world had come apart. She had wanted to believe that Robert would come with them. But his life was bound up with Penrith, and he would chase that dream until the day he died. The land meant more to him than she did.

The loss of him made it impossible to concentrate on anything else. All she wanted to do was crumple into a heap and sob. But what good would self-indulgent tears do? Nothing at all. For two years she had lived her life around him, making every choice based on what Robert wanted. In the end, she hadn't been enough.

Morwenna took a deep breath and squared her shoulders. There was no choice but to seek her own future, one without him. No matter how much it broke her heart.

Lord Holyrede spoke with the guards who allowed them to enter. Nerves caught in her stomach as she imagined what it would be like to finally meet her mother—if Rochelle was, in fact, her mother.

Morwenna stared at the small stone keep, wondering about the people who lived here. The dwelling was smaller than she'd expected, but it appeared orderly. Children ran about, smiling as they chased one another. There was no sense of the tension Lord Penrith had caused at Penrith.

But when she saw a noblewoman standing at the top of the stairs, her heartbeat quickened. Lady Rochelle had her same dark hair, the same eyes. It was like looking at herself twenty years from now, and Morwenna understood why the women at King John's court had recognised her.

Inside, she felt frozen, unable to move or speak. She could only stare at her mother's features, wondering what had happened over the years. She remembered that Lord Banmouth had died a few years ago, but she knew not whether Lady Banmouth had remarried.

Lady Sarah of Holyrede walked forward to greet the matron, and though Lady Banmouth observed the expected courtesies, her gaze moved to rest upon Morwenna. There was a sudden falter in her smile, but she masked it.

Lady Holyrede motioned for Morwenna to dismount and come closer. She did, and a boy took the horse's reins from her. She walked up the stairs and stood slightly below Lady Holyrede.

'My husband and I are travelling south, and we are grateful for your hospitality for the night,' Lady Holyrede said. 'I would like to introduce you to Morwenna, my travelling companion.'

Lady Banmouth paled but gave a nod. 'Come inside and join me for some food and drink. I believe we have a great deal to talk about.'

Morwenna followed them, wondering whether the woman would acknowledge her or not. The lady led them inside and ordered the servants to bring food and drink. Lord and Lady Holyrede took a place at the table, and before long, they were enjoying fresh bread, cheese, and venison, along with a cup of wine. They ate together, and soon, Lady Banmouth turned to Morwenna and asked, 'May we speak alone?'

She nodded and Lady Banmouth excused herself before leading Morwenna towards a corner of the room. She pulled out a stool for her and sat on another. 'I suppose you know who I am, don't you? It wasn't fate that led you back to me.'

'I was hoping for answers,' Morwenna admitted. 'I believe you're my mother.'

Lady Banmouth inclined her head. 'I think that is obvious to everyone. What is it you want to know?'

Everything, she wanted to say. But a part of her was slightly dismayed that her mother did not seem overjoyed to see her. They were strangers to one another, and there was no sense of happiness at the reunion. She didn't know what to think about that.

'How did I end up with the miller and his wife?' Morwenna began.

Her mother paused a moment, and then admitted, 'My husband forced me to give you up.' There was a rise of colour in her cheeks, but she continued, 'I had no choice.' She motioned to a servant who brought more cups of wine. Morwenna took a goblet but only sipped at it.

'What of my brother, Brian?' she asked. 'Is he truly my brother?'

There was a sudden flare of sadness in Rochelle's eyes. 'He is.' But once again, she offered nothing more. Morwenna sensed that she was probing old wounds, so she decided not to push too hard.

'I didn't come here to ask anything of you,' Morwenna began, 'except… I was recognised when we were at the king's camp. They told me you were still alive, and I wanted to see you.'

Rochelle drank her wine, studying her closely. 'I suppose they told you I was the king's mistress. That I seduced him and bore two bastard children.' But from her tone, it sounded as if that wasn't at all the truth.

'What really happened?' Morwenna asked.

Rochelle's expression grew strained. 'John was not yet king then. He was a young and impetuous prince who always got what he wanted. And even though I was married, it mattered not to him. He sent my husband Edmund off to fight, and he demanded that I share his bed. There was no choice at all for me.'

'I'm sorry,' she whispered.

'Edmund was furious that I bore the king a child. For a while, neither of us knew whether you were conceived from the king or whether you were legitimate.'

There was no denying the shame on her mother's face. Morwenna didn't know what to say, but she held her silence to find out more.

'Edmund let me keep you for a few years, to see if we could learn the truth. But then, the king sent for me a second time,' Rochelle continued. 'Brian is King John's bastard son—there is no doubt of that. I don't know about you.' She closed her eyes as if gathering strength. 'But after Brian was born, my husband refused to allow me to keep either of you.' She drained the rest of her cup and took a breath. 'I have another younger son who is the heir to Banmouth, but I never imagined that I'd see you again. What happened to Brian?'

'He went to fight in the Crusades,' Morwenna answered. Although Robert had sent word to the monks, her brother had not returned. Worry knotted within her that she would never see Brian again.

Rochelle glanced at Morwenna's gown. 'I am glad that you received the gown. I didn't know if the miller would sell it or give it to you.'

'He gave it to me a few years ago. But then Brian and I were captured, and I didn't see it for two more years.'

Rochelle paled with shock. 'Dear God.'

She didn't understand the reason for her mother's horror. 'We did escape, thankfully.' She told her mother of the attack and how they had hidden at Stansbury.

But there was a rigid cast to Rochelle's face. 'My husband must have found out where you were.' Her mouth tightened, and she said, 'I received word from Geoffrey, and he wanted coins to support you and Brian. I sent some silver, along with the gown and pendant. A short time after that, Edmund told me he was sending men to fight for the king. But he must have planned to take you both.'

Tears spilled over her eyes, and she fought to

gather control of herself. 'I don't know whether he meant to have you killed or bring you back to me.'

'The king's men were there that night,' Morwenna answered. 'So, your husband did tell you the truth. Four of us were captured, but Robert helped us escape.'

Morwenna flushed as she spoke of him, unable to push back her feelings. But it overwhelmed her to know that Brian had been right. Someone *had* been hunting them. And whether or not the soldiers had meant to kill them or ransom them, it didn't matter any more. Because of it, her life had changed.

'Tell me what you know of this necklace.' Morwenna reached for the pendant, but Rochelle shook her head.

'I've no wish to see that again. I was glad to be rid of it. I only sent it to you, if there was ever a time when you had need of it.'

'It belonged to King John's mother?' she ventured.

'It did. The king gave it to me after you were born.'

Morwenna tucked the pendant back beneath the gown. She didn't know if she would have need of it in the future, but for now, it was enough to have a connection to the king who might be her father. She wasn't certain how to feel about her parentage, but one fact was now certain—she did have noble blood. And whether or not it mattered to anyone else, it strengthened her confidence. She did deserve to wed a nobleman like Robert.

'I was hoping to stay for a time and get acquainted with you,' Morwenna began, 'but if my presence bothers you, I could go.' She had no idea where that would be, but she didn't want to be an unpleasant reminder of the past.

Her mother studied her and replied, 'Perhaps you could stay for a time. As long as the king does not…interfere.'

She now understood Rochelle's hesitation—her mother had been used as a pawn before, and she had no desire to meet with the king again.

Morwenna reassured her, 'He does not know who I am or where I am.'

At that, Lady Banmouth relaxed. Her mother stood and invited her to join the others for a meal. But even as Morwenna took her place, she felt an overwhelming sense of isolation. Lady Holyrede and her husband would continue their travels, and she would be alone here.

But then, she had spent the past few years living for someone else. Perhaps it was time to discover what she wanted.

* * *

After two more days of attempting to gain a private audience with the king, Robert was starting to realise that it might never happen. Morwenna had been right. Without Robert having wealth or soldiers to offer, the king had little interest in granting him an audience.

Frustration darkened his mood. He'd made so many mistakes, believing that he could help his people. Instead, he was caught up in a trap of his own failures. Morwenna had been right to leave him…for what sort of life could he give her?

The night sky was black and clouded, and he sat near a fire, contemplating what to do now. Each day, the king had travelled farther north on his journey towards Scotland. Robert had thought about returning to Penrith to try and organise an uprising. But the men lacked enough food to be strong fighters, and many would die. Aye he'd made a vow to his people, but he couldn't ask them to fight.

No, there were other ways to help them. He could send them food in secret. Perhaps bribe the guards to avoid punishments. There were ways to ensure their survival while he obtained the men and wealth he needed.

Robert drank a horn of ale and walked amid the tents. It was strange not to be with Morwenna any longer. He'd grown accustomed to having her near, listening to her advice. Without her, he felt lost and adrift. It wasn't only her absence— it was the desire to watch over her, to take care of her and see her smile.

She had accused him of choosing Penrith over her, and although she'd been right, he was starting to realise that he'd made the wrong decision.

He'd allowed himself to believe that without land, he was worth nothing at all. That if he could not offer her Penrith, he didn't deserve a woman like her. But he'd gone about it backwards. If Morwenna wasn't with him, nothing else mattered.

She had travelled south to Banmouth, to meet the woman who was supposedly her mother. Although Banmouth was not a large estate, he'd heard that the lady was a widow and had family connections to Normandy.

His mind began turning over possibilities, and he decided it was time to stop standing around doing nothing. He had to adjust his plans and find a way to accomplish his purpose. He had been entirely too reliant upon King John instead of himself.

Not any more.

He'd fallen into the trap of honour, believing that kings and noblemen would obey what was right and just. That way of thinking had been naïve and dangerous. Instead, he needed to change his approach and manipulate the outcome until he got exactly what he wanted. Only then could he get Morwenna back.

He could be ruthless for her sake.

Robert walked past another tent and overheard the sound of disgruntled voices. He knew that many of the nobles were frustrated by King John's taxes. 'He's bleeding us dry,' he heard a man complain.

'It has to stop,' another responded.

Their voices dropped lower so he could hear nothing else. Still, it made him realise that this was the reason why Lord Penrith had gained power. Alfred had given King John a large portion of the rents while the other nobles struggled to pay.

Morwenna had been right all along. He needed to regain wealth and use the gold to buy back the king's favour. In time, he could earn what he needed.

But for now, it was time to fight for what he wanted—and what he wanted most was her.

Chapter Eleven

❦

'I am here to speak with His Excellency,' Robert said when he reached the king's tent.

'The king is no longer granting any audiences,' one of the guards said. 'He will not see you.'

Robert deliberately raised his voice. 'Forgive me. I thought His Highness needed men to fight in Normandy and in France. Or am I wrong?'

The two men exchanged a glance. 'Wait here,' one said, disappearing into the tent.

Robert obeyed, and as he'd predicted, within moments the soldiers stepped aside to let him enter. The king's tent was an elaborate shelter with a large bed, a chair, and a table set with bejewelled goblets. Two women stood against the back wall, wearing only their shifts. Upon the ground was a luxurious woven carpet from the East.

King John sat in another chair, an irritated expression on his face.

'Your Majesty,' Robert greeted the monarch. 'I am grateful for the audience. I will not take much of your time.'

'You have fighting men we can send to France?' he mused. 'And here we thought you were an Englishman, stripped of your lands because of your traitorous father.'

The king obviously intended to waste no time on pleasantries. His doubts were more than evident.

'I believe you are acquainted with the Lady Rochelle of Banmouth,' Robert began. 'Her daughter Morwenna is the woman I intend to marry, and her mother's family is from Normandy.'

At the mention of Lady Banmouth, the king's face grew stony. 'And you somehow believe Rochelle will grant you the men we need?'

'I cannot speak on her behalf. But I believe the Lady Morwenna might be willing to help you. Especially since you may be her father.'

At that, the king grew wary. 'Is that what she told you?'

He met the king's gaze openly. 'I want to marry the lady Morwenna, with your permission. You have my fealty and my vow that I will help you in any way I can.'

'And in return, what do you want?' the king replied.

He could read the monarch's annoyance, so he chose his words carefully. 'My father lost Penrith and paid for it with his life. I don't know what happened, but if I am to take care of Lady Morwenna, I am asking for land of my own. I fought Lord Penrith in the hopes of regaining what was lost. I still hope you would consider granting it to me.'

He paused a moment and studied the king. The man's face remained bored, and Robert sensed he was treading on dangerous ground.

'But if you cannot give Penrith back to me,' he continued, 'I ask for land that you can spare. And in return, I will send whatever men I can to France on your behalf.' He paused a moment. 'I would even fight myself.'

The king remained silent for a long time, considering his choices. Then he regarded Robert. 'Go to Banmouth and bring back your bride and the fighting men we need. If you do this, we will consider your request.'

Three days later

'You have a visitor,' Rochelle told Morwenna. 'Robert of Penrith is here to see you.'

Colour rose to her cheeks, along with a rush of emotion. Though she desperately wanted to believe he'd come for her, Morwenna wondered why he was here. 'I will see him,' she agreed.

Her mother led her to the stone stairs, and Morwenna waited for Robert to approach. Truthfully, she hadn't expected he would ever return.

He wore chainmail armour and dismounted from his horse before approaching. Though she longed to run to him, she forced herself to remain in place. He walked up the stairs and paused a few steps below her.

'Hello, Robert.' She held out her hand, and he raised it to his lips. A warmth slid over her at the memory of his mouth on hers. And her traitorous heart beat even faster when he continued to hold her hand.

'You look beautiful, Morwenna,' he said.

She thanked him, but the compliment made her feel shy. Even though her mother had given her new gowns, it still felt as if she was pretending to be someone else.

'Is there news?' she asked, wondering if he had heard from Brian. 'What of my brother?'

'I do not know where he is. But I needed to speak with you.'

Morwenna grew wary of his intentions, even as her heart was delighted by his presence. 'We can walk around the inner bailey if you wish.' She led him back down the stairs towards the training ground.

He followed her, offering his arm. When they were away from everyone else, at the farthest end, he said, 'I owe you an apology, Morwenna.'

She didn't ask why, though she wanted to ask more questions. Instead, she forced herself to remain silent.

'You were right to be angry with me about Penrith.' He stopped walking and met her gaze. 'I realised I've been waiting on others to solve the problem for me—the king, Lady Gwendoline— and it cannot be that way.'

Her emotions threatened to spill over, but she forced them back. 'What do you plan to do?'

'I have some ideas,' he said, 'but I'll need your help.'

His words startled her, for she'd not expected this. 'Tell me.'

'I want you to return with me to the king's encampment,' he began.

Morwenna waited for him to tell her more, to say something about his feelings for her. But when his next words were about plans to send soldiers to the king and nothing to do with them, her hopes faded. 'I don't see a reason to return with you, Robert. You have enough plans to make without me.'

He sobered and regarded her. 'I've done it all wrong again, haven't I?'

He had, but she wasn't in the mood to tell him all the reasons why. 'If you stop by the kitchens, they'll have food for you. If you'll excuse me…'

Morwenna started walking away, the ache of disappointment pressing down on her. But what had she expected? That he'd come here because he missed her or wanted to be with her? He'd said nothing of the sort.

She returned to the castle keep, nodding to her mother as she passed by. Then she walked up the winding narrow staircase to her bedchamber. Weariness slid over her, and she closed her eyes for a moment. During the past few days, she'd felt more tired than ever, and she had no idea why.

There came a knock at the door, and she called out for the person to enter. To her surprise, it was not a servant, but instead, Robert walked inside. When he saw her lying down, he set down his leather pouch and asked, 'Are you all right, Morwenna?'

'Just tired.' She forced herself to sit up. 'Why did you follow me?'

'Because I said everything all wrong. Penrith means nothing without you at my side.'

Though it was what she wanted to hear, she shielded her heart from him. 'And now you expect me to just return with you and follow wherever you go?' Her heart was already protesting, for she did love this man. And yet, she couldn't bring herself to be a shadow again, always following him with no life for herself.

'I don't want to let you go, Morwenna.' He moved to sit beside her on the bed. 'We're not finished yet.'

'Aren't we?' she asked. 'You chose Penrith.'

'If that were true, I'd be there now.' He reached out and stroked her cheek. Heat rose beneath her skin, and she felt her defences weakening. 'I brought you something. And it's not a shield this time.'

He stood and retrieved something from inside his leather pouch, bringing a squirming kitten to her. The black and white feline was slightly bigger than the palm of his hand, and it emitted a squeaking meow. With one gift, he'd utterly disarmed her.

'Oh, Robert.' Morwenna couldn't stop herself from reaching for the animal, nuzzling him against her throat. Although the kitten was a wonderful gift, the kind she'd hoped for, it didn't mean that Robert understood what she needed. More than anything, she wanted to know his feelings for her.

'I'm not any good at courting women,' he admitted. 'I've made more mistakes than I can count. But I hope this is a good start.' He knelt beside the bed and reached out to touch her cheek. 'I wanted to give you everything, Morwenna. I still do.'

'And what if you cannot get the land again?' she ventured, cuddling the kitten close.

'I may not succeed,' he admitted. 'I did offer a bargain to the king, but he demanded to see you. He also wants men to fight with his armies in Normandy.'

'And how will you get those men?' she asked.

'I intend to offer payment to your mother's soldiers,' he said. 'If they are willing to come with us.'

Her gaze narrowed, for how did he have any money at all? 'Where did you get the silver?'

He grimaced slightly. 'I…sold my father's clothing. Everything I owned, save my armour,' he admitted. 'And then I wagered with some of the king's soldiers to win some more silver.'

She'd never expected him to surrender everything like this. Even so, she had to ask, 'What if the men don't want to fight? What if my mother refuses to let them go?'

'It's a risk,' he admitted. 'But one worth taking.' He took her hand in his. 'And the king wants to see you.'

'He refused to see me the last time. And I don't even know if he's truly my father or whether Lord Banmouth was.' Morwenna didn't want to follow him back to the king's camp, hoping for a shred of occasional affection. 'It's probably better if I stay here. You don't need me.' She continued petting the kitten as a distraction from her own self-doubts.

At that, he took her other hand in his. 'You're wrong. Even if I do somehow reclaim Penrith, it means nothing without you at my side, Morwenna.' He leaned in closer until she felt the warmth of his breath against her mouth. 'The days I spent without you felt wrong somehow. I never realised how much until you were gone.'

His words were an assault against the walls around her heart, completely crumbling her defences. 'What do you want from me, Robert?'

'I want to marry you,' he said against her lips. 'I want to give you children and a home where I wake up beside you each day.'

Morwenna surrendered to his kiss, even as tears spilled over her face. He gripped her in his embrace, and she took comfort in his arms around her. But even though her body cried out for his touch, she pulled back.

'I do love you, Robert,' she answered. 'But I don't want my life centred around Penrith. Not any more.'

He held her close. 'You mean more to me than the land, Morwenna.'

She wanted so badly to believe him, but there was still a chance it could fall apart. 'And what if I asked you to let go of Penrith?'

He drew back, his eyes staring into hers. 'Then I would let it go.' He took her hands in his. 'I can't promise that I wouldn't send food or supplies to my people. But I made the wrong choice before. I won't do it again.'

He leaned in and rested his forehead against hers. 'You never gave me an answer. Will you wed me?'

She wanted so badly to say yes, but fear held her back. 'I will think about it.'

He stole a kiss. 'Then I'll have to convince you.' From the seductive tone in his voice, she knew exactly what his plans were.

She drew back and rested her palms on his chest. 'I won't share your bed again unless we are married.' It was the safest way to guard her heart from being broken.

'Then you're at least thinking of wedding me,' he said. He stole another quick kiss and admitted, 'You're tormenting me, Morwenna. But I will do as you wish.' He sat back, and the kitten began climbing her skirts. 'The king may want to witness our marriage,' he added. 'Will you travel back with me?'

'I will,' she agreed. 'But you'll need to speak with my mother first to ask permission to hire some of her men.' Part of her feared that Rochelle would not agree to his request. And if he did not have the men, what then? Would he change his mind about wanting to wed her?

She wanted to believe that he loved her, though he hadn't said it. But right now, it felt as if she were standing on the edge of a mountain. The slightest breeze of misfortune could send her falling to the ground.

'We're going to succeed in this, Morwenna,' he reassured her. 'I have every faith.'

She only wished she could believe it.

The journey back to the king's encampment lasted nearly a sennight. Lady Rochelle of Banmouth had not been willing to let many of her men go, but Robert had paid a dozen of them to join them for now. He was well aware that the king would not be pleased with so few soldiers, but Robert had sold everything he had to hire the men.

Even then, all this was an illusion. He was taking a grave risk that the king would accept a promise that was not based on truth. The men were here, aye, but for how long?

Morwenna sensed the tension just as he did. He was starting to wonder if she was feeling well. She seemed pale and tired all the time. Even when he'd brought her food during the journey, she had only picked at it.

'His Majesty will see you now,' one of the king's guards informed him. 'Bring the Lady Morwenna and your men.'

Morwenna was wearing a deep-blue silk bliaud, the long sleeves trailing to the ground. Around her throat, she wore the pendant, and her dark hair was braided and pinned up beneath a veil.

'Are you ready?' he asked.

Though she ventured a smile, it did not meet her eyes. 'I don't suppose we have a choice.'

He took her hand and rested it upon his arm as they approached the king's tent. They walked towards a group of noblemen, and Robert overheard them arguing again. This time, it wasn't only about taxes. Something else was wrong, and the rising unrest made him rest his hand upon his weapon. But after he passed them, their conversation died down. Robert continued escorting Morwenna towards the king while his soldiers trailed behind him.

He and Morwenna were granted their audience, but the soldiers had to remain outside the tent. Robert held her hand, but her fingers were like ice.

'Your Majesty,' she murmured, dropping into a curtsy while Robert bowed.

'So, you are Rochelle's daughter,' the king mused. 'We see the resemblance.'

'I am.' She kept her head lowered out of respect.

'And do you believe that you are our daughter?' His words held an edge to them, and Robert tightened his grip on Morwenna's hand in warning.

'I know not if I have that honour,' she answered, 'but… I hope it is true, Your Majesty.'

Her answer seemed to please the king, and he offered her a faint smile. Yet, it was the only reaction he gave. Robert glanced over at Morwenna, and he sensed her disappointment. A part of her had wanted to believe that she meant something to the king. Instead, he was treating her like any other bastard daughter.

Then the king changed the subject. 'We understand you are to be married.'

She faltered a moment but answered, 'Robert has asked for my hand in marriage, yes.'

The king's attention shifted. 'And what if we did not grant you permission to wed him? What if we asked you to wed a nobleman of our choosing instead?'

She hesitated, not knowing what to say. The king's stare was piercing, and Robert nearly intervened, but she answered, 'You would have to search a long time before you would find someone as loyal to you as Robert of Penrith, my lord.'

'His father was not loyal. He refused to send the taxes he owed. And he was part of an uprising against us.' The king's voice held a frigid tone.

'A son cannot be blamed for the sins of his father,' Morwenna said softly. 'He has brought you some of the soldiers that were promised.'

'We want all the soldiers who were promised.'

Robert laughed softly. 'If I were to bring an army of men into your encampment, I would look like a threat to you. No, Your Excellency, it would be better if I send them later, after Morwenna and I are wed.'

The king seemed slightly appeased by that. 'Then give us two hundred fighting men. And in return, we will find a small plot of land you may govern.'

Morwenna exchanged a glance with Robert, and he already knew what she was thinking. Two hundred? Such a number of men was impossible. He'd had enough difficulty gaining a dozen men, much less two hundred. But for now, he would do everything in his power to obey the request.

'I would be grateful, Your Highness.' He had no choice but to accept any land he was given, even if it wasn't Penrith. Only then could he rebuild his father's wealth and send aid in secret to his people.

'We will only grant this land after you have sent the men,' the king remarked. 'Until then, you must wait.' Robert bowed his head, not allowing the king to see his frustration. 'Send them to Portsmouth when you have them. We are building vessels to set sail for France.' King John waved his hand in dismissal. 'You may go.'

Robert bowed again, and Morwenna curtsied. They backed out of the tent, and when they were outside, she murmured, 'Where are we going to get two hundred men, Robert? We have twelve.'

He took her hand in his. 'I wonder if we could get volunteers from Penrith.' Though he spoke in jest, it wasn't entirely meant in teasing.

Morwenna slowed her pace. 'I'm being serious, Robert. If you cannot get the men, how will you get your land?' She tightened her grip on his hand. 'And what is this talk of other land? I thought you only wanted Penrith.'

He stopped to look at her. Worry lined her face, and he understood what this was about. She was afraid he could not provide for her.

He leaned in to kiss her, heedless of the people around them. 'I promise I'll find a place for us to live, Morwenna. And somehow, I'll do whatever I can to help my people. It may take time to build the king an army, but I will find a way.'

Her expression dimmed, and she looked as if she wanted to say something. He'd expected her to say she would stay with him, just as she had before. But now, she appeared uncertain. He didn't know why.

'You never gave me an answer,' he said softly. 'Do you not wish to wed me any more?'

'I don't know what will happen now, Robert.' She'd gone pale again, and she stopped walking, steadying herself as if she were dizzy. 'Things have changed.'

He wondered if her mother was a part of this. Morwenna had learned that she might be the daughter of a king. She didn't have to live as a miller's daughter any more. She could wed a man of her choosing.

He waited for her to say more, but she held her silence. He didn't know what had happened, but she was keeping secrets from him. He pulled her into an embrace, wondering if she would push him away.

Instead, she clung to him, as if it were the last time she would ever hold him in her arms. And that unnerved him even more.

She pulled back and glanced around. 'Robert, where *are* your men? They were outside the king's tent a few moments ago. I don't see them anywhere.'

Her question might have been a means of distraction, though he wasn't certain. 'I don't know.' But his suspicions heightened, for the men were supposed to obey his orders.

'You should probably go and find them.'

Though he wanted to stay with her and press for answers, she was right. The last thing he needed was to lose the only men he had. 'I'll take you back to the women's tent.'

He walked alongside her, while his thoughts remained uncertain about what would become of them. But after they reached the tent, she reached up to embrace him again. 'Be careful,' she warned.

'I will.' He kissed her lightly and then returned outside.

On the way, he walked back towards the king's tent, searching for a glimpse of his hired soldiers. One man thought they had joined others at wagering with dice but could not say for certain.

He had no time to consider it further before he saw a group of noblemen approaching the king's tent. The men appeared angry and resolute. Robert passed by them, but a sudden wariness crept over him. It looked as if a confrontation was about to happen. Although the king had his own personal guard, it might not be enough.

Robert began searching among the tents, hurrying to find the men he'd hired. Eventually, he spied one of them with a mug of ale. 'Gather the others,' he commanded, 'and meet me outside King John's tent. Now.'

The soldier appeared disgruntled, but he sighed and put his mug down. At his reluctance, Robert seized the man by his tunic and said in a low voice, 'The king's life is in danger. And we are going to protect him.'

The man's expression changed, and he gave a single nod. 'I'll find them.'

'Arm yourselves and surround His Majesty's tent,' Robert said. 'Get more of the king's guards if you can. I saw some of the noblemen gathering. It may be nothing, but I would rather be prepared.'

The soldier hurried away, and Robert strode towards the back of the king's tent. There were two guards already there, and Robert joined them. He picked up a shield and stood beside them, waiting. From within the tent, angry voices were rising.

'I think you should go inside to guard His Majesty,' Robert advised. 'My men are on the way. We can defend the perimeter.'

One soldier pushed aside the flap and peered inside. 'He's right. We should go inside.'

The other man followed, and Robert held his position. He heard the sound of arguing and was about to follow the king's guards when he saw a second group of noblemen striding towards the tent. It was clear that they meant to enter and surround the king.

Robert raised his shield, even as he knew he could never hold off that many men. All he could do was defend the entrance.

He called out to the guards inside, but he already knew no one would come. If he was fortunate, some of his own men would arrive. But when he saw the soldier he'd spoken with earlier, the man met his gaze and already knew the danger.

He could only hope that he would survive this fight.

Chapter Twelve

No one spoke to her in the women's tent, and for now, Morwenna was grateful. Her life had been upended during the past few weeks, and now she was left to wonder about whether she was truly a bastard daughter of the king. She could hardly grasp the truth of it.

For a moment, she had felt a sense of disappointment that she meant nothing to John. Though what had she truly expected? She was only another forgotten daughter.

Geoffrey had been the only father she'd ever known—and he was gone. He'd made countless mistakes, but he had done his best to take care of her. He'd also saved the gown and pendant for her, as Rochelle had requested.

Morwenna was starting to realise that it truly didn't matter whether her father was the king or a nobleman. The only difference was that now she felt as if she had the right to desire more than a serf should dare.

She had hesitated to say yes to marrying Robert, not because she didn't wish to wed him—but because she was afraid. They had no land, nowhere to live.

For a moment, she sat in the corner, trying to decide what to do. She hadn't told Robert of her suspicion, but she had already missed her courses. Certain smells bothered her, and she'd nearly retched when she had passed by someone roasting a fresh fish. It was not the sickness during the morning that many women complained of. No, this sickness lasted from the moment she awoke until she fell asleep at night. The only food she could tolerate was bread and cheese but only in small quantities.

One of the women poured wine, and Morwenna stood. Already she felt the familiar nausea, and she didn't want to wait for the women to begin eating something. She needed fresh air and a moment to breathe.

She'd nearly told Robert of her suspicions, but fear had held her back. What if she was wrong, and she was not with child?

He'd promised to find a place for them, and at one time, she'd been eager to live with him—even if it meant travelling from place to place.

But unless he found men willing to fight for the king, they would have nowhere to live, nowhere to raise a child. The safest place for her to remain until she gave birth was with her mother... at least until Robert could find a home for them.

Emotions caught her heart, and she worried about whether he would even want a child with her. What if he decided to hire out his sword? What if he left her?

She stepped outside the tent and took deep breaths, trying to calm herself. Allowing the anxiety to take command would accomplish nothing.

Nearby, she heard the ringing of swords, and suddenly, men began rushing past the tents. Dozens of soldiers joined them, along with noblemen.

'What's happening?' she tried to ask. But the men charged forward, pushing back against the crowds gathering.

A dark premonition caught within her, for they were moving towards the king's tent...where she had left Robert.

Morwenna felt her throat closing up with fear. She pushed back her terror, for that would do no good. Instead, she pushed through the crowds, searching for a glimpse of him. There were so many men, it was impossible to find anyone.

But then she spied a familiar gleam of blonde

hair. Lady Gwendoline was walking beside her father, whose expression was grim. The lady's misery was evident, and though Morwenna wanted to speak with her, she wasn't certain how to help.

But if Gwendoline was alone, then Piers was in danger or already dead.

She quickened her pace until she was behind her friend. Several noblemen were rushing forward, and Morwenna seized her chance. She bumped against the men, and they pushed into Lord Penrith, causing him to stumble to the ground. The earl cursed while he was on his hands and knees, giving her precious seconds to talk to Gwendoline.

While he was on the ground, Morwenna seized her friend's hand. 'Where is Piers?'

'He's a captive.' Gwen's eyes filled with tears. 'Please, ask Robert to help him.'

Morwenna felt terrible, but there was nothing she could do. 'The king is in danger. I think Robert is trying to defend him.' Then she took her friend's hand and led her into the crowd of soldiers and men. 'Robert can't save Piers now... but you could. If you know where he is.' They hurried away from Lord Penrith together, and Morwenna handed Gwen her knife. 'Take this.

And if you can save him, send him to fight for the king.'

With that, Gwendoline disappeared among the tents. Morwenna got caught up in the crowd, and though she tried to push her way through, she nearly lost her balance. She had to remain on the edge of the crowd in order to get closer, and when at last she neared the king's tent, there was no way to reach it.

Robert was fighting hard, and she could barely see him. Only the ring of swords told her that he was still alive. She saw a barrel nearby and tried to climb atop it to see better. Shielding her eyes against the sun, she saw that the dozen men he'd hired were fighting alongside him. The king's men had also formed lines on either side of the tent, but Robert never wavered, never stopped.

He moved like water, shifting from opponent to opponent. Fear caught in her throat, but she couldn't tear her gaze away. In him, she saw the man she loved, fighting for them. He didn't have the men the king wanted, but he was proving his loyalty right now. The crowd surrounded them, but he never once faltered.

Then at last, King John emerged from the tent and stepped forward. 'Enough of this!'

Beside him, more soldiers emerged, along with archers who aimed their bows in both directions. Robert struck his last blow and then lowered his sword in obedience.

For a moment, it seemed as if time stood still. All eyes rested upon the king as he prepared to speak out against the uprising.

But then, Morwenna caught a slight motion, the flash of a blade, just as someone threw a dagger. There was no way of knowing who had aimed the weapon, but Robert threw himself in front of the king.

Only sheer instinct caused him to raise his shield up. The dagger had been thrown so hard it was embedded in the wood. A moment later, a man fell to the ground, shot by an archer.

'Is there another man who wishes to die?' the king demanded. Fury caused his face to redden with colour. 'Return to your tents. And unless you are part of our royal entourage, we want you gone.'

Robert sheathed his sword and started to walk away.

'Not you,' the king said. 'Robert of Penrith, we wish to speak to you.'

He bowed and followed the king back inside the royal tent. Though he'd hoped to see Morwenna, there were far too many people. 'My liege,' he said, dropping to one knee.

'Rise,' the king commanded. 'You fought well this day to guard us. And we understand your men joined mine and stopped the rebellion.' There was a faint crease at the man's forehead, as if he knew the battle was not yet won. 'Were it not for your shield, I would no longer be king.'

Robert could only say, 'My sword is yours, Your Majesty.'

John seemed pleased by that. His gaze rested upon him, and Robert never looked away, hoping that he had done enough to earn the king's favour.

'You want Penrith, don't you?' The king's eyes were discerning, studying him as if to uncover the truth.

These were the words he'd hoped for. It was what he'd dreamed of for the past two years. Although he wanted to say yes, Robert hesitated. He had trained to win back his land, and now that the opportunity was in his hands, it seemed almost unreal.

'Yes, I do want the land,' he admitted. 'I want my people to live without fear. I want to atone for my father's mistakes and become the earl they need.'

The king studied him for a long moment. 'You deserve to be rewarded for saving your king. But Alfred of Penrith has also shown me loyalty. We

cannot repay that by stripping him of his lands.'
He paused a moment. 'But if you were to marry
his daughter…'

'She is already married,' Robert answered,
'to my half-brother Piers. They wed in secret.'

'She will be a widow, soon enough,' the king
said. 'Alfred has demanded the execution of your
bastard brother for kidnapping his daughter and
forcing her into marriage. We have him chained
right now.'

A coldness threaded through Robert at the
thought. No matter how much he wanted Penrith, it was not worth the cost of his brother's life.

Were it not for Piers, he would not be alive
today. And the idea of setting Morwenna aside to
marry Gwendoline? No, that could never happen.
His fierce, beautiful Morwenna belonged to him
and always would. He could never wed another.

And as for Penrith, his half-brother was deeply
tangled up in that land. Piers had been downtrod-
den all his life, a man to whom nothing had been
given. He had always coveted Robert's inher-
itance. But more than that, he understood the
people of Penrith in a way Robert never could.
Piers had been raised among them, labouring
alongside the people during his childhood and
adolescence.

Now that he had dared to marry Lady Gwendoline, his own life was at stake. He would die unless Robert intervened.

'I am honoured by your offer, Your Highness. But I don't want my brother to die. He saved my life. And were it not for him, I could not have guarded you, my king.'

The king's expression held wariness, and Robert choose his words carefully, so as not to offend him. 'I have had a change of heart. If you were to grant me Penrith, it might cause greater complications for you. I would also prefer to wed Morwenna, instead of Lady Gwendoline.' Before the king could argue with him, Robert continued, 'If you have another plot of land where you have need of a loyal subject—even if it is small, I would be grateful.'

The king seemed to consider his request. Then he gave a nod. 'The nobleman who dared to throw the dagger at me is now dead. And he has no son.' He pondered the matter and said, 'We will grant you his lands, if you are willing to live a great distance from here.'

Robert wanted to ask the king more, but he forced himself to remain silent. The king answered his unspoken question. 'The lands are in Ireland. You will return to Dunbough and claim it. And once you are settled, we still expect you to send as many soldiers as you can

for our cause.' He motioned to one of his men
and commanded, 'See to it that Robert becomes
Earl of Dunbough, and I will set my seal upon
the orders later.'

Robert bowed deeply. 'I am most grateful,
Your Excellency.'

There was movement at the edge of the tent,
and two soldiers entered with Morwenna. Robert held out his arm, and she went to him, embracing him hard. He breathed in her scent, so
grateful she was safe.

'You're alive,' she whispered. 'I was so afraid
of losing you.'

'Is it still your wish to marry this man?' the
king demanded. 'I could arrange another match
with another nobleman.'

Robert held her waist, hoping she would agree.
They had endured so much…captivity, poverty,
and fighting…to be together. There was no other
woman he could imagine sharing his life with,
but Morwenna had not said yes.

She drew back from him and dropped into
a deep curtsy. 'Your Majesty, there is no man I
wish to wed more than Robert.'

Her words filled him with a blend of relief
and joy. Though he wanted to crush her into his
arms, he held restraint before the king.

The king motioned for her to rise. 'I grant my

blessing upon your marriage, then. After you are wed, you will depart with him to his lands.'

She offered the king a soft smile. 'Thank you.'

Only then, did Robert give in to the urge, and he pulled Morwenna into a hard embrace, stealing a kiss. Behind him, he heard the king's amusement, but he simply didn't care. She had agreed to marry him, and it was all that mattered.

Robert took her hand in his, but before they could leave, he heard the sound of someone arguing.

'I will see the king!'

Robert unsheathed his sword, prepared to defend King John, if needed, but it was Lord Penrith who entered the tent. His face was nearly purple with rage.

'My prisoner is gone and my daughter with him,' Penrith spat. 'I suspect this man set him free.'

Robert kept his sword at the ready, uncertain of what the earl intended. He didn't trust Penrith at all.

'Lord Robert has been with us this entire time,' the king remarked. 'He defended us when you could not be bothered.' His cool tone held a warning. 'Take your troubles elsewhere. If you could not keep your own prisoner, this is not our responsibility.'

'I demand justice,' Penrith insisted.

'You do not make demands of us,' the king said in an iron tone. He nodded to his soldiers to take the earl. 'Escort him out and see to it that he returns to Penrith. We have no further need of him.'

The earl looked as if he wanted to argue, but as the soldiers closed in on him the king added, 'If you make another threat, it will be your last.'

Alfred paled and turned away. Only after he was gone did Robert sheathe his sword once again.

The king's face revealed his approval. 'You were prepared to defend us again, were you not?'

'Indeed, Your Highness.'

'Take the Lady Morwenna and marry her,' the king commanded. 'Then journey to Trim Castle in Ireland. I will send my command to Lord William de Lacy. He will have orders to send men to help you take Dunbough.'

'Thank you, Your Highness.' Robert paused a moment. 'There is something else I would ask, if I may.'

The king waited, and Robert added, 'Do not send men in pursuit of Piers, my liege. My brother is no threat to you, and he did nothing wrong except to marry Lady Gwendoline without permission. If you allow him the chance, he will prove his loyalty.'

King John appeared uncertain about it, but he shrugged. 'Whatever fight your brother has with Lord Penrith is his own to face.'

'Thank you, Your Excellency.' Robert bowed again, and Morwenna dropped into a curtsy once more. The king waved his hand in dismissal, and they left the tent.

As soon as they were outside, Robert picked her up by the waist and swung her around slowly.

'What are you doing?' she laughed.

'You said yes.' Slowly, he let her slide down, and her eyes held happiness as he stole another kiss. 'You agreed to wed me.'

'I did.' She framed his face with her hands. 'And I cannot wait to be your wife.'

It was growing dark, and Robert led her away from the inner tents to one that lay on the outskirts. He opened it and spoke to two of the soldiers, offering them silver coins. 'Find another place to sleep tonight.'

They departed, and Morwenna turned to him. 'I was so worried about you, Robert.'

He pulled her close and kissed her with all the desperation he felt. His heart pounded as Morwenna's tongue threaded with his, and a surge of lust gathered within him. He needed to lie with her this night, to show her how much he loved her.

'Would that I could marry you this very moment,' he said. 'Do you still plan to make me wait?'

She laughed, kissing him again. 'Robert, there is only one thing I want to be, more than your wife.'

He nipped at her mouth. 'What is it you want?'

'To be naked with your skin on mine.' She pulled at the laces of her gown, her gaze fixed upon his. 'I almost lost you again today, and I don't want to wait.'

She let the gown fall to the ground until she was wearing only her shift. And when she pulled it off and stood naked before him, he lost sight of any words he'd wanted to say.

'I am going to claim this night for myself,' she murmured.

She was beautiful in the last light of evening, her skin golden. Her breasts jutted out from her body, the nipples puckered in the cool night air. Her body was lean and muscled, and she took his breath away.

She rested her hands on his chest and stared at him. 'Unless you want me to stop?'

Never in a thousand years. In answer, he stripped away his own tunic, pulling her until they were skin to skin. 'I'm going to give you everything you want, Morwenna. Now, and always.'

Desire roared through him, and Robert surrendered to it. He claimed her mouth, devouring her while his hands slid down her curves. She gasped when he touched a sensitive place, and he forced himself to slow down, gentling his kiss.

He took her hand and led her to a pile of sleeping furs. Then he stripped off his remaining clothes and drew her to lie down. 'I'm in love with you, Morwenna. And God willing, I want to spend the rest of my life with you.'

He couldn't imagine being apart from her any more. He didn't know what Ireland would be like or what challenges they would face. But it didn't matter, so long as they were together.

'I love you, too,' she said, as her tears broke free. But they were tears of joy, not sorrow. And right now, he wanted her with a desperation beyond reason. He needed to bring her pleasure and watch her fall apart. The memory of the first night he'd claimed her innocence haunted him still.

Morwenna brought his hands to her breasts. Her skin was cool, and when he palmed her nipples, she gripped his shoulders, her eyes closing. 'That feels good.'

Her voice held a breathy sigh, and he experimented with caressing her. With every touch he found his own need growing stronger, harder to control. She moaned when he gently rolled the tips between his fingers. He bent to kiss one breast, and she let out a shuddering gasp. With his tongue, he continued exploring her sweet flesh while he stroked the other breast.

She was so sensitive, she cried out. Morwenna clenched his hair and adjusted her position so she was seated with her legs open. All he had to do was lift her hips and he could be inside her. But he wanted to draw out her pleasure.

'Show me,' he commanded, taking her hand. 'Tell me where you want to be touched.'

Her face was flushed, and she bit her lip as she guided his hand lower, between her legs. He slid his hand over the soft hair to the wetness there. He remembered how she had touched herself in the past, and his body went rigid as his fingers dipped into the warm folds.

She reached for him then, her palm gripping his erection. She squeezed him gently, and the intense pleasure roared through him. He showed her how to move her hand, and as she did, he slid two fingers inside her. He entered and withdrew, and she echoed the movement with her own hand. The ecstasy built up inside him until he realised he was losing control like an eager adolescent.

He took her hand from his manhood. 'Morwenna, wait. Lie down.'

She could hardly catch her breath. But she obeyed his command and lay back on the furs, raising her knees up. Her body had come alive, flooded with needs she hadn't known she possessed.

In her heart, she had already spoken silent vows before the priest on the night Piers had married Gwendoline. And now, she intended to seize this moment for herself.

Robert's hungry gaze swept over her like an invisible caress. Once again, he kissed her breasts, and the heat of his mouth brought a fierce ache between her legs. She didn't understand what he wanted at first, and then he brought her hand atop his. 'I want you to show me what to do. Show me what brings you pleasure.'

She felt a wave of embarrassment, but then she realised he had relaxed his fingers. He wanted her to pleasure herself, using his touch. It was a shocking sensation, but she brought his fingertips against her hooded flesh. Gently, she showed him the pressure that brought her the most intense yearning. She was shocked at the sensual heat that rose hotter as she taught him what she liked. He caught on quickly, and soon enough, she could barely catch her breath. He circled her in a rhythmic movement.

Then he shocked her when he continued the caress while sliding a finger inside her. She was clenching her hands, writhing against him, when suddenly her body erupted in a storm of release. She gripped his finger, her body alive as the pleasure flooded her.

Morwenna pressed Robert to his back and straddled him, wanting him inside her. She brought his rigid length to her swollen opening. She was so wet, and she wanted him to feel the same release.

She raised up, positioning him at her entrance. Slowly, she lowered herself upon him with her knees on either side of his waist. He was so thick and hard, it stretched her to take him. But he reached up to caress her breasts, and somehow, she took him deeper.

He was gentle, allowing her to go slowly, but it felt so good, she needed more. She moved against him, and Robert let out a low hiss.

'I'm sorry,' she apologised. 'Did I hurt you?'

'No. Do it again.' He closed his eyes, still

stroking her nipples while she continued to move. He took her hips and guided her in a rhythm. Her shallow penetrations echoed deeply in her womb, and the rising pleasure started to rebuild inside her.

She loved this man, loved that they could share this moment. He was breathing hard, his hands cupping her bottom. She didn't know what to do, but a moment later, he thrust against her, and she squeezed his length.

'God above, I won't last if you keep doing that.'

'Do you like it?' she whispered, trying again.

'I love it, just as I love you.'

The words filled her with such happiness, Morwenna could hardly bear it. 'I love you, too.'

Robert lifted her hips slightly and lowered her to take him. She felt the ache rising harder, and as she met his thrusts, her own desire rekindled. But she wanted him to take control now. This time, she withdrew from him and moved to her back, raising her knees. He understood what she wanted, and he palmed her bottom, thrusting deep. The new position gave him the chance to take what he wanted, and she surrendered to him, trembling as he took her higher.

She couldn't stop herself from meeting his penetrations, and when he took her nipple in his mouth again, he ground against her. She utterly shattered in his arms, crying out as he quickened his tempo. Over and over, he thrust, until he uttered a guttural cry and spilled himself inside her.

She locked her legs around his waist, her body still quaking with aftershocks. He relaxed atop her, and she was so grateful to have the man she loved.

'Do you want to be married at Banmouth?' he asked, kissing her lips.

She thought a moment and then shook her head. 'I think we should invite your uncle Oswald to hear our vows. And though I would wed you anywhere, we could marry at Stansbury where we lived and trained. It's where I fell in love with you the first time.'

He rested his nose against hers. 'I'll make the arrangements.'

A sudden shyness overcame her, and she added, 'We should marry soon, Robert. I don't want to wait long.' She drew his hand to her stomach and met his gaze. 'I've already missed my courses once.'

A look of joy came over his face. 'A child?'

'It's too soon to tell, but I believe so.'

He kept his hand upon her stomach and stroked

it, as if to offer love to their baby. She kissed him again, so thankful for the gift of this man.

And the years yet to come.

Robert stood among the ruins at Stansbury, waiting beside his uncle. The morning air was cool, but the sun shone brightly above them. Although he was eager to wed Morwenna, his anticipation heightened with every moment. He had made the preparations for their journey to Ireland, and he was eager to reach their new home. A few of the Banmouth soldiers had decided to accompany them to Dunbough, and they stood at intervals within the courtyard.

His half-brother Piers came to stand beside him. 'I am glad for you and Morwenna,' he said. 'I hope you will find happiness together.'

Robert clapped his brother on the back. 'And I am glad you came to join in our celebration.' His gaze turned serious. 'Will you and Gwendoline be all right?' Although he'd won the king's consent not to send men to pursue them, Robert sensed that the danger was still there.

Piers nodded. 'Our fight isn't over yet. But her father will never change.'

'If you ever have need of sanctuary, you are always welcome in Ireland.' And he meant the words.

'Not until we've brought peace to the people of Penrith,' Piers answered. 'I made you a promise, and I intend to keep it.' His brother turned serious. 'I owe you a debt I can never repay.'

'If you restore their freedom, that will be payment enough,' Robert answered.

Their conversation ended when Morwenna appeared at the entrance to a stone archway. Gwendoline and Rochelle stood on each side of her. His bride wore the crimson gown Lady Gwendoline had given her, and the sight of her stole his breath. She walked towards him slowly, her hair flowing free down her back. She'd let it grow, and it fell in soft curls below her shoulders. She wore a crown of pink wildflowers, and her smile held the same love that he felt for her.

Robert took her hands in his, and as his uncle began the marriage rite, all he could think of was how fortunate he was. He would start anew with Morwenna in Ireland, and they would build a life together.

Even now, their child might be growing inside her. He had never imagined having a wife or a family of his own, and as he gave his vows, he made a promise to always protect her.

Afterwards, he leaned in for a kiss of peace. Morwenna's face was radiant with happiness, and he felt the same as his uncle began the familiar Latin words of the Mass. Amid the ruined fortress, Robert remembered the days he and Piers had trained here while Morwenna had watched. Sometimes, she and Brian had joined them. He could almost hear the ring of their swords in his memory and the laughter at the end of the day.

He leaned in close and whispered, 'I wish your brother could have been here. I tried to find him.'

Her eyes grew sad. 'I know. I pray that one day he'll return.'

'He will. I have faith in that.'

After the Mass ended, he took her hand in his and their guests cheered. Even Morwenna's mother dabbed at her eyes with a handkerchief. Although she was still getting acquainted with her daughter, Rochelle had wanted to be here. She had also brought the kitten back with her in a small basket, and Morwenna had been delighted at its return.

'I will come to visit you in Ireland,' her mother promised as she embraced her. 'In the spring.' Her smile grew knowing, and Robert suspected Morwenna had told her about the baby.

Gwendoline came next, and she hugged them both. 'I wish you both all the happiness in the world.' To Morwenna she added, 'And I am glad that Piers and Robert are half-brothers. For now, we can truly be sisters.'

'If you ever need our help with Penrith, you have it,' Morwenna promised.

Piers put his arm around his wife's waist. 'Thank you.'

The monks joined them in a simple feast of bread, cheese, mutton, and fish. They also shared a platter of fresh blackberries.

After hours of storytelling, singing, and even dancing while one of the monks played a lute, nightfall drifted across the landscape. Soon after they lit several fires to warm the courtyard, they said their farewells. Gwendoline gave her a small gift and Morwenna thanked her for it.

Robert led her away from the ruins to a small overlook. She set down the bundle and went to stand beside him. All around them, hundreds of stars gleamed in the sky. 'It's beautiful,' Morwenna said, lifting her face upward.

'Very beautiful,' he agreed, but his gaze was fixed upon her.

He kissed her again, and she wrapped her arms around him. Then after a moment, she pulled back. 'I have a wedding gift for you, Robert.'

'You already gave me a wedding gift,' he answered, sliding his hand down to her womb. 'Though it will have to wait for some time.'

'Not that. Though I pray it is true.' She smiled and took his hands in hers. 'No, there's something else. I asked Gwendoline to look in the castle for some of your belongings.' Morwenna retrieved the small bundle and gave it to him. 'She found these and gave them to me just now.'

He unwrapped it and found a wooden fish that his father had carved for him. There was also a small prayer book that must have belonged to his mother. But the last gift was the woven linen cloth they were wrapped in. It was embroidered with a delicate thread, and Morwenna marvelled at its softness.

'I believe my grandmother might have woven this,' he remarked. 'We'll keep it for the baby.'

'I wanted you to have some things from your past,' she murmured, 'Since we're starting over, and you have to leave it behind.'

'It doesn't matter any more,' he said. 'No matter what lies ahead, we have each other.' He set the gifts aside and took her in his arms once more. 'Once, all I could think of was reclaiming Penrith. It was the only thing that meant anything to me.' He framed her face with his hands. 'But I was blind and could not see that everything I needed was right here.'

'I love you, Robert.' She leaned in to kiss him again. 'And whatever happens in Ireland, we will make a home for our family.'

And for him, it was enough.

Epilogue

Morwenna shielded her eyes against the afternoon son. Her three-year-old son Nicholas was playing with a tiny wooden sword, swinging it as he grunted and pretended to be a soldier.

It appeared that a lone rider was approaching, and she wondered who it was. Her daughter had a fist in her mouth, and Robert came to stand beside them. He dropped a kiss upon Eleanor's cheek and then reached down to swing Nicholas into his arms. Their son giggled, and Robert lifted the boy up high before settling him against his chainmail armour.

'Who is the rider?' she asked.

'My men sighted him a short time ago. Come and meet our guest.'

She wasn't expecting anyone, but she followed Robert. Over the past few years, he had transformed Dunbough into a massive fortress by the sea. They had protected it against invasion with high stone walls, and he had taken the time to know every person who lived there. The people had not welcomed them at first, despite the king's decree, but Robert had won them over in time. The land was more difficult to farm, but they had sheep and cattle, along with fish from the sea. No one went hungry any more, and Morwenna loved nothing more than to stand on the battlements and watch the waves crash against the stones below.

But who was this rider? The man drew closer, and when she started to recognise him, her heart began pounding. Then she started to run, clutching the baby as she did.

'Brian!' she cried out, the tears of joy spilling over her cheeks. 'My brother!'

He'd grown so tall she had to tilt her head up to look at him. His skin held the bronzed tan of the sun, and there was no doubt that he'd been to Jerusalem and back again. He dismounted, and she wept as she reached for him. Robert took the baby so she could embrace her brother.

Brian held her close, stroking back her hair. 'I returned to the abbey, and Uncle Oswald told me where you were.' He glanced over at Robert. 'I thought you were dead on the night we tried to rescue Morwenna. It was my fault.'

'No, you were right to attack. I should have done so sooner,' Robert admitted. 'I only wish you had stayed at the abbey a little longer.'

But Morwenna knew her brother had left to face his own demons. Joining the Crusaders had given him a purpose, but she didn't miss the shadows in his eyes when she drew back from the embrace.

'I never thought you would give up your lands at Penrith,' Brian said to Robert.

'I found something of greater value,' he answered. Morwenna smiled and just then, her daughter began to sob. Robert put Eleanor to his shoulder, soothing her and patting her back. From the way the infant kept suckling her fist, Morwenna knew she was hungry.

Her son's face twisted with worry, as if he somehow believed the stranger had made his sister cry. But Brian only smiled and knelt down to Nicholas. 'I am your uncle Brian, young lad. What's your name?'

'Nicholas,' the boy answered.

He appeared uncertain, and Morwenna smoothed his hair to offer reassurance. 'He's my brother, sweeting. Just as you are Eleanor's brother.'

At that, her son seemed to understand. He

tugged at her skirts and informed her, 'I need to play.'

'Go on, then.' Brian patted his shoulder and then met her gaze. 'You look happy, my sister.'

'I am. More so, now that I know you're safe.' She had worried about him for so long, wondering if she would ever see him again. The years had transformed him from an adolescent into a man. He had a quiet strength about him, as if he had witnessed the horrors of war.

Robert pressed his hand against her spine, and asked, 'Have you to come to live with us, Brian? We would be glad to have you stay.'

Her brother smiled. 'I will visit for a time, but I have my own debt to repay.'

'What sort of debt?' Morwenna asked. 'Do you need our help?'

Brian only shook his head. 'Not one that involves silver. The debt was my life.'

'You have our help, should you need it,' Robert promised. 'Come and join us for a meal.'

They walked together towards the keep, and as they passed the people, Morwenna saw Dunbough through her brother's eyes. They had taken a neglected estate and rebuilt it into a place of prosperity. She had taken her place as its lady and although sometimes she felt uncertain about her decisions, Robert was always by her side.

'I need to feed the baby,' she told him when they drew closer to the entrance. 'I will join you afterwards.'

Robert kissed her, letting his hand linger at her waist. 'I'll be waiting.'

As she took the baby and walked towards the stone stairs, she paused to look back. Once, she had been a scared girl, fighting to survive. And now, she was surrounded by those she loved. With Robert by her side, they had formed a life together. She cradled her daughter, marvelling that an act of love kept bringing more love into the world.

Her husband met her gaze, echoing her silent message. She loved this man with her very soul. There was nothing in the world she wouldn't do for him, and she knew he would lay down his life for all of them.

And this was only the beginning.

* * * * *

COMING SOON!

We really hope you enjoyed reading this book.
If you're looking for more romance, be sure to
head to the shops when new books are
available on

Thursday 26th
May

To see which titles are coming soon, please visit
millsandboon.co.uk/nextmonth

MILLS & BOON®

Coming next month

HOW TO CATCH A VISCOUNT
Annie Burrows

"You and I must part here," Betsy informed him.

"No. I mean, I am sure I can get Socks, that is, my mare, across this wall."

"That is not it. This is the boundary to my father's land. Once I am on the other side of it, I will be, more or less, home."

His face fell. Then brightened. "You know, if your father really is as knowledgeable about the feelings of the folk in these parts, and so influential, I really ought to visit him and make myself known to him."

"No! I mean, not today, anyway. Or at least, not with me. Not like this! Please!"

He tilted his head to one side. "You really don't want anyone to know we have been alone out here, do you?"

"No!" Her reputation was in a precarious enough state as it was. "You are bound to meet him at church on Sunday. Can you not wait until then? And meet him in a perfectly natural fashion? Everyone is bound to want to know who you are, and once Father learns why you have come here he is bound to want to further your acquaintance, since the state of the Earl's holdings had been vexing him for years."

"If that is the case, could I not simply call on him and pay my respects?"

She turned her back on him and began to scramble over the wall. Even though she could manage perfectly well, and had done on many occasions, he seemed to think he needed to place his hands at her waist to steady her, lest she take a tumble.

It was all she could do to turn and face him once she was safely on the other side. Her body still burned where his hands had been, as if he had left a fiery imprint. And warm tingles were spreading to the rest of her body. She'd never experienced anything like it. Men had touched her before, when helping her alight from a carriage, or during the measures of a dance. But none of their hands had felt as if they'd seared their way through every single layer of clothing she wore.

"P...please don't," she found herself begging him. In regard to what he'd said, rather than what he'd done. "If you were to turn up at the house, I would be sure to give away the fact that I already knew you, by blushing, or being unable to meet your eye, or something of the sort. And Mother, who is a veritable bloodhound when it comes to that sort of thing, would be bound to sniff out the truth, somehow."

"Then, to spare your blushes," he said, giving her that mischievous smile once more, "I shall wait to present myself to your father until Sunday."

"Thank you," she breathed.

"I shall be counting the days," he said.

"I...I..." She would be too, she realised. Not that she could tell him so. Or even let him guess she might be thinking such a thing.

Her head in a whirl, her body tingling, and her heart pounding, Betsy turned away from him, and pelted down the hillside.

Continue reading
HOW TO CATCH A VISCOUNT
Annie Burrows

Available next month
www.millsandboon.co.uk

MILLS & BOON

THE HEART OF ROMANCE

A ROMANCE FOR EVERY READER

MODERN

Prepare to be swept off your feet by sophisticated, sexy and seductive heroes, in some of the world's most glamourous and romantic locations, where power and passion collide.

HISTORICAL

Escape with historical heroes from time gone by. Whether your passion is for wicked Regency Rakes, muscled Vikings or rugged Highlanders, awaken the romance of the past.

MEDICAL

Set your pulse racing with dedicated, delectable doctors in the high-pressure world of medicine, where emotions run high and passion, comfort and love are the best medicine.

True Love

Celebrate true love with tender stories of heartfelt romance, from the rush of falling in love to the joy a new baby can bring, and a focus on the emotional heart of a relationship.

Desire

Indulge in secrets and scandal, intense drama and plenty of sizzling hot action with powerful and passionate heroes who have it all: wealth, status, good looks…everything but the right woman.

HEROES

Experience all the excitement of a gripping thriller, with an intense romance at its heart. Resourceful, true-to-life women and strong, fearless men face danger and desire - a killer combination!

To see which titles are coming soon, please visit

millsandboon.co.uk/nextmonth

JOIN US ON SOCIAL MEDIA!

Stay up to date with our latest releases, author
news and gossip, special offers and discounts, and
all the behind-the-scenes action
from Mills & Boon...

 millsandboon

 millsandboonuk

 millsandboon

It might just be true love...

MILLS & BOON
True Love
Romance from the Heart

Celebrate true love with tender stories of heartfelt romance, from the rush of falling in love to the joy a new baby can bring, and a focus on the emotional heart of a relationship.